DAY
BOY

Books by Trent Jamieson

The Stone Road (Erewhon Books)

Death Works
Death Most Definite
Managing Death
The Business of Death

Nightbound Land
Roil
Night's Engines

DAY BOY

BOY

TRENT JAMIESON

Erewhon Books

Day Boy
Copyright © 2022 by Trent Jamieson

First published in 2015 by Text Publishing (Melbourne, Australia)
First published in North America and Canada by Erewhon Books, LLC, in 2022

Edited by Liz Gorinsky and Mandy Brett

Erewhon Books
2 W. 29th Street, Suite 3S
New York, NY 10001
www.erewhonbooks.com

Erewhon books are available at special discounts when purchased in bulk for premiums and sales promotions as well as for fundraising or educational use. Special editions or book excerpts can also be created to specification. For details, send an email to specialmarkets@workman.com. Books available in Canada for retailers at University of Toronto Press, representation by Hornblower Group.

Library of Congress Control Number: 2022938696

ISBN 978-1-64566-026-2 (hardcover)
ISBN 978-1-64566-036-1 (ebook)

Cover art by Qistina Khalidah
Interior design by Liz Gorinsky and Cassandra Farrin
"Underline" by Caputo from NounProject.com

Printed in the United States of America

First US Edition: August 2022
10 9 8 7 6 5 4 3 2 1

For Sophie Hamley,
who pulled this story from me word by word,
sentence by sentence, paragraph by paragraph,
and chapter by chapter.
This is your book.

I learned to be a man from a monster.

You need to know that if you're to understand anything that follows.

I am, I believe, a good man, so was he—but the monster was always there.

I learned to be a man from a monster; there's no escaping that.

But the god-honest truth is that I miss him.

Part One

Imperatives

You will not wound another.
You will wield no weapons unless so sanctioned.
You will not harm our servants.
You will not bar your doors or windows.
You will not hide.
We will visit and you will welcome us in.
The night is not yours.
Our ways must not be walked.
Do not dissemble.
You will be found out.
Do not try to run.
We will catch you.

Every story should start with a fight. Fists bunched, all knuckles, blood in the mouth and laughter.

Every story should start with a hand clenched around a bit of chalk, marking the circle and the seven upon a front door. A door that can't be locked on any account.

The Sun, I draw it in chalk. I draw it simply (a circle the size of my palm, the seven lines that radiate from it) in the style of the Day Boys. Big enough that there's no mistaking it. That Sun means my Master is coming to see you: coming for his measure of blood. Your door will open, and he will enter, talk a while, if the mood takes him, and then he will drink.

In truth, for Midfield, and the rest of the towns east and west that cleave to the City's rule, a single line scratched across the door would be enough. No one but a Day Boy would dare to make the chalk mark.

It's a courtesy, nothing more, but courtesies hold weight in this town.

I'm just finished with my circle and seven when I spy George, done from his day at Saul's Butchery. He gives me a wave. He's a big bloke, three times my size at least. The grin he gives me is lit with weariness; the steps up to his verandah creak under him.

"That time again?" He drops onto the bench on his verandah; it, too, creaks beneath his weight. He rests his hands by his sides, neat and particular, like a lot of big men. I can smell the day's work on him, sweat, and honey. He tends a hive in the hills when he has time. There's a mark on his cheek from a sting.

Folk are always surprised when their turn comes round; I guess time surprises us all. Even if it's only twice a month. The beats of the day pass by unnoticed until they hit you.

"Yes. He'll be here tonight." I slip the chalk back into my pocket.

George wipes his hands on his pants. "You thirsty?"

It's a hot day, but I won't be drinking, not here. I get a prickle, a little premonition of hard words from Dain. I can't hide my desire, though, or the thinking better of it. Dain says I'm an open book, and Master Dain knows all about books.

George lifts his hat, his hair thin beneath. Scratches his scalp. "It's all right, boy, I won't hold you. When I was your age, the day was a million directions, all of them herding me, all of them saying, 'This way, come here!' Days like this, long as they are, they're even worse. Go and get yourself in trouble."

That's George, good old George. I don't give him time to rethink the sentiment.

But I'm barely a block away, sucking back on a smoke that I've rolled pretty swell, when Twitcher calls out to me. "Mark!"

First I mistake him for a crow, caw, caw, cawing. Then he's caught me up.

"Mark, Dougie's after you."

Trouble. Always got its sights on me. Better Dougie than a Hunter, is what I always say. But Hunters never come into a town like ours really; they wouldn't dare. The monsters they stalk are in the south and north, remnants of that last war.

"Dougie." I puff myself up. "After me, is he?"

Twitch rolls his eyes; he just wants this done. This heat brings out every kind of impatience. "Says you know where to go."

"Not the cave then?"

"Not that kind of meeting."

I cast a glance back to George's place, but he's gone inside. Should have taken him up on that drink. I take another puff of my smoke, flick it to the ground all casual.

If Dougie's got a fight in mind, which he has, he'll be waiting by the field on the edge of town. No idea what I've done this time, but we Day Boys take our insults and challenges seriously. I grin at Twitcher. "Will you be joining me?"

Twitch gives me a flat look, not a twinkle to be seen. He kicks at a stone. "I better," he says.

"What'd I do?"

Twitch shrugs. That passes for conversation in these situations. He walks close to me, like he's frightened I'll run away. Run away where? Day Boys don't run. I crack my knuckles, lope a bit, swing those knuckles low and parallel to the cracked earth. Try to get a laugh out of Twitch.

The boy's as grave as blood; chills my guts a little. So I straighten up, and we walk all funereal, him and me, in silence, kicking our boots in the dirt. I stop to piss, but then I can't, feel it draw up in me. What a misery! All that discomfort and not a drop of release. Twitch finds a bit of humour in that.

"Should I fight you first?" I ask.

He shakes his head, quick, lifts his hands high. "Might wanna keep your strength."

"True that."

And we're both smiling, despite what's coming. And that's how it is when we turn the last bend in the road, heat and dust rising from everything ahead and behind.

Dougie's waiting for me on the beginnings of the dirt road that heads out of town. Nothing more than a trail now, barely that, but it leads out and out to the elsewhere of Hunters and the monsters they stalk, out beyond the calm of the towns that run along the line to the City. North and south are the Bad Lands, and here is just before they start.

Right where Dougie and the other boys are. Standing on the edge of safety. He's curling his fingers closed, then opening them, giving a nail a bit of a chew, his stovepipe hat pulled low over his face so I can't see his eyes. I try not to squint. I turn my head, spit on the ground.

He whistles a little tune, then stops, pretends startlement. "You took your time." His voice is soft, and polite like a fillet knife.

"Such a beautiful afternoon." I smile in the dusty heat, my belly cold, and swing a fist into his face.

You get the first punch in. Sometimes you might not get another.

Dain says we fight to breathe. We fight to be born, and forever after we're all rage at the brevity of the world and its multitudes of cruelties. I'm not sure about that. But we fight. And we Day Boys fight like we're men angry and sanguine. Little soldiers marking doors with chalk, sketching the seven-pointed Sun upon the wood. Working and walking, all strut and talk—until we fight. And then the talk doesn't matter anymore.

My punch catches him in the mouth. The force of it runs up my arm; his teeth clack together. And he stumbles backwards, hat flying. But he recovers almost at once. I stand there a moment to see what I have done, shaking my sore hand. Dougie blinks a slow blink and touches his lip, a little hesitant, but only I'm close enough to read that. He studies the blood on his fingers. Then he rolls his shoulders.

I start swinging again, but he's ready. I've had my shot and he's coming at me. And I'm not fast enough for those fists. Not the first hit or the second or the one after.

All I can do is grin and take it. Day Boys don't run.

I don't know what Dougie's problem was before, but he's mad as a snake now. I shouldn't be showing my teeth like I am. But the bastard looks like an idiot when he swings his heavy fists: knuckles gritty with chalk. He shouldn't look so dumb because those knuckles offer a hell of a lot of hurt. But then again, pain can be funny. And you gotta laugh, don't you?

There's nothing worse than the dog that's not the top, but wants to be, and that grin of mine makes him swing harder. I spit blood in his face, and he snarls at me, offended: A beaten boy should just take it.

I'm on my rear, and the sun's beating down almost as hard as Dougie, and blood's flowing, nose, split lip, grazed cheek, and every time I try and get up, Dougie pushes me back onto that hard-packed earth. And I sit up again: blinking out sweat and dust and the cruel sun.

I give myself a glance past the prick.

There's his stovepipe hat, skew-whiff in the dirt. An affectation, Dain calls it. Well, I belted that affectation right off his skull.

Past that sad old hat it seems like half the town's youth are watching. Two circles—orbits Dain would say, and it's always what Dain says, he's the one that sees how the town works. Two circles like they're two worlds, and they are. A circle of Day Boys. And in a wider circle, the other lads of Midfield—keeping back, all big eyes and gentle bones, and I don't blame them. To be such a boy, possessed of such timidity, scared of the dark, scared of what might be coming, rising with the night, and creeping through the window.

I know what's coming. Oh, I know! All us Day Boys do. And it doesn't creep.

There's a few girls there, too, but I don't see Anne. I don't see Grove, either. Interesting. Chief Day Boy, and he isn't here to see my beating.

There's another orbit further out. So far, we can't see it, beyond the dry woods, circling where the cold children are in their ditches and drains long forgotten. There's always things circling.

I blink. And I blink.

"Are you done?" Dougie asks, his lip fat because I got in that good hit myself—just the one. But I'll take my delights where I can, and that swelling mouth of his is a joy to see; a radiant hurt that I've made, me and my raw stinging fists. He lifts me by my shirtfront, the cotton tearing, and growls straight in my face, all hot foul breath. "You done?"

I'd not done anything, far as I can tell. I spit another gob of blood in his face, and he thumps me again, twice, and then drops me so I can't help but fall. I'm seeing constellations, and I'm hitting that dirt hard with my spine, and laughing. True. I still can't stop laughing.

He takes another swing, and I kick him in the shin. "Stupid little shit," Dougie hisses, and I kick out at him again. He's ready for it, gives me a good boot back, and it knocks the wind from me.

I scramble away best I can, trying to draw breath; and Dougie picks up a bit of wood, solid bit of wood, two by four. I close my eyes, raise my hands, wait for it to come.

It doesn't.

I crack those lids a bit. There's Grove. My mate Grove, standing over Dougie. There's a hardness to Grove's eyes that you don't often see with him, a look of disgust. No, disappointment. He holds the two by four in one hand; an accusation. Taps it hard into his palm with a satisfying sort of a slap.

"Enough," Grove says. He's got a good foot of height over Dougie, and he isn't tired from thrashing me.

I thought I'd seen Dougie mad, but I hadn't seen anything. He's back on his feet, snarling and spitting (not a drop of blood in that spit, even with his fat lip). Grove pushes him back down. Easy. Like he could do it all day, and Dougie lands hard, and winded. He stays there. Pinned beneath Grove's glaring eyes.

"Enough," Grove says, and Dougie nods.

Grove's my best mate. If we're allowed such things, which we shouldn't be since his Master, Egan, and mine rarely see eye to eye. He offers me his hand, and I take it. Trust is the only thank you I can give him. He yanks me to my feet and it hurts a bit, but I don't show it. Grove's still got a good grip on that two by four with his other hand.

He waves it in Dougie's direction. "Stay down, Dougie." Dougie seems to think about it, but not for long. He does as he's told. I can see it's killing him, and I try not to smile, I really do, but I can't help it.

"Stay down," I say.

Grove frowns at me, pushes me in front of him. "Get walking, Mark."

"You weak little boy," Dougie shouts. "Like your Master. Hating what you are. Come back and fight me fair."

"Keep walking," Grove says, looking capable with that two by four in his hands, looking like he knows what to do, because Grove always does, even if it's the wrong thing. He's slowing his stride for me like he does. I always feel like I'm playing catch-up with Grove.

His slowing burns me a little. How can kindness be an insult? Grove's like that, though. That's what gets him into trouble, because there's all sorts of ways trouble will find you. And kindness is one of them.

"Thank you," I say. I have to say something.

"You'd do the same for me, Mark."

No, I wouldn't. We both know that, but I nod all the same. Hell, maybe I would.

"You all right?" he asks.

I've got a bit of a limp, there's bruises and lumps fattening up all over. And flies keep scrabbling at my juicy lip; it hurts when I brush them away. "I'm all right."

"You gotta stop doing that."

"Stop what?"

"You know."

But I can't say that I do.

Dain's on the roof. The sound of him striding about up there in the dark is louder than a possum and more sure-footed. There's no need to pretend he's got any need for stealth. There's no weight to him, it's his presence that shifts the iron roof sheeting; it bends and shudders beneath him. They do that, they change the world just by being, and the world rushes to fit them, to do their bidding. That is their Mastery.

He descends, pushing his mood before him, and I can tell he's aggrieved. He doesn't conceal the clatter in his bones, there's no fluid to him right now. He's chosen to discard it and I can feel the certainty of trouble. He descends and I don't bother hiding; there's nowhere to hide. Not from him.

The night's hot and bright, and there's a moon shining in the window. He's caught in it for a moment, and there's him cast across the room like a scattering of deeper night given shoulders, and long, long arms. A head dipping towards me. Then he's through the window.

I lie in bed staring (been too hot for sleeping anyway) and he lifts me up. Hefts me easily, as if I don't weigh anything at all. "I know you're awake. I—" His eyes widen, and then narrow; it would be comic on someone more human. "There's blood on you, you—"

Dain knows blood. He's defined by it, you might say, it is his food and fury. There's blood on him, too, I can smell it. Fresh from George.

"Nothing, it's nothing," I say.

"Doesn't look like it."

Dain lets me drop. Back onto the bed, and none too gently.

I sit up with some effort, not much of it exaggerated.

"Come with me," he says, and I follow him downstairs and into the kitchen.

He clicks his tongue at the mess. The unwashed plates, two-day-old stack. Most of it mine. The Master takes his teas, his liquors, his thin broths, but scarcely any real food passes his lips. He has no need of it. Doesn't mean he hasn't taught me to cook. The Masters don't eat as we do, but they like the smell of good food cooking, and fine brandy; well, Dain does, and I've seen Sobel guzzling his dusty old wines down by the bottle. Dain's a good host, on the rare occasion it's called for, which means I have to be, too, so I'm set the task of practising most nights.

Doesn't mean I like cleaning up after.

"Why didn't you drink with him, boy?" His voice is all clear in my ears, all insinuated there, working its way deeper. All those Masters' voices settle in you, threat and terror and charm.

I don't blame George for telling him. The feed loosens their tongues, and Dain would have drawn it out of him along with the blood. Dain's always with the questions. Did my boy treat you well? Was he respectful?

"I was busy." I look down at my feet.

"You were busy at things you had no right to be busy at, when you could have been keeping one of mine company." He crouches down, and peers at my bruised face. Clicks his tongue, again. "Unlike that—there's no shame to be had in compassion. No more than there's shame to be felt in what we do."

"But I feel it." And he can't tell me it isn't the same for him. Dain's lying to both of us if he thinks that.

"'Course you do, you're a good boy." He stands slowly. "I raised you that way. You'll go to George's tomorrow, you'll see that he is looked after."

Dain expects the civilities to be observed because the core of him is most uncivil indeed. Anne once asked me, one of the few times she was being serious, what it's like, being a party to all that terror, the Master and his hungers, being his Day Boy. And I told her it's very well-mannered. Because I know the history of it, how much greater the terror was before. The Dark coming to town, swirling in all unchecked after that final last war was lost. The doors broken down if you locked them, and if you didn't, sometimes that was just as bad. Things weren't at all civilised then. And there was nowhere to run, because it was that way everywhere.

Dain holds my chin, jerks me this way and that as he examines my bruises. My skin's hot and sore, his fingers cold and soothing for all their hardness. His eyes are dark with disapproval, and the slightest flicker of restlessness. My Master's been that way of late. "You've got to stop doing this." Everything's an echo today. I think of Grove and his disappointment.

"Doing what? Bruising when Dougie hits me?" It hurts to move my mouth.

Dain's face darkens, but he's already softening; there's no

violence to him tonight. He's at his most human when he is full of blood. "Provoking him. The boy's as mean-tempered as his Master, and not nearly as calculating."

"It were just a grin."

Dain's eyes shift darker still. "I know your smiles. Didn't Dav teach you anything?"

"Dav is long gone." Dav was the boy before me. Gone to the City in the Shadow of the Mountain when his time was done. He'd taught me much, all right, but some things don't stick and anyway, Dav was good at trouble, too. Just he had an awful good knack for not being found out. Even now Dain speaks fondly of him. Dav did this better, or Dav would never . . . Makes a fella sick with jealousy, sometimes.

"You've a lot of learning to do. And not much time to do it in. A year with me, perhaps two if I go cap in hand to the City and ask for an extension, and then your tenure's done. I want you to think on that, Mark." He brings his full gaze to bear on me, and I'm swept up in it, my limbs shaking, till he turns his attention away. "Your future, be it constabulary work, or something . . . lesser—that's dependent on your actions as much as any sponsorship of mine."

He ruffles my hair.

"Regardless, there'll be a trip to the City in the Shadow of the Mountain. You need to see what futures lie ahead for you. I'm not sure you understand the possibilities. You've never been one to think more than a day ahead, if that." He wrinkles his nose. "Now, clean this kitchen, it's starting to smell."

And he's gone to his study and the book he's always scratching at.

Something lesser? What about something greater?

Dav took Change, got his official letter, and went to the City five years back. I know there's not much chance they'd offer it twice in a row. I'll be sent to the City, to work there. At the university maybe; apprentice to a tradie.

Which isn't as bad as it could be. Mastery's a grim sort of gift. Dain isn't one that loves his kind. He's set himself apart from them all the years I've known him, says what he has is a curse, not a blessing.

I stack those dishes, one by one; everything's hot to touch. Time's slow, grown liquid like honey with twice the stick.

And I stand there, in soapy water to my elbows. And despite myself, I imagine what Dav was given. Mastery and the shaping of the earth to his will, and the fighting of monsters, and the walking of boundaries. And Day Boys of his own! And all those years and hungers! And to see so clearly in the darkest of dark. And it gets so much that my head is buzzing. But it isn't mine to be thinking of. There's all the time in the world.

I've a year to impress or to disappoint, to see if I'm worthy of anything better than drudgery. It's too much. Too long.

I pull the plug, watch the water drain, and I'm all tired again, and tomorrow's looming. And I can't help yawning.

A year's all kinds of forever.

———

You never know when they're coming. But they will come, and they will drink, and you might drown in all that drinking. People die, and their deaths are whispered. And their deaths are seen as the consequence.

Their funerals are quiet affairs, with none but family there—if there's family left.

Lots of bodies in that cemetery, and that's just the way it is, I guess. Cemeteries have a habit of filling up. They always do. Patient bloody things, accommodating, and wide.

Egan and the Moon

This is how Grove tells it. Standing before us all. Face grown to seriousness, and a deep remembering. He likes to get the words proper and in the right order. You can see his mind working them, well before his mouth. I reckon we all have a better memory of it than him. But he still says it.

We all know these stories; they're the stories we tell when we gather in the old cave—our secret meeting place (as if there were any secrets from our Masters). We tell these stories with no embellishments. Well, very little. But Grove says it perfect. The rest of us might change a word, or a scene or a beat in our stories. Some of us might throw in some comedy, who doesn't like a laugh? But he won't have any of that. This is Egan's story. Egan is his Master, and my Master's enemy, and this was how he told it to him. So this is how we hear it.

And I remember it still. Word for word.

Egan is old; you all know that, don't you? Oldest, maybe, amongst the new. Why is he out here in our little town, so far from the heart and the city dark? Whys and wherefores, that's all messed. Don't you all be looking at me. Egan's my Master, but he don't share much. Just the chores, like the rest of you fellows, a bit of learning. Not that I took to the classroom. Stop your smiling Twitch or I'll clobber you.

Stop it.

But Egan tells me; he fell in love with the moon.

Back in those days of engines breaking, the sky grown loud and supple and cruel. Back when the world was bigger and smaller, which is how they put it, bigger and smaller.

That's how the world shook out, I guess. Back then, he fell in love with the moon.

He left his life, his once lovers, why he even left his phone, and they were magical things with everything in the world in them. He rolled up his belongings. Kissed his past goodbye, and he took to the road. You know them roads. They were threads of black; they went everywhere, not only east to west. But that's where he went. West. He followed the moon.

How do you catch the moon?

'Course, you don't. It's up there, and we're down here. You can't catch that. Once maybe, but even then they'd lost those great fires, those massive engines that could get there. All the great fires were burning down, and no one cared to blow on those embers, and build 'em up.

So my Master travelled. Threaded his way through all the falling down and burning, through a night pitched as dark as ever been. He met others, but none could help him. He might have been mad. Might have stunk with fear. He crossed bridges. He marked the earth with his blood. He walked through his shoes till his heels found the hard earth, and a time came when he walked barefoot. His feet grown horny and black. Clothes on his flesh ragged, not much flesh to cover. The road had hardened and thinned him. He was a shadow: a hungry shadow.

You wouldn't have recognised him. Maybe you would. And he chased that moon.

How do you catch the moon? Moon catches you. If it wants to. It led him to the Mountain.

You know it. You all see it in your dreams sometime. The whispering Mountain where the winds go. Wasn't no city in its shadow then. Not much but a few shacks.

Others had followed the moon. And my Master was great in his envy of them. But they were frightened, bent low by the Mountain. Scared of what had drawn them. It was the Master that went down.

It was him that went into the Mountain. It was him that came back, and he weren't like them anymore.

And then, of course, he met Dain, and those two found trouble between them. But Egan was always the first.

———

All I remember *that makes sense is him.*

He's my youth. The voice of me growing up. He tended my wounds, you see; they're not just the makers of wounds. He saw to my tears (and he was more tolerant than most folks would be, I guess; I was a weepy sort of kid), and he taught me. Of the past before the Masters came, of the secret past that was there all along. Of the crack in the world, and the way deals were made.

"Everything's a negotiation," Dain said. "The past and a place relative to it. To live or to die. We all make choices within a greater matrix of choices. Those that brought this world on us made choices they thought were the right ones."

"What do you think?"

"Everything's a negotiation."

Dain liked his lessons. History, maths, English. I found it all too slippery, but he never let up on it. He'd been a teacher once. "You learn to think, boy, and you might get yourself out of trouble almost as much as you get yourself into it."

The other Masters called him the Professor. Their boys, too, when he wasn't around. I know he doesn't like it. I never use it, don't think it's worth the hard clip beneath the ear. Some things I know I can get away with, other fights just aren't worth having. Dain taught me that. He's taught me most things, be it direct or in silence. You pick your fights: You pick the ones you reckon you'll win.

There's some fights you're never going to win, no matter what.

I'm out the door, stomping my way through a morning that's already getting old, but lunch is hours off, and there's work done, and work to be done.

Day's spiking my back with sweat, and I've yesterday's hurt to contend with. I try not to limp, out along West Street then on to Main where the jacarandas are drooping. They're all green; they've lost their blooms weeks ago. Out of the sun and into shade, shirt clinging to my back. I'd ride my bike, but I'm still too sore. The baker's door is swinging, the heavy screen of the butcher's black with flies, as are the scabbed corners of my lips. Keep brushing them away, and they keep coming back. Stomp, stomp: I'm weighed down with the weight of the sun, and the dead weight of my boots. This is a day for bare feet, but I'm working. Like Dain says, we're boys, not animals. Come back with the soles of my feet black and a clip under the ear'd be my earning.

Down the dust of Main, past a couple of tired horses, waiting for their owners to finish buying supplies. I have some stubs of carrot, kept special: Both snuffle them up. Horses aren't that proud. Feel their wet lips against my palms, the soft weight of their eyes. Never ridden a horse in all my life, but I know how to treat them, and they seem to know that I know.

When I'm out of carrots, I move on. There's things to attend to.

I turn left into East Street, and he's standing there like he's been waiting, as I suppose he has, in the middle of the road, his feet bare, stovepipe hat at an angle. There's a bruise under his chin; that makes me happy at least.

"Mark," Dougie says.

I fix a smile on my much-more bruised-up-than-his face. No matter what Dain says, I can't help it. Dougie holds his botheration inside him. There's a lump of ice he's chewing on, got a red slick of blood through it like a filament of ruby. The only ice in town comes from the butcher's, shipped here on the Night Train, weeping as it's carted off.

Dougie doesn't mind the blood. You can't be queasy, not in our line of business. It's good practice, all that red. I don't have any of that ice for my split knuckles. Flex my fingers a little.

"I've work to attend to," I say. "Master's work."

Dougie takes a long suck of that ice, nods his head. Puts out his hand. "No hard feelings."

I look down at it, the water that beads a palm as tough and worn as my own. "No hard feelings," I say, though I'm never going to shake it.

Now it's Dougie who's smiling, like I've given him validation, like he's the bigger man, and he is: no contest. "Fair enough," he says. "We accounted for ourselves."

"Some of us more than others."

Dougie laughs, pops the ice back in his mouth, and then, almost as an afterthought, he spits it back onto his palm. "You see that Grove, you tell him that, too. No hard feelings."

Poor Grove, getting into trouble on account of me. "I see him, and I will."

Dougie nods, and gets back to his ice. Those blue eyes staring hard at me.

I leave him on East, get onto Brickell. Walk past Mary's house; there's a piano playing. Anne. Plays better than anyone in town, and I can't find a sweeter happiness than the thought of her. I'd sneak a longer listen, but I've work to do. Always the rod at my back.

George is a while answering his door, which means he was out back. But he comes. He knows who's knocking, and you don't make us wait.

He stands there and yawns, eyes still crusted with sleep, pupils still hunting for the compass points of the day. "Morning, Mark."

"You all right, George?"

"Maybe I should be asking you that." He gestures at my bruises with the slightest shadow of my Master's disappointment there. We're all echoes of them that rule.

And I give him such a don't-want-to-talk-about-it look that he shakes his head. "Dougie?"

I shrug.

George sits heavy on that bench, lids fluttering a little. The bandage on his wrist is weeping. "The boy's bad news, all pumped up on his own pride. Sobel's never kept him in line. You keep your distance from him."

"Not me I'm concerned with. You all right?"

"Just weary," he says. "I'll lay myself here and rest. Gets me worse in summer. Maybe I'm getting old."

George has years ahead. Still, he looks old today. Smaller.

They always do.

I get him a pillow, put it under his head. "Sorry I didn't drink with you yesterday."

"He tell you that did he? What I said?" I nod.

"Sorry, boy. He asked, I had no choice. You know how it is. He comes and he talks, gentle, but there's no give to him. The blood and the words just flow somehow, and you're all of a sudden babbling, and he's listening even as he feeds." His voice is all dozy. "If you'd stayed, I'd've saved you trouble, on both counts." He rouses a little. "Not just me doing the talking, neither. Your Master's worried for you, your last year of working. You going to go to the City?"

I give a shrug that ducks the question. "No need for sorries or worries," I say, "and the bruises would have come anyway. That was something that was coming no matter what."

George is snoring. I fetch him a clay jug of water for when he wakes. And then I work in the yard, clearing and stacking rubbish. His gutters are clogged, so I get up there, and clean those out. Find a brown snake, and there's a little stand-off before it decides I'm not worth it and retreats, quick and haughty, off the roof. I win that round. Me and the snakes have an agreement, mostly. I keep away, and they do, too. Dougie, he likes to break their backs. I can't fathom such pointlessness. Snakes have a beauty all their own.

Up here I can see out to the forested edge of town, and the ridge that swings up in the east, first serious rise towards the Dividing Range. West is just farms and flat, interrupted by the odd low hill that's erupted from the earth, and the dark thin line of the railroad. I stand a moment in that heat. Enjoy the view. Then back to work.

There's a gate hanging on its hinges, I give that some sweat too; and a creaking floorboard (nothing under, because I checked). Gutters, gates, floorboards uncreaked, George has done all right out of his visitor: a rough night for a gentle day.

I wait till he wakes, look at his books, nothing too salacious. And when he wakes, we drink. Get him some more cold water, up from the basement.

"Your Master doesn't take much," George says, "but it hurts and wearies anyway, that little bit."

He doesn't take much. He takes everything.

———

Most of them sleep in wine cellars, our Masters curled up there, far, far older than the grog, but Dain don't. He lies in a bed. Likes to be close to the air.

"Something comes for me, boy—it'll do just as well down or up."

I don't reckon there's a single boy who hasn't snuck in to see their Master sleeping. It's deeper than sleep. They're like stone. No breath, just an awful stillness. I slapped Dain's face once, and he didn't even move. That's why they need us. They sleep so deep, they sleep in the memory of their past, and that's an awful big chink in their armour. Still, even then killing one would be hard. Asleep, their skin is stony, breaks most knives, turns or blunts most sharp things. They can be dragged out into the light, of course; burn away that way.

Best time for killing's the gloaming, we reckon. Skin's supple, penetrable, as Dain says, and they're dozy for an hour or two, not quite awake. Though they're quick to wake if they sense a threat to them and theirs.

We boys talk about such things. Boastful like. As though we could kill our Masters, as though they wouldn't have their hands—or worse—round our necks quick smart, snapping and snarling and seeing us out of such stupidity.

I've seen Dain leave by the cellar window, I've seen him flow cross the night like some dark breath blown by the moon. He's fast in the way an eagle's fast, in its effortless diving flight and endless hunger. You don't kill that. Much easier dying, and many have, many folk much stronger than me.

I sleep in the room next over, and I wake with his passage. That darkness coming and going, it's stronger than a change in the air, or a smell, though it's both (he can't hide his smell, the raw meat odor of him). It's electric. Makes your hair stand on end.

I'm a Day Boy, but it don't preclude night works.

I'm still moving slow by nightfall. My skin's too tight, my bones too sore. Dain's home, watching me, going to work on his book like he does most nights when he's not visiting or swinging wide circles around the town, keeping guard against the monsters. He has a distracted look. He's still angry with me, and more.

He calls for a sherry—purely to be difficult, I'm sure—and I bring it quick smart. Put it on the table by his desk. There's a drop of the reddish liquid on the edge of the glass; I wipe it away lest it drip on all that scrawled-on paper, stacked neat and to one side of him. His study's always neat, that chair, his desk with the stack of papers that grows steadily, but never by much. He writes in ink, scratching away on one side only, and most of those sheets find the bin. He goes through so much of it. I'm sent least once a month to pick up a box of paper when the Night Train comes.

Dain looks over at me, reading again the story of the bruises, and I feel the shame of them rising in my face. There's a softening takes place in his eyes, the sharp line of his mouth finds a smudge. He puts down his pen. "Nothing but thugs, most of those boys. Except Egan's. Grove, that one's been raised right; I know he's settling on making him a Master. The rest are not shown any other way to be, they're left to run wild. Don't make me think I've failed you."

How is it that Dain can talk about his failure, and make me feel it's mine? Because it is, I suppose. I could have left that fight, I could have run, been marked as a coward, though. What does Dain know of cowardice?

"You've never failed me," I say. "But this world's the rough one into which I'm thrown."

"And I can throw you out of it," Dain says, swiping a hand at me, though not without affection. I dart all a-wince backwards.

"You've time to heal now," Dain mumbles, waving an arm at some vague sentiment in the air. "But it won't always be the case. This is not a time for you to start feuding. The days are running down. And you must be more careful." Dain rubs at his lip, his face grown long. He sniffs at the air and draws in a breath that he doesn't need. "Now fetch me some paper, and refill my good pen. And a finger of whisky, the black label, you know the one."

I do, and I know it means he's going to spend the night working on that book of his. Means I've got more grump headed my way. He takes the whisky. Sips a little, rolls it in his mouth, sighs. Picks up his pen again, then puts it down.

"Why do you set yourself at failure, boy, with a myriad other paths laid out before you? You are a prince of these dry streets. You've the gifts of your station, and you cast it all aside with a smile. Never has a child been more determined for ruin. Why? The love of falling? Is that it?"

"I don't know. I try—"

"Then don't! Stop trying." He lifts a hand in disgust. "You can go to bed now. There'll be a list as long as both your arms tomorrow."

I groan.

"Twice as long!"

———

Hot nights like this, all you can do is toss and turn, the sheets all rasp and ruin. There's night birds calling, and the town feels small; huddled against the greater dark. The day's grown smaller, they say, and the night's grown huge and toothy. You know what it's like when you can't sleep, and each aching fragment of the night passes slow and steady, and the late hours lumber, full of thoughts that you wouldn't think when your brain's Sunlit.

Most days I wish I was cleverer than I am. Cleverer and less mouthy. Grove gets into trouble because he doesn't know better, and thinks too kindly of the world. I get into trouble because I'm too impatient with it.

And time is running down. There's a city calling me, and I'll see it if I'm lucky, but I'm feeling my luck run thin, feeling old, too. Choices heaped ahead of me, and I feel so ill-equipped to make them.

I like to hold things in my hand, get a good grip of them. Like to work them out and solve them. There's nothing of that now, no answers in this nighttime murk.

The Night Train comes and goes, its cargo unladen, its whistle calling out, and I'm still awake. Still thinking. Thinking. Thinking.

When I tumble to sleep, it's a lean sort of thing, no meat or fat to the bones, just a gristle of drinks not drunk, of girls not kissed, and a tall man with a taste for civility, who's disappointed with what he raised.

———

Do the Masters *sleep deep during the day, as their god traverses the heavens? How can they not be stirred by the day, the furious quickener of blood? Yet I have seen Dain abed, flesh hard as stone, flesh that you could not pierce with a knife. I've placed a mirror to his lips and seen not a breath. I've called his name and he has not stirred.*

But do they rest?

He told me once what they dream of.

"The Sun, blessed and pure, a long shore, a wave that breaks, and the hunt. These are the endless things, so deep in us that we are nothing without them. We dream of a place that is all predation; a place between the light and the dark where the blood is hot and sweet, and everything is possessed of purity. We dream of that perfection. But it retreats from us; no matter how we reach out or run, we cannot catch it.

"Oh, and sometimes in our dreams, when a boy is foolish enough—and he has to have a lot of foolish in his veins—we hear him call our name." Dain's face lost a good bit of its whimsy. "Do not call me in my sleep. Do not disturb my dreams."

Sometimes I looked in his eyes and all I could see was that shore, receding, receding, but never quite gone. You can see time in their eyes, a stream of moments shrugged off. "What do we have without the oppression of time?" Dain once asked. "We've all the crystalline perfection of forever."

It's the sea that calls them, and the sun that rises out of it.

I shouldn't have been here by the river, and I should've been watching, what with the fact that this place is off-limits to me, and also rightly dangerous. It's past the borders that the Masters define as safe, and it's territory that is none of my business. But I've been here before, and nothing went wrong. Just looking for yabbies in the dirty water. You get a bunch of them, cook them up (all squealing, the damn things cry for mercy no matter what Dain says), and they're tasty. I had a hunger for them today, and there was already a bunch of them on the grass beside me; insecty legs twitching. All that sweet meat not knowing what I had planned for it.

But I'm tired. And tired's halfway to blind, which is why I shouldn't have been here.

I almost miss the fella that comes out of the grass by the river. Slick and fast as a snake. I get just a flash of that movement in the corner of my eye, and I roll and bolt straight into the water. So I'm only touched by the briefest passing of the knife; a slice, skin parting, blood spilling, but I'm not spitted on it, which was what the bastard was aiming for. Then water soaks me, or blood, or both.

He grunts behind me, and I'm already scrambling deep into water, fast as the fire in that cut, fast as fear into the reeds and rocks, and they're all slapping and scratching at my feet, maybe even a big old catfish having a nibble as I crash past.

Don't have much on me. Just my pocketknife and the piss in my pants.

I shouldn't have been there, but I was.

Dain would be mad—even more than he is already. But that is a black cloud on the horizon of later. Now is a knife at my back and the heavy breaths of a man giving chase.

I've a choice: Left or right?

Left leads against the flow of the river, and out of town. Right swings back around, heads towards Handly Bridge. I've jumped off its edge often enough, but the man's already crashing that way. I can swim, but not that fast. And left there's bulrushes and cover. So I go that way, hoping there's no one else. I slap against the weight of the river, already up against my thighs, flicking my gaze back.

The man's giving chase with a machete in one thick-fingered hand. He's bearded, round at the belly, arms thick as my legs. I know the type. I can smell the grog even from here, drinks to keep himself brave. It'll make him clumsy, though. Probably been watching me and mine, waiting for the right time. Waiting for one of us to do something stupid.

And it had to be me.

I think of Dougie, Grove, the Parson boys, those crazy twins with the wild eyes, and Twitch nervous and laughing, always running or riding or worrying. I'm faster on my feet than all of them, and I'm the one's going to get gutted by a drunk with a big knife.

Not yet. Not yet.

The reeds close around me, and I run where I know they're thickest and the water's deepest, shouting: *Got a knife, too. Cut you if you come closer.*

He grunts again, but he doesn't come through the reeds, and I find myself a hidey hole, been playing and hiding in these waters since I can remember—no matter that I shouldn'ta been there. Been clipped under the ear for it many times, too, given a bloody nose and a head ringing. Dain's not cruel, not in that way, but some things he wants to make stick, he says, since he can't watch over me when the sun rises. Boys are allowed some mischiefs, but they're not allowed everything. That'd be anarchy, plain and simple.

Back's sore where he cut me, but I've had worse. No breath whistling through the wound; no taste of blood—just snot, maybe tears. You'd cry, too. I'm not immune to terrors just cause of whose roof shelters me. I'm as scared as you, beneath the strut. This is the only time I'll tell you that. But it's there, remember that; it never goes.

The man's circling round. I can hear him. But he doesn't come closer. His moves are a Hunter's, but they don't do this. They don't hunt boys. There's a madness in this one. And here I am alone to face it. I have a knife, but it's not like the machete that he's carrying. Just a thing for cutting soft wire; gutting fish, not men.

Dain says a man should always keep something with an edge to it. Women, too, at that. It's the edge that makes us what we are, he said once, clever apes, clever cutting creatures. I asked him what knife he carries, and his lips curled up, tight against his gums. He keeps his edge within him, he said, all superior. He's no ape, not any longer, but he's *all* kinds of clever.

Not that it will do me any good.

I'm here, and he's still in the black dark, hiding from the sun.

I shouldn't have been there. But I was, 'course I was. Never where I'm supposed to be. What's the fun in that?

Chipped a tooth last year cause of what Dain likes to call my misadventures, cracked a leg bad, a few years back, blood swelled it and darkened. He nursed me through the bitter agonies and the sweats—and I know what that cost him, me being weak and all, hardly any use to anyone, let alone the likes of him, but he did it. Can't nurse me through death, though, and I know I'm in for a bloody hiding if I get through this all right. A hiding at the least.

For an hour I'm crouching in that water, clutching my knife. Twice a catfish brushes my legs, and it's an awful cruel thing that I can't slide my fingers under it and flip it free of the river—make a good meal, and Dain says I need fattening up. There's gunshots in the distance, like a storm that's building. The hunt's on round the Summer Tree. Deer being culled in the heat.

A different sort of hunt to what this fella engages in.

"Not here to kill you." The voice comes clear through the reeds, and it's all I can do not to let out a cry, and an accusation: *The cut says otherwise.* I'm shivering a bit, and the catfish takes a tiny nibble at my calf just then, and I nearly yelp again. "You're near to being at your end of work. And I've need of a new boy. My last been kilt, down in the Southern Darks.

"Could kill you easy enough." There's a slur to his words—still drinking. You don't drink like that unless you mean to kill something, even if it's just yourself. "You'll see the truth of it soon enough."

My teeth chatter.

"I'm patient," the Hunter says, telling me that he isn't. "You don't live in the places south and north of the line without being patient."

I can't help but find a sliver of hope in that, forget awhile the chill seeping into me. I stay where I am in the brown muck of the river, still as still can be.

"He won't find you," the Hunter says. "We'll both wait out here until you or me dies. I don't intend dying today."

Neither do I. No one ever does.

But every day holds its own terrors, its own surprises. That's why the Masters have us Day Boys. The ones that keep the wheels spinning even while that sun's burning. We run their chores. See to their business and make it our own.

And I'm doing none of it, stuck here in silt and menace. There's another hour. Just me, and his voice calling; and I'm not moving, barely breathing. That's a hard labour all itself.

There's another nibble at my toes.

Sometimes staying still can almost drive you out of your skull when all you want is to be running, all your head is saying is RUN RUN RUN. And I'm not a stay-still kind of lad. Never been that.

"What you've got to hide for, boy?" More slur. Which leans the odds to my advantage. The time's coming, as I see it. "You know I'm not the bad man."

Not the worst man, no. But there's all different types of bad. He's got bad enough in him.

I hear him moving through the reeds; he doesn't feel he needs to hide—brazen as a bloody Master. I move, and he'll find me. He's too far to the left.

RUN RUN RUN.

But I stay still.

Something motors down the river. Mayor Aldridge's dinghy. I want to call out to him, but by the time he comes, my throat'll be sliced into a second smile. No one ever expects to die. Death is death, and I'm in no hurry for it.

The Hunter curses. I hear him back away. And still I don't move.

I wait. I wait.

And the hours pass.

Slow. They pass so slow, and the reeds move around me, as a wind picks up from the west with the dust from the west, and I can smell the river and the riverbank, and the slow passage of time, which Dain says is just an illusion, that if I saw it as he saw it, I would know it was just an illusion.

Catfish nibbles, and I let it and don't jump. I don't hardly breathe.

I wait till the sun's past setting, and then I move.

Slow. Almost as silent as breath. I get to the bank. Take a step onto firm dry land, and another. And the machete slides under my chin.

"**Not a word,** not a squeak," comes the voice in my ear; grog breath washing over me.

I nod, feel that blade cut my skin, just a touch. My heart's beating so fast, blood pumping so hard I'm surprised I don't pop.

"Drop your knife," he says. And I drop it.

"Now you're coming along with me. Slow. There's a boat ten minutes down the river. You'll walk with me."

"There's no boat," I say.

The machete presses tighter, I can feel its longing, the yearning to sink into flesh, to cut and carve its frustrations into me. I turn my gaze a little. He has a tattoo on his wrist, a spiral. A mark I've not seen before. It catches my eye and holds it.

The machete shivers. "Walk."

And that's what I do.

"Eight years in the wilderness. Time to take on an apprentice," the Hunter says. A rush of words after the hours of silence. "Eight years of solitary mindfulness. You'll sign my papers, and then I'll have you. Even them night things respect those papers. Nice, eh? Monster's child groomed to kill the dark and the hungry things."

I'm not signing anything. I don't care what he says, I can feel the death in him.

—

Ten minutes, twenty more like! Along the river, neither fast nor slow. Just how he wants me to go. Once I hear a dog barking that I reckon might be Petri over at Paul Certain's farm. Certain would be good in this kind of trouble, that's a man who's known it. But there's a hard mile between here and there.

The Hunter freezes up, stands there still a moment, that machete getting closer to my veins. But there's no more barking, and we're walking again. And he's mumbling about monsters. Storm birds call, and it's the kind of sound that makes you ache. Always calling. Always storms coming, and falling away.

Earliest sound I remember. Might be my last, too.

At this rate we'll be walking until after the Night Train pauses on its way to the City in the west, drops off the ice and fuel, and picks up the produce. The odd head of cattle, grain, honey and ash. Mr. Stevens waiting at the signal tower watching the east, waiting for it to arrive. Of course, I'll be dead by then, bled white and gutted. Nothing happens in Midfield. Nothing of consequence. Not really, we're just the bit between here and there, between the City and the sea. My death won't mean much. Won't trouble the City folk, won't bring on much of a tear. Maybe Anne'll miss me. Maybe not.

I snuffle a bit at the thought. "Stop yer cryin'," the Hunter says. Can't even wipe my nose.

Sometime along, we startle a few deer. It's late in the season for them to be so close to the river, maybe the gunshots have driven them here. They crash into the undergrowth and leave us both panting. We stop for a second or two, before the Hunter's pushing me hard in the back, driving me on. A little from the river, cause the land grows thick around, but we curve back.

He pauses, hesitates at the bank. Curses, crouches down, machete still against my neck, his knees popping, and looks at the rope, cut neat through. And a river clear of any boat, just brown water, in either direction. He drops the rope, gets back to his feet. And I can see the knowledge in his white-rimmed eyes.

"'S not here," he says.

"Of course it isn't," comes a familiar voice from the dark, an insinuating voice, angry, and my skin crawls. I can't help it—feel a bit ungrateful—but it does.

I drive my elbow into the Hunter's gut, and the blade drops from his hand, and I'm bolting free, but not before I feel his piss stream down my back. I'm swearing, rolling forward, then scrambling backwards smelling of his terror, and there's a goodly bit of mine there, too. Death's one thing, but there's deaths and there are deaths.

"Don't look," Dain commands. "Don't look, boy."

But I catch a glimpse anyway, of a man-shaped darkness.

Darker than the night, eyes glowing like a fresh-stoked fire. The Hunter's stepping backwards, one arm flung out, other hand around his throat, blood spilling through the fingers. He's turning, starting to run, if such a broken motion could be called running. But the dark and the fire is upon him.

And I feel the fits rising in me, feel the shakes. But it passes.

It passes, and the whole world stills.

I close my eyes, and the screaming starts. I squeeze them shut as silence washes over me, a silence of small sounds. Bones breaking, skin tearing.

"Go home," the Dark says, voice down low. "Go home, you've chores to do. I'll deal with you later."

I hesitate.

"Go!"

And then, for the first time in forever, I'm running, running, like the Devil's at my back.

And he may as well be.

———

Home through Midfield. Down Main Street, and west along Zephyr, past picket fences and tall houses, brick and wood and verandahs edging every one, bringing each the comfort of shadows. Past jacaranda trees full and leafy, and loud with the scratch of cicadas. The smell of lawns freshly cut, a few lights lit in windows, a few shadows moving. Flying foxes sweep across the sky, screeching when they find a tree fruiting, real foxes calling out in the hills.

The town is winding into sleep. But there's blood in my head, thoughts rushing, and my back's sore where I was cut, and I'm sticky with piss and sweat.

The Sewills are sitting on their verandah, and they wave at me. Night isn't full deep yet, and there I am walking in the middle of the road. I wave back like it's any other day.

And it is, I guess.

Tomorrow, in fact, I'll be marking their door. Glance at their lawn—too long—and I'll be the one to mow it. Pushing their damn mower that's never sharp enough no matter how I sharpen it. Going to wear me out, but maybe I need that.

I don't see any Day Boys, and that's a relief. But I catch a shape that might be Egan, a darkness leaping between roofs. It sees me, two circles of fire regard me, and then it's gone. It still gives me a shiver. There was enough hate in it that I'm certain it was Egan.

I make it home, check that the fire's burning clear, and it's not. So I get to fixing that. And then I drop to bed. Need a bath. Infections are getting worse these days, Dain says. But I'm too knackered to be drawing one.

I doubt Dain will talk to me tonight. His talking to me later will stretch across days.

Isn't the easiest sleep I find, but I find it anyway.

———

"We need to talk, boy," Dain says, pulling me from dreams of water and fish that nibble at my toes until the flesh is all gone, and they're nothing but bones. Can't be too much more than a few hours since I made it home. Glad I'm not stuck there, but not so happy to wake to those fiery eyes.

I yawn. My body's sore and hot. Should have drawn that bath.

Dain sniffs. "He cut you, Mark?"

I nod. My shirt's stiff and stuck to my back. "Then you will bathe, and then we will talk."

I groan. All that work! Dain pats my arm. "Strangely enough, I appear to have drawn a bath." And I think of him, my Master, drawing a bath. Heating the water in the copper, taking it bucket by bucket and pouring it into the tub. A steady, serious sort of labour for a man like him. "It will go to waste otherwise, and you know how I feel about waste."

I stagger to the bathroom, strip, and sink into the water. It turns a little rusty, and where I was cut, it burns. But then the aches subside, and I'm sinking my head under the water (which tastes of salt) and looking up at the single burning lamp, and wondering if this is at all like the sea in the books I get to read, or is that brown like the river?

Comes a knock at the bathroom door.

"Hurry, boy," Dain says, though there's little hurry in his voice. The night is his.

I'm as reluctant to get out as I was to get in, but I do.

Dain's waiting for me in the kitchen. His face long, his elbows resting against the hard table—Formica, he says. All I know is that it's crooked and old, and he's far too attached to it. "He was from the Red City—the city of iron and dust—not the City in the Shadow of the Mountain, though they sometimes are, that place can turn a bitterness in a man." Dain says that last bit as though it still surprises him. "He told me so much, a flood. But he was addled." He sips a brandy, washing the taint away. Hunter and hunted, both of them been at the drink. Didn't help the hunted, and I'm still hearing that bone crunch. I'd winced at the smell of the grog when I'd poured Dain's glass, hand pinched over my nose until he'd slapped it away.

"Enough of that pantomime! You shouldn't have been there, Mark. Do I not keep you busy enough?"

"Never seen a Hunter there before."

Dain's rage rises. "And you would argue the point? You'd argue it even after a blade's been pressed under your throat?"

"I'm not unacquainted with terrors."

Dain laughs the chillest sort of laugh. I lower my head, and I don't look up until he stops. And there he is, staring.

"So, you've chores a-plenty tomorrow," Dain says, eyes serene unless you know him like I do and can see the rage in him. I keep waiting for the back of that hand. It's been a long time since I was struck, but I know you're never too old for a clip under the ear.

He passes me a list, longer than what I was expecting this morning, and I try not to cringe. He looms over me, all storm front and night lightning. Hairs on the back of my neck try to run off. Instead I get the cold shivers.

"He would have killed you," Dain says.

"I know." I don't look him in the eye. "I didn't see him coming."

"Which is why you do not go there, by that part of the river. The edges of things are deadly."

I shrug.

Big mistake. Do I ever learn my lesson?

He lifts me with one arm as if I weighed nothing, pulls me close to his face. "As much as it pains me to say it, I do not want you dead. You've earned more than that, and the future holds possibility—so, please, do not betray my trust."

There, so close to grinding jaws, eyes death black—all the fire gone out of them—and empty, I find it hard to trust in his affections. I try to speak, and he gives me such a withering look that I do not.

He lets me drop. I land with a whoomph, and by the time I've caught my breath he's gone, and I'm left holding his list. And I remember that tattoo, the spiral. Was going to ask on it, but then, it's nothing. 'Course it is, and I've lots of chores, two days' worth at least. I'll be up with the dawn, visiting homes, gathering ash, bagging it, getting it ready for the train.

Never going to sleep. My head full of things. But back to bed I go. Got to at least try.

And damned if I don't sleep despite it all.

I dream again of Hunters and spirals that gyre up from torn wrists, and catfish.

Wake up hungry for fish.

So I go back out there, and catch that nibbler, and it's not easy, gives as big a fight for its life as I would and no Master to rescue it. Me and the other boys, all six of us, feasting on that plump fella. Dougie, the Parson Boys stick thin and laughing, Grove and Twitcher. Big fish, big party. And I told them my story, but not as I'm telling you, more swagger, less piss in pants. We're Day Boys, we're brave and foolish, and we don't ever let on that we're not.

We shouldn't have been there, but it's the shouldn'ts that are the sweetest.

Shouldn't be monsters. But there are.

———

They worship the Sun *because it is the only god as cruel as them.*

You see it on them, the circle with its radiants. They cannot let the Sun touch them, not without, as they say it, Severe Consequence. But it marks them just the same. The bangles they have fashioned, the tattoos scratched with bone—because it scores permanent—and ash—because it burns permanent—into their cold skin.

Some of them find shame in this fascination; Dain, at times, seems embarrassed. But it doesn't stop him praying to the fire, playing old knuckle bones—carved with the Sun—through his fingers. Fire'll kill them just like sunlight. And ash will burn their skin.

But they love both, even in the heat of the middle summer, cicadas calling and burring, gotta keep that fire lit. Only Kast fears an open flame; says he dreamed of a time when it consumed him.

Keeps an oil burner instead. The other Masters mock him. Dain reckons he's a fool, that the oil's more dangerous than any open flame.

Dain often sits by his fire. Reading, staring into the flames. Don't know what he reads there in the blaze, but his look goes distant. Not predatory, but calm. I could almost imagine him a man, in the way his head tilts, and his fingers tap against his wrists, as though he's playing some musical instrument.

But he isn't a man. Most times there's no mistaking that. Long fingers curving to fists, a lip that will pull tight and reveal the compact mass of cutting teeth beneath. Most times there's no way of forgetting what he is.

Two nights later and things are nearly normal, if they can ever be. I could almost forget what had happened, but the world, as they say, always thinks otherwise. Dain shakes me awake, a gentle touch, but insistent. I open my eyes, squeeze them shut again, in no mood for consciousness. Body heals quickly, or maybe it's that the days pass so slow: There's a cruelty and a tenderness to that. I'm a little sore, but Dain has to wake me because sleep's coming easier again.

Wind's turned cool, shifted west to east, down from Mount Pleasant. The air doesn't quicken the blood, but stills it, and I'm worn out and not happy at the waking. But that doesn't matter.

How I feel doesn't matter. Not really.

Dark eyes regard me; pale, almost luminous skin, like he's part of the moon come down all ghostly to walk amongst us. A sharp-toothed sliver, and like the moon it's aglow with a dark heart. I blink back at that gaze, wipe my crusted eyes.

"Wake. Wake," he says. "We've work to do, boy."

"What?"

"Your answer is always a question, isn't it? A strength and weakness. The correct response is yes."

I don't tell him that he was the one that taught me to do so. I don't think argument would do me well tonight. "Wear your suit," he says. "The good one."

And I know where we're going. Only one place in the night requires that.

"Really?"

"Yes," Dain says. "And if you do not hurry, we will be late, and that will not look good. I've called the Court of the Night to order, and we, most of all, must be seen to take it seriously. You, Mark, you must be seen to take it seriously, so hurry. I've let you sleep too long. I should have woken you early. Now all we have time for is haste, and that is rarely a good thing."

I'm already pulling on my clothes, in that awkward half-asleep way. The suit's only six months old, and it doesn't quite fit across the shoulders, and my wrists poke out, and rupture the formality with skin, tendons and knobs of bone. My right wrist is bruised.

Dain tilts his head, purses his lips, frowns. All hurt to me offends him. All such hurt he feels as his responsibility. Doesn't he get that I'm the one meant to be looking after him?

His eyes drop to my feet.

"Matching socks," Dain says. "Matching socks, if you please, Mark."

I don't please to do anything except fall back into bed and never get up again. But I grunt, squint into my drawer, and make sure my socks square up—how does he know? How can he tell? But he's always right—and that my shoes are shining (after a last bit of spit'n'polish).

"Quick, boy," Dain says.

I was, and I am! Wasn't he watching? "Quick!"

The wind's got up, the sky's clear, and the moon's setting itself to wane. No one's about, but you wouldn't be at this time of night. It can be seen as an open invitation if a Master's in a mood—and they always are, of one sort or another. Moody as the storm-thrashed spring, Dain says, every single one of them. The Night Train's come and gone, not even an echo on the horizon or a beat on the tracks.

Town Hall's on Main, near the square. The Constabulary's part of it, built into the western edge. It's an old white building—far older than the troubles—always smelling of fresh paint. People got pride in this town; as long as there's paint, this hall will be painted.

We aren't the last to the meeting, but we're not the first either, and I can tell that annoys Dain. But he's been tetchy all the last few nights, like a prickle in a sock. Like the one in my sock, the matching one, digging in, and I can't even scratch the bugger.

Two Masters come in late, smelling of blood, eyes as wide as plates, neck veins thick. And the Parson twins are dressed shabby: One of them hasn't even managed to match his shoes. I flash them a grin a touch superior, until Egan gives me a look that would freeze the blood of a normal boy and chills mine right enough.

Five Masters together, in Town Hall. What a dark splendid thing! There hasn't been a meeting in months, and certainly not one that required me or the other boys to be here. The floorboards creak and crack with their footsteps; the gravity of such inhuman men. They can be as light as breath, but here they are weighty. The windows are misting. The Masters are darkness and luminosity, and that shifts, depending on their mood. They're marked with ash-burned Suns, their bangles clatter, and their eyes give out their radiance.

Here they are: Egan, Dain, Sobel, Kast and Tennyson. The uncontested rulers of this town, have been for generations. And there it is in them, that displeasure, the intensity with which I'm considered.

Everyone knows why we're here.

There's five Day Boys looking at me, eyes sticky with sleep. They appreciate this about as much as me, only I'm the one to blame. Even Grove is giving me surly looks.

It's Egan that gets the meeting started, being the senior. Grove stands behind him. Sobel and Dougie to his left. The rest of us around on the other side of the table. Dain has his enemies, even here, even in this small town. And I think what that must be like, to have those enemies, to have them so close across all the centuries. I couldn't bear Dougie for six weeks, let alone a century.

"Time," Egan says, his voice so smooth it could grease a rusted lock. "Gentlemen, it is time. Our dear moon has found her breath at the top of her climb, and now, past pause, she falls."

The room shifts, broadens and narrows like it's grown alive, like it's moved back a ways, but is focusing hard on us. Sometimes the sky feels like that. Dain says that predatory sky's one of the reasons why they need us: You need a monster to keep a monster from the gate. I don't know. But it makes my skin crawl, that gaze, and I'm used to it.

"We are here, we are the room and the walls, we are the table and the chairs, and the air that billows lungs. We are the Court of the Night, called to session by one of our brothers."

They pull chairs from the table and sit, and we stand behind them, perfectly still for a heartbeat or two.

"Dain," Egan says. "You have the floor."

Dain stands silent, eyes cast out to the other four.

"My boy was visited with violence, by a Hunter," Dain says. "You all know this. He was taken out of town, taken to a boat hidden in the south, to be smuggled west. Well, he would have been if I hadn't got there first. I have few memories of such a threat, and they were long ago, at that. Before any of these boys, before the lot that preceded them. Hunters know where our edges are, and they do not cross them. Or they haven't until now." Egan stands, the whole hall shivers, there's a rustling murmur in the air. Dain's hands drop to the table. It creaks beneath his grip; he isn't steadying himself, but the table itself.

With all these Masters here, and words heated, the hall and its objects seem skittish.

"It's a half-truth, an exaggeration and a folly," Egan says. "There are always troublesome elements, those that don't do as they are told. But I think we know who crossed the line." He looks at me direct. All the niceties are undone.

"This was more than troublesome elements." Dain stands steady, but there's an edge to his voice, an effort underlying. "Much more. I believe that we need deeper attention given."

A sound somewhere in the hall; near the kitchen. A door slams. Dain doesn't lift his hands.

Egan grins. "Ah, the Professor and his *deeper study*. The wind blows wrong half a night and you call for it. And you would have us draw the attention of the Council of Teeth? We've tangles enough without that web. It is a small town, our little exile here, surely we can manage such troubles?"

And he says it like Dain is a child, a nuisance to be placated with the barest of kindnesses. There's heat in my face, and it is building. Dain is no fool. They've no right to treat him as such. And then I realise they can speak to him that way because of me, and I feel the shame of it.

Tennyson, Sobel, and Kast are nodding their heads.

Dain seems surprised, or angry, or both. He gestures at the others, palms open; the table shudders, released. But the others just smile. Three faces of open mockery. I can see he knows that he's been ambushed. "When there is an open threat, the Council of Teeth should know. This is Court business."

Egan laughs. "The Council of Teeth complicates everything. Besides, we are its teeth, are we not? Do you think it cares for us as long as we bite?"

"It cares for the Imperatives. It cares that we don't capsize the peace we have, or cast ourselves into the Outer Dark."

Egan's got one of those cat-with-the-cream grins, and I understand the poison of a smile. "As do we all." He turns his all-too-clever eyes to me. "Trouble comes from within, in my experience, not without. Why were you at the river, boy?"

"Wanted to cool my toes." Not the whole truth, but I've no desire to point out previous indiscretions.

"Yes, but that place. You know the dangers of that place."

"Big old catfish there," I say.

"There are catfish in the turns and shadows of any river. That the Hunter found you, suggests you frequent that place forbidden. That he was expecting you."

"I—"

"Don't lie to me, boy. I can see the workings of a lie like the pulse that beats within the prey. You lie to a Master, and you will find a Master's sharp punishment."

I lower my gaze to my hands, they've a bit of a shake in them.

"Look up at me, boy." Of course he would demand that. His eyes are snarled with a cruel, cold grip. I can't look away.

Everything is a plummet, a background noise, a narrowing and falling away. Just those damn eyes.

"You frequent that place?" I can't even tell if he's speaking, or if those eyes are asking.

"Yes."

"In fact, you have been there since, have you not?"

"This is not an interrogation," Dain interrupts, and I can hear the anger in his voice. "We are not here to question the boy."

"Why not?" Egan's gaze slides to Dain, and my heart starts beating again. "*They* will question the boy; the Council of Teeth will be much more demanding. All motives and possibilities will be explored; they are the kings of snares and winding avenues, and one does not rule with threadbare truths. They will grind it down, then build it back up. Boy, why would you seek out such a place? What does a boy do all alone?"

Twitcher sniggers. Dougie winks at me, from behind Sobel, and Grove turns away. Even the Parson twins got big stupid smiles across their faces.

"I was not!"

"So you say." I don't need no eyes directed at me, to feel my cheeks burn. How can such a sweet voice speak so sour? "But you are of age. Your time is nearly upon you, such concerns are the concerns of boys. You seek solitude, the release of crude urges. Perfectly normal, isn't it? Is that what you were doing?"

"I was not!" And I stare back at Egan long as I can. There's a heat to my gaze, and I feel it returned, a flash and the false light of after, and Egan almost turns his head, as though he's forgotten who's the Master. But he hasn't, and I'm the first to break that stare. And I realise that he was just baiting the hook. Egan raises his hand, all calming, almost gentle. "I was mocking you. You're a Day Boy, you should recognise it.

"Mockery is a tool, is it not? So this Hunter came upon you while you were alone?"

"Yes."

"By the reeds he waited, unseen by you."

"Yes."

Egan nods. "I could smell his fear there, and the drink he had taken to drown it. That was a night later, and it was still strong."

"He were drunk, that's for sure."

"And yet you could not evade him? Didn't even notice until he was upon you?"

"Drunk and persistent," I say.

"My boy's skills are not on trial here," Dain says.

"Of course not," Egan says. "Nothing is on trial here. We are just talking. Enjoying the cut and thrust of conversation. Surely, Professor, you are familiar with sophistry. Deception can lead to truth, can it not?"

Dain's jaw juts, his hands press hard against the tabletop, wood groans, but he nods his head.

"Yes."

"Then I shall continue, shall I? If that is all right with you?" Egan looks to me. "So he caught you, and then . . . ?"

"Said he was going to take me away, to his boat. He was taking me as an apprentice, or something like."

"Which is not unheard of. The Hunters are unruly, their ways peculiar. His boat? Did you see this boat? Either of you."

"It had been cut loose," Dain says. "And not by me."

"I don't think he meant what he said. I think he meant to kill me."

"Would that he were still alive," Egan says. "Oh, then we might have a surer idea of his motives."

"I spoke to him," Dain says.

"Did he seek to kill your boy?"

"He was . . . muddled. I don't—"

Egan rises to his full height. Rises up with all that effortless grace. "You don't know? Could I submit that he wasn't a Hunter, but rather a different sort of predator? The sort that enjoys the death of boys. And that he was drunk, and his muddlement was the muddlement of liquor and desires. Did you drink of him?"

"Yes."

"Did you eat?"

"I was enraged."

"Could such rage have muddled you?"

"No."

"Always the scholar. The most rigorous and thoughtful of us all. Except we know that not to be true. We need not even look to your boy to see that. Here, in this mess, is all the evidence we need of your shortcomings. The Hunter is dead. We have no truth, only familiar mysteries. Small-town mysteries. Either there is a conspiracy involving the murder of Day Boys and, by extension, us. Or there is not."

"Which is what we need to know. The answer lies in the City."

"But what other boy has been so threatened? Just yours, one near enough to his last days to know better." Egan smiles. "And you talk so fondly of those that cast us out. As though they hold answers. Do you really trust our tormentors so? Did they not ruin you, as they ruined us?"

Dain's lips grow ever so thin. "They were wise to send me here."

And there we have the enmity between them. Egan never missing the chance to blame Dain, to remind him that they could still be in the City. Dain reminding him it wasn't as simple as that.

"Always so reasonable. Always so respectful. Do not even begin to think that we share your fondness for those in the City, for that Council of Teeth. Do not make that mistake."

"I would never think such a thing of you."

Egan frowns. "Michael, you overstep. The miles are long between here and the City, and the Sun . . . well, you know about the Sun."

Dain almost rises from his chair. The hall is a-creak with the internal pressures. A window rattles in its pane, then stops. The air cools till it's stinging. "You'd threaten me? Stephen?"

There's a slight gasp. Old names. Old names and so publicly spoken.

Egan ignores it, in fact he lifts a hand, all dismissive, but he keeps talking like Dain isn't even there. "No, no! Nothing of the sort." His gaze takes them all in. "And what do you think, my fellows? Yes or no to whimpering and begging for our over-lords' indulgence? Do we crawl on our bellies at the slightest trouble, like snakes to our makers?"

"Nay." There is no need for a second vote. Dain lowers his head.

"This is for us to deal with," Egan says. "As the townfolk cull the deer, so we shall cull those Hunters who dare approach this town. We will extend our territories a little. The fate of our servants is ours to deal with. Let these Hunters seek out others, not little boys who should know better. Now, there are other matters to attend to. The ridge is to be made off-limits to all those of mortal blood. As is the river east of the last turn, as it always was. Do I need to remind you that our word is law, boys? Well, do I?"

"No, Master," we chorus.

He looks at me, belts away my breath again, and all I am is a bird, caught in fingers that could crush it. "There's some I be-lieve less than others. But we shall see."

The meeting lasts a full hour before we're out, and deep in that summer night, low clouds passing over. And the other boys and their Masters heading to their homes. Just me and Dain walking together in the dark.

"Overindulgent," Dain grumbles. "Overindulgent, says he, standing shoulder to shoulder with the Master of Thuggery. I've long known he's no patience with Sobel, and yet he hurls that at me. Bad blood's rising between us again, so be it. And the rest . . . Fools, every single one of them. May the Sea take them all. There's new webs in the making, so you best look out for spiders." He clenches his fists, looks east to Mount Pleasance, and growls. "This isn't an ending, boy, this is a beginning. To bed with you. There's work in the morning."

I take a step towards the house, and his hands fall upon my shoulders, and he turns me to him, crouching low, like he did when I was younger, scarcely out of napkins. When Dav was around, teaching me the tricks, keeping me on my toes.

"You be careful now," Dain warns. "Eyes are watching, waiting for you to fail. You've enemies. We've enemies here in this town."

"We ever had friends?"

Dain laughs. "No. But I feel I've grown complacent. Careful, you must tread as careful as a fly on the web."

"I will," I say.

Dain laughs again, and it is like the cold wind running before a summer storm, a blessed relief and a threat, too. "Oh, if I could believe it!"

The last of the clouds gives out and the sky is bright above us. We stand in the dark awhile, looking up.

"You know, the stars were less bright once. We dulled them with our own bright works. Light was a pollution, can you believe it?" Then he is rising, and walking into the brilliance of the night (for there's hours of it still ahead), and I'm stumbling back to my bed, where I know sleep has been kicked clear to the next town away, and all that remains is a ragged thread of cruel, dark-eyed dreams and a wind that blows to the west, hard and fast and gossipy.

———

All I remember is Dain.

Nah, that's not true. There's a grey fuzz of memory; a before, but it ends pretty quick. Dain's worn the memory from me, taken the pain of those first few years. Eight years with Dain; first two with Dav as well. Before that, no faces. Just a warmth, a smile, the smell of some summer flower that I can't quite place.

Dain took me as all Day Boys are took—well, except City boys raised in the Crèche or the Academy—a fairy-tale snatching. Dain reads me them sometimes: those stories from Grimm and Andersen. Some child snatched from some distant town, a bed left empty—and me to never know which one. But why should I? That is just how it is. And when the world thinks otherwise, it'll tell you.

People fear the Masters. Fear them more than the Imperatives of Truth they lay down for us to follow. Dain says that's how he knows my kind are weak. He'll ruffle my hair with those cold hands of his as he says it, even say fondly: I was the same, Mark. I was just the same. It's how we rule, through human weakness.

Of course, there's more to it than that.

There's three councils of Law in the land. The Day Council, the Court of the Night, and the Council of Teeth. The Day is for roads, and civil laws—every community has one. There's always one of us there, once a week, except in emergencies—and there are a few of those each year, fires, plagues and whatnot. The Court of the Night is the Masters, once a month it's run, and by a different Master each time. It's a court of blood and promises, and those things which the

Day Council can't decide. Then there's the Council of Teeth that rules from afar. It's the Sun and the moon. It's the proclamations that appear, mysterious, on pillar and post.

It's the Imperatives, it's the voice of the wind, and the dark reason behind it.

And it's the auditors that are sent to pass on night's justice deep into the day.

Kast the Storm

Those Parson boys. They're always snapping at each other, brothers scratching and chasing each other's tails. Dougie fights dirty, but those boys are crueler to each other than you could imagine, a big tangle of cruelty and love in the way they'll look out for the other, or finish a sentence, racing and rushing to make sure that their twin doesn't fall. That's how those Parson boys are.

Gotta respect that, and fear it, too. They could easily run this town, if it weren't for Grove's strength and Dougie's guile.

And this is how they tell Kast's story.

It was a storm. Big one. One of those big ones.
Maybe the biggest.

> *Definitely the biggest, worse even than that storm a*
> *year back. Worse even than that fella.*

Maybe.

> *Lightning thrown across the sky in sheets. Lightning*
> *that lasted. No little flash, but a sky-bright-burn. I've*
> *never seen such a thing.*

Me neither.

It was a storm.

He had fought for it.

*He had fought for his family. He had done all right.
But wasn't a time for all rights. Was a lean time, a
storm-thrashed time.*

And his family died. He was—

Was burying his sons.

They'd sickened.

*The Angry Gods had come, and made them
dance and die.*

*And he was the last, and weak, and sickly himself,
but he took up that shovel, and dug. Bent his back
to the labour of his grief.*

*He buried them in that storm. Shovel biting the
earth, hard and dry, then soft and sticky as the rain
fell. He'd bundled them in sheets, and towels.*

Both of them.

He was sad.

'Course he was.

But he was angrier than that storm.

*Angry like that storm, in fire and rage and mad-
ness. Angry and wanting death.*

The world bubbled and spat and fell.

He brought his boys down into the liquid earth. He buried their flesh and their bones, and the world cut its fire and shadow around him. And when he was done, panting and weary, the Dark whispered in his ear. The Dark brought its teeth. The Dark bit.

They say the Change is easy for some. Wasn't easy for him. He fought it.

Let me tell this story.

He fought it. He raged against it. But rage is nothing to the new blood, the new birth, and what's rage when your boys are dead? What's rage to a storm? A storm laughs at your rage, and the biting Dark laughs with it.

Was a while he walked the earth, buried himself when the sun came up. But he took to the roads. He took to the roads, and he wasn't all cruel.

The Imperatives bound him, even then.

If I hadn't been all busy yawning and grumbling under my breath, I'd have seen it before it hit me. Might have been able to duck, but no. I fell on my bum, blinking, and the missile bounced off me and rolled away. I'm up quick, and there's a laugh not too far away, a laugh I know well. One that brings a bit of heat to my face.

"Very funny," I yell, eyes scanning the trees on the edge of the property, rubbing my head where the half-ripe peach struck it.

A small shape drops from the tree nearest, as light-footed as she's deadly with a peach. She's holding another and grinning, fierce as any Day Boy.

Takes a bite. "Thought you'd fancy some breakfast," she says between crunches.

"No time for playing, Anne."

Anne throws the peach at me. This time I'm ready, but it nearly gets me regardless. "Won't be brushed off by the likes of you," she says.

She's a hard one to cross, and a friend as good as any I got. Mary's daughter. Mary who owns the grocery. Whom I need to visit this afternoon, because I need milk because ours has gone off. Always forgetting the milk. Anne's da, no one talks about him.

I shrug. "Master's got me chored to the teeth today," I say.

"No time for fishing then?"

"You at school today?"

She glares at me. "If I was at school, would I be here?"

I shake my head. "No time."

"You want a hand?"

Give another shrug. But she's already gunning for the gutter, clambering up the ladder and onto the roof faster than me. "These won't clean themselves."

"Don't you fall," I say.

"Falling's the best thing!" Anne says.

I clear my throat. "I don't want Mary coming after me."

Anne's head juts over the roof, eyes that trip me up and make me fall myself. "And she would, you know. My ma's got a backbone all right."

Two people that Dain doesn't ever get me to mark their doors. Certain's one of them, Mary's the other. I know Dain visits her, but I don't draw the seven at all there. He says they have other arrangements.

I don't know what her ma thinks about her coming and helping: probably take a dim view on it. But Anne's her own girl, no Master to lord it over her. I like her. I don't know if she likes me.

A handful of leaves finds my head, and then another. "I can take down that ladder," I say.

"And I'll just jump on your head. Thick enough from all accounts."

Yeah, yeah, she's right. Chores are easier shared. If she wants to share them with me, I'm not fighting her. And she's good: She's a worker. She can hold a tune, too, and I like listening to her sing. Sometimes I like watching her sing when she don't think I am: I don't think I've ever known such earnestness.

We're done with those gutters in under an hour, and a good thing, too, because the sun's fierce this morning. Then there's the lawn, and the garden and the raking, and the verandah to be swept and cleared. By the time we're done, the sun's well past noon. And we're lying on the grass in the shade of those leafy trees, looking at the clouds, and I've pulled two cool drinks from the cellar. Anne won't go down there with me, she thinks it's where Dain is sleeping, and I won't make her no wiser. Some lines I won't cross for no one, no matter how much I might want to impress. Besides, Anne's stronger and mostly tougher than me: It's nice to show a bit of bravery to her.

Sweet cider, a blue sky streaked with clouds and the smell of fresh-cut grass.

"Useless, you Day Boys. Tits on a bull," Anne says, drinking deep. Eyes fixed on me.

"You know it," I say. A bit stung.

"Never understood why there weren't Day Girls."

"Same as why there aren't woman Masters."

"Mistresses," Anne corrects. I wince, feel heat in my face, hotter than the day.

"The women come out all crooked; it breaks them, burns 'em up. Girls is a bit different, Dain says."

Anne puts her glass down, brings her face close to mine. I swallow; try not breathe her in. Try not to look like it anyway.

My skin prickles, my head is light, like I could just float into that blue sky.

"You know what I think?" she asks.

"I guess I will in a moment."

"I think they're frightened of us. And . . ." I look in her eyes, dark as the sky in the middle of the night. "They should be."

She smiles, touches my nose with a finger, swings back from me and picks up her drink. The day's slowed. My heart's beating hardly at all, I reckon. I take a breath, and another. I can feel her so close, a thousand miles away.

"Nearly was killed last week," I say.

Anne frowns. "You been annoying Master Dain again?"

"Again?"

"You're trouble and everyone knows it," Anne says. "Only a matter of time till you're et, if not by him, then one of the others."

I laugh, low and easy. "Who says?"

"No one." Anne's lips thin. "Maybe Sally Dalton."

"Sally Dalton don't even know me." Feel my cheeks go hot all over again.

"Makes big enough eyes at you."

"Never seen that," I say, though I probably have. We're Day Boys, we expect big eyes. "She's most likely right, but . . . No, it weren't Dain, but a Hunter."

"From the City? You wandering where you shouldn't be."

"Where else?" I take another swig. Drag a finger across my neck. "He was going to slit my throat."

"And you're sitting here all calm."

"Dain saved me, but not that I needed him. Cool as this cider I was."

Anne snorts, and I know I've taken it one brag too far.

I pull out a ciggie and offer her one, and her face falls. "That'll kill ya just as good as any Hunter."

"Nothing going to kill me," I say. "Not Hunter, certainly not plain old smoke."

"You're a damn fool," she says.

"Maybe I am." But I put the ciggie away.

"There's never any maybes with you," she says. "Sun and Sea take you!"

And I don't know how to feel about her anger.

No time for reflection anyway because just then the world thinks otherwise. A green ant stings my arse. They've got a damn lot of venom in them, and I'm up and jigging like a maniac trying to get the bloody thing out of my shorts. Not the way to impress a lady. Not even close. Anne leaves me to my misery, her laughter stinging even more.

I didn't even get a chance to thank her for her work. Just watch her leave with a tightness in my belly, and my skin turning dull and tired.

———

Soon he'll have to make a decision, and my thoughts don't come into it.

Put me out into the town, or out of the town altogether, and have me trained for other work or draw me up to become what he is. Send me to the City in the Shadow of the Mountain to learn my lessons, a year or two, then into the Change. But that's a most unlikely option. I'm no Dav. Even I know my edges are too rough. So more than one option; that's something, I guess. But knowing it only adds to the uncertainty: the pain in the belly and the prickle under the skin. I doubt there's much likelihood of the Change being offered. And if he's intent on sending me away, well, he should have just let the Hunter have me.

I've known what I was since I could know such things. And now I don't. There's a deal of hurt in that.

I don't know what I want. I guess I don't want anything much, but the choice isn't mine to make. I would have nothing change, but the older I get, the more I see it. Everything changes, whether I want it to or not.

Dain raised me. And he didn't raise me stupid. It wasn't just facts he hammered into my skull.

There's a wind blowing in after the night, hot from the west and whispering when Certain comes to visit, Petri waiting outside like the good dog she is. Certain doesn't always spend his time on the farm, and he's good mates with Dain. He's an Old Boy, one of them who was once a Day Boy but didn't take, wasn't offered, the Change. Certain was allowed to live on the edge of town, given land and an occupation. If it rubs him the wrong way, he doesn't show it. We don't get many visitors; it's usually Dain that does the visiting.

Certain's arms are long and ropey. His smile a thin slash that you'd be hard to see as warmth. He is wide across the chest, but he limps, favours his left leg more than his right: You can see the scar a quarter-inch above the knee if you look hard enough.

"World tackles you, boy," he'd told me once when I stared too long. "Sometimes you get up fine, sometimes you get up a little broke."

I've had my share of breaks.

"Here to see your Master," Certain says, standing at the door, and he's dressed up a little. Shirt and long pants, shoes that are too long gone for buffing to bring out much good in them, but they're cracked and comfortable.

"Business or pleasure?"

"Bit of both. Mainly for that whisky sour he's got, I guess. You do have lemons, don't you? Sugar?"

I don't understand whisky, tried it once and it made me sick. Give me a cider any day. I pull a face.

"You can come in, I guess."

"He out, is he?"

"Not fer much longer."

I pour him a glass of that rough stuff, squeeze in some lemon juice.

Certain raises his glass, peers at me through it. "Could do with some ice." So I'm down to the cellar and the ice chest. Shaving bits off the old brick down there. Bring him back his glass.

He takes a good long sip. "That's the stuff," he says. Leans back in his chair. "You given much thought to your what-comes-afters?"

"What do you think?" I ask.

"I think time's moving fast. My last years did. Faster than I'd ever thought they could."

"I'll be all right," I say.

"Keep to that thought. Hold it, and you might just be. There's coming a time when you'll make decisions, even if it don't feel like you are. What kind of man you'll be. Or perhaps not a man."

I snort. "No chance of that."

Certain rattles the ice in his glass. "More peculiar things have happened. Man or monster. There's different types of both."

"I'll decide," I say.

"Funny thing is, you never stop deciding. Never wanted to stay in this town, but that's the way it turned out. And I've found I'm glad of the fact." He takes another sip. "Right now, you are what your Master decides, but one day . . ." Certain looks into his glass. "This is empty. A refill, if you please."

Like I have a choice in that!

⸺

"You weren't the only one here today. And I'm not talking about our evening caller," Dain says, an hour after he's finished his drinking with Certain, not even noticing the verandah, but you can bet he would have if I hadn't tidied it.

"Just me and Anne."

Dain frowns. "You are not to consort with the child."

He don't like it, and neither does Mary, though she's polite enough with me.

"I don't consort with no one, she helped with my chores."

"She should be at school, not with you. And I think her mother would agree."

"I don't encourage it." I fold my arms. Dain raises an eyebrow.

"Your mere presence encourages trouble. You're a beacon for it, boy. Trouble sees you as it comes down off Mount Pleasant, and it gets a little jump in its step," Dain says, but not without some fondness today. He ruffles my hair, and my scalp tingles with the cold touch of him.

He bends down to my height, and I can see the dark of his eyes, and the ring of fire they contain, the only thing that separates the pupil from the outer dark—his kind don't have no whites of the eye. That ring's burning bright.

"She is not to come around here, by which I mean, you're

78

not to encourage it. As in, you are to discourage it. Understood?" He says it in a tone that has no room for argument, which is his tone most times, so I don't argue. Too tired for it, tonight.

Doesn't mean I'm going to do what he says.

———

Sometimes you'll hear the rumble of a distant machinery. Once I saw a shape fly overhead, rigid, not a bird. Moved as fast as it was still.

From the City, Dougie said matter-of-fact when I told him . . .

I believed him, but it could have just as well been a dream of a sky that had once been crowded with such things aeronautical. The world remembers everything, and sometimes those memories bump up against the now. The past haunts everything. The Before was before, but it's also now.

What happens to Day Boys gone old? Just what they tell us. We never see it, not Dav nor the other ones I remember, Peter and Sil, and Craver. Other Masters pass through, boys do on occasion as well. But they're from different towns, same Imperatives, different rules. Certain is the only Old Boy I know of. But he's a quieter sort.

I don't know where Peter is. Or Sil. They were old when I was young. Moderates in their way, they didn't treat me bad. They sighed and sang, they ruled in ways louder than any of us.

Dougie often says they were real boys, gentlemen. And we'll not see their like again—which is funny coming from him.

Wherever they are, they are gone. Sent south or north, or deep into the belly of the Mountain. Grown into Masters or auditors or constables.

Or maybe they're buried somewhere just out of town.

Nothing comes of that hot west wind. Nothing that I can see, and the town settles in the heat, in the dust, and the slow passage of the summer. Nothing happening until it does.

Back from marking another door, I catch Dougie smashing at Grove's bike, kicking it to bits, his hat wobbling on his head. Have to try not to laugh. Still too sore for fighting. Always been something scratchy between him and Grove, but this time my mate must have done something particularly sour. Thing with Grove is, he probably wouldn't have even noticed it. Dougie's a boy of sensitivities. Grove's Master being the most senior rankles him.

"Don't you tell him," Dougie says to me, boots bending frame and breaking gears.

"I won't." I don't know what's going on, but I know enough that Dougie needs this. Sometimes the right thing's not the right thing at all. And Dougie's near the top of the tree, and it's sure not my place to challenge him. Not in this. The past binds all of us together. Done stuff together, sat in our Masters' halls and made faces. They sleep heavy, and you can get away with a lot. Sure we're respectful, but we're Day Boys, got limits to stretch. And Dougie and his Master Sobel possess the cruelest sentiments.

"Grove finds this out, he'll be coming for you."

Dougie laughs. "What do you think I am? Stupid or something?" He drags the bike behind the shrubs on Marriott Street. Grove'll find it. "But you ain't gonna tell him, and neither am I."

I'm with Grove when he finds his bike, didn't mean to be, but the world wanted otherwise. He frowns and shrugs. Can see he's hurt, but he hides it well.

"Not the end of the world," I say, and he almost laughs.

Not quite. Still, he says the words. "*Cause that's already happened. You'll help me fix it?*"

"'Course," I say.

It isn't so much fixing as remaking, but we get it done.

Grove mostly, but he calls me when he needs a hand.

And when you fix a bike, you have to ride it. Don't you? And you have to give it a good ride, test it out. And if you don't, it'll sit there looking sad. Expectant. Until you do.

Two days of rain, and we don't have the chance. I'm talking real rain, the stuff that slides in from the south of a summer and just dumps until the river starts looking wild and white-edged and breaks its banks a little or a lot. So that's how anxious Grove is to ride it.

And I can't blame him. Since its ruin and resurrection, it's grown a damn sight more impressive. He's painted flames down one side, there's a new set of gears and tires that Egan brought in special for him from the City in the Shadow of the Mountain.

I've trouble keeping up, down Main, and as we start on the steady slope, it only gets harder. But I can't bear Grove no ill will.

Grove's just what he is. There's something about him to make a girl swoon, or a boy if that's his taste. Grove does something and you want to do it, too. Makes anything seem possible. He cut his hair finger-length short a few years back, and we were all doing it a week later. He's a good boy in his way, can smile himself out of trouble with that wide grin he has—see, not every smile's an arrow pointed at disaster.

Grove doesn't do the things we do. Grove works harder for his Master than any of us, he won't be at smoking or fighting—though he's plenty of fight in him. And he can give you such a look of sad disappointment when you do, you feel it for near half a day. I've had whole afternoons ruined by that frown. Only afternoons, mind. I'm not Grove.

Mary has a fond spot for the boy, says his heart's big enough for all of us. I reckon it's easy enough to have a big heart when you're a fella like Grove, when everything comes easy to you.

We pass Sally Dalton coming home from the schoolyard. She waves, but I don't stop. Thinking about her thinking about my end of days. Still I give her the brightest smile I have—pure dazzlement. And there's boys, too, walking back from the yard, watching us with wide eyes. Sometimes I forget they exist, these other boys, normal lads who don't have Masters but mums, dads. We don't mix, they seem timid things to us. They're not, not really, they just don't have the freedom of brazenness. They pay a higher price and they pay it in blood. They never get the heights we have, they're not driven to them. It's just the steady beat of their lives and their quiet dreams. I wonder if I can dream like them? Could be I'll find out soon enough.

Grove's laughing as we hit Wembley Road heading out of town. And I'm laughing, too, coming onto another edge of our Masters' domain.

We ride on a bit to where the road thins and becomes a trail. They say it used to broaden, but it doesn't anymore. The Masters don't encourage travel; only tolerate it along the line, on the Night Train to the Red City, the Mountain or the coast.

So the trail's rough going, but our bikes can handle it, till we get to the part where the ground softens, grows silty and wheel-sucking, and we sit on our bikes there beyond the edge of the town, sweating and panting.

Midfield behind us, next to nothing but scrub and plains ahead. The old rotting wood of the Patterson Yards—used to be cattle there, now there's just termite mounds and fence posts sagging. There's roos in the distance, tracking the shade. Keeping out of the sun.

Grove frowns, starts to look a bit green, and then I catch it. The stink of death.

We know enough of that to recognise it right away.

Off those bikes we get and follow the scent like two hounds, hesitant because we know what's at the source, or at least part of it. Every death's a damn story, even when it's not your own. And every death can lead to another.

We find a clearing a short walk from the trail, and there's a shallow grave that some dingo or fox has dug up, unmarked but by the hunger of beasts. We catch bits of flesh and bone, and the boil of ants and maggots that dead things draw. Something's had a good chew. Almost could imagine a bear. But there's no bears in this country of ours, other than the slow sort that sit small and grunting in the trees at night, and chew on leaves. Dougie reckons otherwise, says there was zoos and circuses, and the bears and the like got out, but I've seen not a-one of them.

Would like to. A bear now, or a tiger, what a thing to see. "Rain's been heavy, and the wind's been blowing the wrong way, or we'd not be the first to find it," Grove says.

"Not for us to dig it up. Wind's turning."

"Yeah, so when the Masters find it, they scent us, too, right? We need to get the word out, take responsibility for the finding." Grove isn't one for slinking around anyway, but there's a slyness to his thinking now that gives me a new bit of respect for him.

"What, you reckon there's killers amongst us?" We both laugh. 'Course there are!

Grove gives me a look. "You thinking on killing me?"

I pat my chest. "Got a knife on me here somewhere."

There's a growling in the undergrowth, deep and low. And none too distant. Grove and me aren't laughing anymore, we're bolting back to our bikes. Something heavy moves slow behind us. I get the feeling it could catch us up in a few big steps, and I can't help myself, I look back at where we've been, still running, but gawking, too. I don't catch nothing but a darkness moving between trees, moving away.

"Watch it," Grove says. Cause I've nearly hit him from behind. Then we're on the bikes and round the bend, and there's no looking back.

We're back on Main before we stop, and even then it's only because we nearly collide. I hit a bump, end up arse over tit on my back, and panting.

"You right?" Grove says. Big hand reaching down to help me up.

I squint at him, winded a bit. "Right," I manage.

"Just a dog," Grove says.

"A dog from Hell."

"Just a plain and simple dog. Maybe Certain's."

"Petri don't growl like that," I say. "Been chased out his farm enough times to know that."

"Just a grumpy old dog," Grove says. "If that's what you reckon."

"'S what I know."

We're to Town Hall. The constable there squints at the pair of us. Name of Mick Jones, he don't like me much, but there you go. He's laughing at some sort of joke. He laughs a lot, but he stops when he sees us.

"You two look like ghosts."

"Seen a shallow grave out near the Patterson Yards," Grove says.

Mick gets out of his chair. He's a big fella, bald head spotted with the sun, has a long knife strapped to his belt.

"You boys gonna show me?" We nod.

"You disturb anything?" We shake our heads.

"Something out there," Grove says. "Something that growled. Not that we would have poked around anyway, but we for damn sure didn't hang around."

Mick juts out his bottom lip. "Growled, you say?"

He jangles some keys in his pockets. Walks in the room behind. Comes back with a rifle and a shovel. Flat-headed.

"You didn't see this, boys." Guns aren't exactly banned, but they're not encouraged. Maybe seen three of them before, outside of the deer hunt, all owned by auditors, come in from hunting vagrants and the like.

"See what?" Grove says. I blink and look at him. That's a sight more subtle than Grove usually gets. Mick reaches out to ruffle his hair. Stops mid-movement, realises what he's doing. Pulls his hand back, and laughs deep and low.

"Exactly," Mick says. "Exactly."

Mick on his horse Charliegirl, us on our bikes, back the way we came. Mick doesn't say a word, except some low whispers to Charliegirl. This time we can smell it long before we see it, like we're attuned. The horse gets skittish and eye-rollery, but she keeps going, and Mick's whispering gets louder. All *It's OK, girl* and *Settle darlin', settle*.

We reach the edge of the road, and Mick drops to the ground.

"You boys stay back," Mick says. "I don't want none of you in this."

We stay on our bikes.

Mick grabs the shovel and the rifle. Walks to the grave, looks down, and something big and dark comes rushing at him. Mick's fast. Fella knows how to shoot, was City-trained. He lifts that rifle and fires. Once and twice. And the big thing's howling and dropped on the ground. Mick's face is white, he aims careful and fires one more time, and it's silent. Stops moving.

And I get the feeling that we're at the end of another story, that it ended bad, and tragic. And that its coming into ours was only to falter and die.

Maybe all stories end that way.

Mick sniffs, spits at his feet. "You all right, boys?" We don't say nothing, he can see we're all right.

He pushes the dog aside with a boot. Then makes gentle work with the shovel. A hiss of breath comes out of him when he uncovers them.

"Is that a babe?" Grove asks. "Is that a woman holding a babe all dead in that earth?"

"You boys go on home," Mick says. But we don't move.

"I said go." There's a hardness to his voice, but he gentles it quick. "You've work to do for your Masters. And I've work to do here. Stop on by the hall and send Jane out to me. Tell her to bring her gear. She'll know what I mean."

We hover there, looking at his work. "Don't try my patience!"

And we're on our bikes and riding.

———

Dain wakes me that night. "I heard what you did, and what you found," he says. "You should have told me."

I shrug, sleepy-eyed.

"The world scars you ten times more if you hold such things inside. If you don't share them."

Says the man who doesn't give away a thing.

"We found a shallow grave," I say. And all the time I'm thinking that we wouldn't have if it weren't for Dougie busting up Grove's bike. And I'm thinking I'd like to bust up Dougie right now. But I know how that ends.

"You found a mother and child," Dain says. "You found their corpses. It is a terrible thing."

"Will you find who did it?"

Dain shakes his head. "They're long gone. Not even the auditors could find them now."

"So they're not here?"

"No, murderers of this sort fear our kind too much to linger." Dain lowers himself onto the end of the bed. "But not enough to stop them from doing this. A mother and a babe, and the mother scarcely more than a child herself. This is a dark place made darker by monsters and fools."

Dain touches my hair, quick and light. "But we are still a part of it." He sighs. "I better get back to my book."

Feels Dain's been writing that book since forever. I asked him once if it were about those last days, when words were powerful.

He just laughed. "Words were powerful, yes. Lightning quick. And judgments flickered across the earth. In those last days, we had screens that we drowned in. They led everywhere, but mostly we only saw our own reflection in them. And then the dreams changed, and then they stopped being dreams.

"Mark, I sometimes wonder . . . if that isn't true. If I just never woke. But then why would I dream of you?"

Well—why wouldn't he?

Two days later, there's visitors that come from Hadentown in a cart horse-drawn. Two men: thin, armed with knives. They come at noon, to Town Hall. Mick's waiting, and he guides them inside. They leave almost at once—their faces dark and heavy. Two small coffins set on the back. One of the men doesn't bother hiding his tears, and it's a hard thing to see.

I'm there gawping with Dougie: The fella knows where the action is. Called me to it, from my work at the Sewills'.

Mick glares at us. "You two, move on." We do—if a trifle slow.

"There was a woman missing from Hadentown. Woman and a baby," Dougie tells me, because Dougie knows most of anything, and when he's in a good mood, he's fine company. Likes to gossip as much as destroy bikes or lay his fists upon you.

"What's it all mean?" I wonder.

Dougie looks at me. "Means there's a murderer about. Or there was." He shrugs. "Maybe it doesn't mean anything, but the world's a damn awful cruel place."

———

Dain's not from here. He wasn't born to this town. I don't know where he came from, some other place of the before here-nows. But he was tenured to the university in the City in the Shadow of the Mountain. I've asked him why he isn't working there still.

And he said the place was a poison and a joy. But the poison was worse. So he left, was assigned, or banished (depending on his mood), to Midfield. His kind don't get much of a choice in where they're sent. But he says he still loves the place, that it suits him more than he would have believed. The City must be fed, and it is the Masters who ensure it is. Who keep the manufactories running, who keep away the other monsters that bleed the towns, as the townsfolk themselves are bled.

But I know he misses his books. I know he misses the conversations. The Grand Conversation, he said, that is the confluence of all that thought. I asked him once if he was afraid to go back, or that they might make him go back. "My people are cruel," he says, "but it's a clever cruelty. I know it; I possess it, too. It would do them no service to bring me back, I was too good at the game. It was why I left."

That's about the best answer I got. Never quite understood what the game was, when he told me this. But I think I do now, having been a piece in it.

Part Two

Country Mice

Of All the Sins Beneath Lord Sun
Of All the Sinners, the Worst, They Run.

It's a month since that Hunter's knife. The wound don't pull so much now. And the sting and the shame of that meeting is dulling. Been a week since me and Grove found that shallow grave. Dain looks me over, sends me protesting for a haircut, and tells me I'm to wash. He has suitcases packed in his room. And a note for me to take them down to the front room. They're heavy, but I get them down those stairs.

Another note says, *Pack for hot and cold, and four days at least.*

I don't have much, but I pack my best. The long-sleeved shirts and the vest. And a cap that Dain gave me last year on my birthday with *NYC* embroidered on its face.

That night he wakes me. Big bright moon in the sky.

"Up, boy, up. We don't have much time." He's holding his bags like they're light as air, not a single hint of strain. The bags themselves creak and grumble like all things when the Masters touch them; they quicken—not quite alive.

"Where we going?"

"You know where we're going," he says. And my heart races. I know. I know. The City in the Shadow of the Mountain.

The city of them. The city of the Masters. Only two places we'd ever go. The City or the sea. Never been to either. And now.

"Best fetch my comb," I say.

He ruffles my hair. "I've packed it for you already."

We're quick to the center of town, and the station.

There's folk already waiting. Certain nods at us, Petri at heel. There's men and women, getting wagons ready. The Parson twins are waiting for a barrel of oil for Kast's burner. They scowl and growl at me, and I give them a good scowl right back, and Dain clips me under the ear—how that sets them laughing. Mary's there with a list long as her arm. Supplies coming in.

"Shipment of paper expected for you, Master Dain," she says.

Dain nods. "I'll send the boy for it as soon as we get back."

"Make sure there's plenty of sweets," I tell her.

Dain's taken his bags, and is talking low to Certain.

Petri's rolled onto her back, and Dain scratches her belly.

"I would if people paid for them rather than just slipping them in their mouth," she says.

"I'm no thief," I say, puffing up my chest.

"No, a thief'd get away with it."

Anne's there, too, and she laughs, until Mary gives her a hard look. And I know I best step careful. Think of it as practice for where I'm going. Mary gets called over to Mr. Stevens, Anne doesn't follow. She's about the most wonderful thing I've ever seen today, she's more radiant than that moon, and her eyes are darker than the sky between the stars. And then she grins.

A smile with an edge like glass. "Off to the City, I am," I say.

Anne nods. "Explains why your hair's combed flat like a wet carpet. Look like a lost country boy who hardly knows what end of a brush to use."

Heat in my face, and my words all drop to my feet, no good to me there.

There's a shrill whistle in the near distance. A building cry of machinery at furious work.

"I—"

"'Course, that's what you are," Anne says. "Be careful in that dark city, they've little liking of country boys except their blood. But there will be music," and her eyes have taken a far-away cast, and I feel the strangest jealousy till she's gazing at me again. "Find the music for me, Mark, and when you do, close your eyes, and think of me."

"I—"

"Yes, I know you will." Then she's off talking to her Ma, looking down the list, and I'm watching her, my blood running hot and cold, and faster than it was.

"What did I say about her?" Dain places the bags at my boots. "When will you listen to me?"

"I listen all the time."

"Schoolyard semantics invite a schoolboy caning," he says, and I wince, but he's smiling again. "No one likes a smart mouth, Mark. Particularly when it is not nearly as clever as it thinks it is."

My mouth's been all types of stupid today. But I'm wise enough to keep it closed for a while after that.

Night Train comes into town all a-racket, brakes screaming out their halt. Mr. Stevens stands watching from a distance, comes over and talks to the driver. Dark shapes dart from carriage top to carriage top. Fish all covered in ice are taken from the rear cars. Bags of grain loaded into the car next over. Manifests are signed off, and trades accounted for. It's a few mad minutes of frenzied industry.

A fella, a Master I don't know, drops lightly from the roof of the nearest carriage, dressed in a long coat, a fedora on his head. "You got your tickets?"

We're the only folk heading to the City from Midfield.

"Of course I have, Frederick," Dain says. "Have you ever known me not to follow protocol?"

The Ticket Master laughs. But he inspects Dain's papers and checks me, too. He holds my jaw, tilts my head and peers into my eyes like he's looking into my skull. Not much in there. Not much at all. Just music, and the way Anne walked to her mum, like she knew I was watching.

The Ticket Master's eyes narrow.

"Frederick!" Dain glares at him, hard as a glare can be.

"Never be too careful," Frederick says. "Could be strung up with bombs."

"The time of bombs is past. He's mine," Dain says.

"Sorry, Professor," the Ticket Master says, without a hint of sorry, and tips his hat, and picks up Dain's bag. Mr. Stevens is already running back to his tower, and a bell starts ringing, and the engines are building up steam.

The nearest door opens, and we step into the train. Me in a train; in the Night Train at that! There's a long hallway that runs down the carriage's belly, rooms closed tight. Though there's noises, music and cries, and laughter. I stop at one door where a fine tune's playing, fiddles and what sounds like a guitar. Music's a bait that catches me, already thinking of Anne's instructions. I put my head against the door.

Dain clips me under the ear. "Keep moving, boy."

We find our room. A bench chair and a bed. I sit down, and the train starts moving, slow at first, but faster with each clack of the wheels. So fast that the dark slides by, and the town with it. And the night's in motion all around us, as though it's drawing the train on and pushing it away. In a few minutes we're farther from home than I've been in my whole life. Farther away from Anne. And I'm feeling a gloom settle in me.

"Boy, listen to me, now," Dain says. "And watch." He taps the bed in three places, and it opens. There's a man-sized space beneath, dark and narrow.

"Just so you know. Not that I need to use it this time, we'll be there before dawn," Dain says. "I've rooms at my old university. But I will take you around the city, too. It is time you knew it better, knew the options that await you, low and high. You'll see little of me for much of the trip. I've errands to run. There is some research I need to engage in concerning this book."

"Well, you'll have plenty of paper for when you get back," I say.

Dain looks at me. "Is that mockery I hear?"

I shake my head. "Will we be there too long?"

"Put away that sad face, we'll be home soon enough. Don't you want to see the city?"

Of course I do! Who wouldn't?

Dain rings a bell and a man comes, hair cut short, tattoos of the Sun on his wrists.

He's all politeness, can't tell if that's truly him or the job. "Take Mark here to the library," Dain says. "He's to have one book, and nothing salacious. And do you have any broadsheets?"

The fella nods. "I'll bring them back with the boy." He takes me down the long corridor that runs through the Night Train.

I feel like I'm in the belly of a snake. We pass locked doors. Behind them I can hear crying, or prayers to gods that I don't know. Old ones, though not as old as the Sun. And there's that music again.

The man frowns when I stop to listen.

"Hurry, young bloke," he says. "We've no time for loitering. These are folk just like you, headed for the Mountain or the Red City that surrounds it. First rule of that place worth practising: Never seem to take an interest in anything; study everything real close."

These might be regular folk, but they're not like me. Well, most of them at any rate. They're not Day Boys. But I do what he says. Been in enough trouble lately.

Finally, we come to the library. Oh, I've never seen anything like this. Books and books and books! There's a dozen shelves of them. Books on everything. I run my fingers over their spines. Some are cracked, some don't even look like they've ever been opened.

"You'll like these ones." The man gestures towards one wall. "They're the stories."

I pick one about a boy and a dragon, or a thing that seems to be a boy. After all, he's only made of words. The paper's yellow and curling. The spine's coming away a bit, sure sign that it's a good one.

"I never knew that there was so many books."

"This?" the man says, picking up the latest broadsheet and folding it under his arm. "This is nothing."

And he might be right, but it's the grandest thing I've ever seen.

"You thank your Master," the man says. "He's a good one." And I do.

"And thank you, good man," Dain says and waves his hand dismissively.

When we are alone, Dain gives me a look. Hard, direct. "There are many things about the city that we must speak of. Too many, and most I am sure you will forget or ignore, but you must know this, and it is paramount. Are you listening, boy?"

"Yes," I say.

"Good. Firstly, know that in the city, I am at my weakest, for there are so many of my kind. In the city there is great danger. From the moment you pass through her doors, you must be careful. And you must not leave her without me. Once those steel doors that guard her close, you must remain within. No diurnal adventures for you. Do you know what diurnal means?"

I nod. "'Course I do! It's the story of my life." Dain gives a little chuckle at that.

"You're a wanderer, Mark, but there is to be no wandering in that city. Everything you do will reflect upon me. And it is forbidden for your kind to leave the Mountain and walk the Red City unaccompanied."

"As if I would," I say, "I hear it's a dangerous place."

"You do not know the half of it. You are my Day Boy, my servant, my responsibility. You break this rule, then trouble will be heaped upon us. You know too much, and you might just know something that those folk in the Red City desire."

"Makes me a powerful sort of fella," I say.

Dain shakes his head. "Makes you someone that they'd happily pull the bones from till you sang. Secrets go into the City in the Shadow of the Mountain, they do not come out of her. Are we understood?"

"Yes."

"Good lad." Dain smiles. He buries his head in his broadsheet, and me in my book, and the night slides by. The land quickly grows dry. Lit by that bright moon, one time I think I see a flash of forms that might be the cold children. Might just be my eyes getting all tricksy.

The train stops twice on the way to the City. Two towns, both about as big as Midfield. The last town, I get off to stretch my legs.

There's a lad watching me, walking towards the train, with that wolfish lope I feel in my own limbs. Day Boy like me. We nod, he grins, and it's like looking in a mirror.

If a reflection could cut you.

I go to talk to him, and Dain grabs my shoulders.

"Loose lips sink ships," he says. I give him a look, then the whistle's blowing.

"Professor and ward," the Ticket Master says. "The train's waiting . . . and it doesn't wait."

We get ourselves back inside, the train moving the moment my feet hit the stairs.

"It's lean living out here," Dain says, as we sit down. "Midfield's paradise compared to these old dry places. Our town is as gentle as it is narrow."

And we leave that lean village, with its wolfish boys, and settle into the rhythm of the tracks, and I find myself drifting off. There's a city waiting, but we've miles yet.

I'm being shook awake. Feel the world's moved on around me, and the Night Train's slowing, starting on a slight rise, and then it's picking up speed again.

"So what do you think of her?" Dain asks.

I blink. Things are shining low in the sky, great shapes are circling the Mountain like cyclopean beasts of the air. And to the east is a dull red light.

And then we are passing low buildings, streets lit with yellow light and busy with folk, the smell of dust dry and hard and coming through the windows. It's a blur that passes right quick, and into the Mountain we go, past the steel Gates of Dawn. And I have to blink away tears.

Morning's coming, Dain's already looking sluggish, his eyes dim. Darkness or not, come the morning he will sleep, like they all must until the sun settles down in the west again. He gestures out the window. "The City. What do you think of the City, boy?"

"It's gloriously bright," I say.

I've never seen so much light. There's no darkness here. Everything is illuminated by beams of light that look like they've been plucked from the sun itself, if such a harvest could be made, and perhaps it can. The ground throbs, I can feel it through the tracks, as though the earth itself has a pulse. A great beating life in them continental plates.

"You know, there are some who would kill to come here," Dain says, almost to himself, like he's lost to some argument that the City's pulled out of him anew. "And they are fools. Holding to the dream that this dark heart is anything, that it's important." He shoots me a glance. "It's not. It's the hollow core of a beast rotting itself to death. Took me a long while to work that out, and even longer to believe it. Don't be fooled by the glamour of it, Mark. Though we both will for a while, that is the nature of the City, part of its shadow. Monsters can be charming, my lad. If the City is offered you, I want you to come to it with your eyes open. Open and narrow."

Nothing's ever simple with Dain—as if it's my choice. I will get a letter, and I will attend to its summons. I suppose my eyes are already narrow. But here we are!

Out we go into dry hot air. And the smell of smoke, and things cooking, and the hint of blood.

The station is crowded, so many Masters amongst the regular folk. More than I've ever seen, and this is just one platform in this city dark.

Though why it is called a city dark is beyond me. I've never seen Masters more clear, more lit. Their pale flesh reflects the light, their skin shivers in it. Their limbs move too fast. And there is an urgency here, no lingering, time's running out. Day is coming.

We are met at the station by a tall Master, long limbed, almost a spider made into a man. He's dressed in outrageous finery, a cloak that flows with his movements, a top hat that makes a mockery of Dougie's. He looks at me haughty-like, as though he has no truck with Day Boys, but he's polite enough with my Master.

"It is good to see you again, Professor," he says.

"Madigan, it has been far too long." Dain makes it sound like the opposite is true, and Madigan's face hardens. But I can see an affection there, too.

"Yes. Yes." He hoists our bags and leads us to a carriage. "You know what's coming," he says. "We must hurry." He doesn't move with any urgency. His limbs make him fast enough. I'm all a-sweat keeping up.

Dain jumps into the carriage, pulls me in, too, and Madigan taps the roof. Down busy streets we go; everywhere there are the symbols of the Sun. We pass what must be a church of the Sun, for both Dain and Madigan dip their heads towards it.

Such a wonderful thing. Dain's warning is already slipping from my mind. This city, in this hollowed out Mountain, is all grandness and gravity. Walls of rock rise overhead like clouds and descend in fists of stone. And all of it is lit, believe me. I've never seen shadows so pale and thin. We're on a road wide enough for four carriages, and turn into the searing bright streets of the inner city, and here we approach a building bigger than Main Street, red brick and a roof halfway to the stony ceiling of the Mountain.

"My college," Dain says, and he sounds all of a sudden whimsical. "It has been a long time."

Into it we are bustled, through long halls and past a library whose first antechamber does indeed put the library in the Night Train to shame. I take a peek and all I can see is wall after wall of books, receding into the distance.

"Come now," Dain says. "There'll be time to explore later."

We come to rooms that smell of dust newly disturbed and soaps and other astringents.

"Nothing is changed," Dain says, picking up a vase and putting it down again, running a finger along a shelf, weighted with old books. I can't tell if that pleases him or not.

"Yes, the same old battles, the same old knives buried in the same backs. Still, there is endless gossip," Madigan says. "And you, still at odds with Egan?"

Dain raises his hand. "A harmless rivalry."

Madigan looks at his pocket watch, pure affectation, Masters are themselves clocks; they feel the movement of the sun with their entire being. "We will talk of them this evening."

Madigan leaves us, and I open little wooden doors to a narrow brick balcony, and look back out at the city. In the distance, where we have come from, but not too far away, the steel Gates of Dawn are closing. Shutting out the light of the Sun that all of them here worship. It shuts entirely, and Dain finds a bit of wake to him. He lays a hand on my shoulder. "I am weary. You must be, too," he says. "Sleep, and then wait for me. This city isn't safe for the likes of you."

Dain walks to his room, shuts the door behind him, and there are the clockish turnings of complicated machines. Here, in the heart of the City in the Shadow of the Mountain, he locks his doors. I go to my room. There's a lock on the door that's too complex for me to figure out. And there's some sort of timer. I shut the door, and the mechanism whirrs locked—and starts ticking.

Well, I'm stuck here then.

Dain didn't trouble to tell me this would happen. My Master didn't trust me. I don't blame him, of course. There's a city to explore. How else might I be stopped from exploring it? I walk to the bed, and I can't stop yawning, but first I circle around the room. Notice the small door that leads, I suppose, to my Master's room.

There's a table next to my bed, and on it a small pile of books, a note beside them:

Mark—Things you might like.

I look at the books as I crawl into the bed. They're old, with yellow-edged pages. There's one on the solar system, pictures that I can scarce believe. There's a book with talking bears in it and a brave girl. And there's one about a boy and a monster: a girl that's a Master, like a cold child. Pages have been underlined in that one.

I scarcely give each more than a flick before I'm laying my head on the pillow and sleeping.

Day Boys, we sleep when our Masters wish it. Even if we don't sleep too easy.

The Gates of Dawn open, their steel bulk thunderous as they part to admit the night. The evening bell starts its tolling. Six slow beats. And the city's lights are lit. Bright, then brighter, and brighter still. They say a cloud of bats leaves the city when that gate opens, comes back when it closes. I race to the balcony and watch, and sure enough, there's the dark spiralling out into the night beyond. All those shrieks and hisses fading skyward; it's a frenzied, beautiful thing, and it makes my hairs stand on end.

When I go in, Dain is up. A swift waking. His eyes are huge. "No sleep like that under the Mountain. Are you rested boy?"

I give him a nod. Not really, but I've been up for hours, reading and waiting. I've a city pulling me to wakefulness. I want it all.

"Good, we'll be busy this night. We've the Tower of Law to visit, first step in seeing the Council. There's always hoops to jump."

Madigan's waiting at our door. "That chat," Dain says, "will have to wait. I've too much to do this evening."

Madigan nods. "Just don't let it wait too long."

The City's warmer than I expect. Warmer than anything Dain had led me to prepare for.

Hot air and the murmuring of pigeons. Trapped in here, all but blind. And there's rats, you can smell them, there's shit as long and white as worms. And everywhere there are Masters, walking, and there are men and women, too, pale as bone in this sunless place. Here the tooth rules, and the pen, the scratching of notes and learning onto paper. There's the long halls of the universities. The brick and steel buildings that run in parallel tracks deep into the belly of the Mountain.

I'd got some view through the window in my room after I found I could open the glass a decent crack.

During the day, it's silent but for the hurried wanderings of servants, the whispered talk. Somewhere near the Temple of the Sun, there is the Crèche, where those best and brightest of boys are raised, all clever and learned in the various necessary arts. I've never set foot in there, too delicate. Too dumb.

But I'd fancy a peek, to measure myself against those new-taught lads, young and unknowing of the world, for all their books and lessons.

My shirt's stuck to my back soon as we walk out onto the street. And it catches me again, all that light, big hot lamps, and at the center of the City is the Temple of the Sun, its grand old brass orb lit up so bright that it hurts to look at it. Which you aren't supposed to anyway, less you were a Master, but I look anyway, of course I do. Right up at that faux brass Sun, the Luminance.

Dain slaps the back of my skull—with his hand, not the cane he's holding in the other one. "Turn your gaze," he hisses. "The wrong folk see you, and they'll have your throat."

And I do, but I'm blinking and blind.

"Fool," he says. "Why must your understanding always be found in self-hurt? You need your sight here. You need to watch, and you need to think. Your eyes can't handle that light, any more than they could handle the Sun."

"I can't see," I moan.

Dain snorts. "You'll get it back soon enough. You barely peeked."

It's a blurry sort of walk we have, and Dain holds my hand like I was still a child after I trip that first time, nearly landing on my face. Can't see, but I can hear, the rumbles of those distant engines, the beating heart of industries.

There's music everywhere: It fills the city. Songs, pianos playing from bars deep in the Mountain. Oh, Anne would love it!

And one time I hear it: the choir. A low singing that builds and rises, that reaches into my chest deep as any kiss. The sound makes me stop, and Dain with me. It's pure, and reaching to the ceiling of the Mountain. There may not be stars above us, but this song has stars in it. And all at once I am crying. Like some baby, sniffling and snuffling.

"Beautiful. Beautiful," Dain says.

"Never heard its like," I say.

"Well, now you have, boy. And I am glad I could share it with you. That's the Luminance's Choir, the Sun church's choir, all Crèche-raised boys. Girls, too. There's heaven in it. The Orchestral Hall is that building nearest the temple.

"They adore their sounds here," Dain says, like he isn't one of them. "Sun, Sea, Song, that's the core of my kind. The things lost, and the things that remind us."

"And what's it remind you of?" I ask him, all blink and tear.

"That we're but a sunrise from obliteration. There's something gorgeous in the ruination of us all."

"Not in any hurry for ruination," I mumble.

Dain squeezes my hand. "Give it time."

It's a bit of walking before I can see more than splodges, and by then we're almost at the tower.

And I catch sight of the cages, rows of them, extending from the Tower of Law, down East Street, and West. And within them are folk, sickly looking folk, three to a cage. And in some of them, there are others. Feeding.

"Who are these?"

"Vagrants. Criminals. Food. Life isn't easy here." Dain looks to me, drops to his knee. "Some of my kind have taken to calling you the Feast. I do not think it appropriate."

"But it's what we are, isn't it?"

Dain doesn't answer. And then he doesn't have time. There's the smash of a fallen tile. And the sound of angry talk. Men drop from the roof like possums grown light and deadly.

The first swings out at me. And Dain is in the way. I see the knife go in, but it doesn't go out. Dain holds it there. His hands reach out, grip his attacker by the neck, and he squeezes. Bone cracks, gristle snaps, the fellow drops, and Dain is already turning, pulling the knife from him; there's a puff of blood, dark and putrid. He runs the blade under the second one's neck, draws a spray of true blood out. The black shape topples.

There's another one dropping, and Dain, hardly even looking, strikes him in the head with his cane. He hits the ground and stays there.

It's over so fast.

There's a distant whistle blowing. "Are you all right?" Dain asks.

"Yes. What about you?"

Dain coughs, lays a heavy hand on me. "I'm wounded, true, but I've suffered greater hurts."

The constables find us there in that tangle of bodies, all embraced by ruination; my Master leaning on me like he is an old man.

They hesitate, and Dain raises a hand. "It's all right," he says.

And then he slumps against me. "Master's been stabbed," I say.

"Does he need care?" the senior—well, the best-dressed—constable asks.

"Do you?" I whisper.

Dain grimaces. "Already the wounds are healing," he says nice and low. "Weakness cannot be seen."

"I'll see to him," I say. "You gentlemen see to this."

Dain leans on my arm. Guides me down one street, then another.

There's a Master waiting at the heavy door, and he does something that I've never seen before. He bends low, a true gen-uflection.

"Master Dain," he says. "A pleasure, an honest pleasure."

("Boy," Dain whispers. "Trust least those that bow the deepest. There's no effort to be had in bending the back, and even the slightest of us has teeth.")

"Up with you, Master Dargel," Dain says. "Up with you quick."

Master Dargel lifts his head; there's a touch of umbrage in his eyes.

Dain laughs. "Oh, don't play hurt, my dear friend. Don't play hurt."

Dargel sniffs. "There is blood on you."

"An altercation, nothing more."

"There's always an element of wildness these days," Dargel says. "But to attack one of us, such is the folly of our feuding kind."

Dain smiles. "I am merely scratched."

Dargel nods. "And how goes your book?"

Dain clears his throat. "It goes. It goes. I've little patience for chatter this night. Things need doing, deeper talks are required."

"Of course," Dargel says. "Why, you nearly built the place single-handed."

I give Dain such a look, and my Master pats my hand. "He exaggerates. I was but one of many."

"Your Master was among the first, he's been our kind for longer than this is old. He set up the schools, he spoke for the new ones. He went below, a hundred times they say. He was one of many, but he was hardly the least."

"Enough, Dargel, enough," Dain says.

"Of course, of course, I forget that is how you are, and now more than ever, though why you would come here—"

"I have my reasons," Dain says.

Not a Master in the world didn't have reasons.

My eyes snap open with the sound of the door mechanism releasing. My dreams were full of ticking clocks and alien moons, of snow and bears and girls with sharp teeth. I'm up and out of bed, quick smart. Hardly slept, still on edge after that attack. Not sure I'll ever relax in this city, which would make Dain happy for sure.

I turn the handle and go out.

There's a table set there with food. Fruit and some cold meats, bread and cheese. I eat it, and all of it's good, fresh food, but it's not what I'm used to. And in that I find another niggle of homesickness.

There's a clock on the wall, 12:30 p.m. Still a long time until night. Maybe there's something wrong with the mechanism: the ticks and the tocks not quite right.

Maybe we Day Boys are meant to wander even here.

I eat a little more because I'm hungry. I'm always hungry, what boy isn't?

Then I put my ear to the door, strain to hear what's going on outside. Nothing. I push the door a crack, peek down first left, then right. Long hallway, not a soul in it. Only me.

I shut the door, walk back into my room and shut that door, too.

The lock slips back into its ticking place, but I no longer trust it.

I grab the book on the solar system and read. Still reading when Dain wakes.

"Where did you get those books?" Dain asks me.

"I thought you organised it."

Dain picks up the one about the boy and the girl, and the cold city, and his face twists.

"Someone is having a joke with us." He takes that book to his room, then comes back, and his face is a little brighter. "What did you think about the book on the solar system?"

I want to tell him about all the things I've seen, the planets in that dark above our head, all those worlds, but I can't. All I can think about is why the books were there, and who put them there. That novel could be the death of someone, why would they risk it? I'm just a Day Boy, and here in the City in the Shadow of the Mountain, that's less than nothing.

"You weren't lying," I say. "Those stars and planets are right huge."

And I know at once that I've said the wrong thing. How can I hope to survive this place if I can't even read my own Master?

"No." He pulls his coat over his shoulders. "I wasn't." And grabs his hat and almost yanks it down over his head. "I am going out tonight. I've business to attend to. You're to stay here. Do not leave these rooms. You hear me?"

"Of course, I do."

"Then heed me. Listen to these words. This city is dangerous, you are not to leave under any circumstances until I return. If you do, you will be punished, and believe me when I say that you will wish it was me that did the punishing. This is a city of predation, this is a city of the hunt; it is not safe for you. Do not mistake its dangers for those of Midfield." He sighs, straightens his hat, getting the brim just so. "Things are far more complex here."

He leaves me to the rooms, and at least I have those other books.

Three hours I'm reading. Then another three. I walk to the narrow balcony and close my hands over the hard cold steel of the ironwork, and I look down. There's lights and steam engines throbbing somewhere, like the pain in my temple. I can see the streets below, the folks walking through it all as though it were nothing, and maybe it is nothing. But I can't look at this place and see it without the threat Dain has suggested. It's there in the lights and shadows. From here, all the way down to the Wide Circle Road where the statues of the Fallen Dark stand, lit and featureless, as the sun once made them.

I feel a gaze settle on me, and I stare down at the streets, and see the red glow of eyes, a head turning, a figure walking away fast.

I reckon since that Hunter chased me, I've felt on the run, as though I had a target painted on my back, and there's all manner of folks chasing me for it.

And the paranoias strike me, and I think that maybe Dain has left me here. That he isn't coming back, that I'm some price paid whether I want it or not. Everything has a cost, Dain says. Maybe I'm that cost.

When I walk back inside, someone's waiting in the room.

Give a little yelp, before I'm jutting out my jaw.

I'm out with my knife quick smart, and the man smiles at me. "Put the stabber away, little man." Madigan bares his fangs. "I'm not here to bleed you."

I slide the knife into my boot, but I keep the handle clear and in easy reach. "Why are you here then?"

"Your Master has left a message. He will not be returning this night, but you are to expect him tomorrow evening."

"Where's he gone?"

"It is not for you or me to ask such things, nor expect an answer." I grimace at that, and he flashes me another toothful smile. "Deeper in the Mountain, I suspect. There is a meeting of the Council, and your Master has been invited. Just as you do not question him, he cannot question them."

But I've questions all right. This fella smiles again, once, then is out the door almost faster than I can see. It shuts, and I lock it, though it'll not do me much good.

Night, and there's doors closing, slamming. There's airs moving. I can feel the breath of the old building. I open one window a crack, catch the fires on the slope to the west, and see the long shadows. Stir crazy I am, two long days in this room, and longer nights without Dain. Books only hold so much comfort when you're as worried as I am.

There's screams, and laughter, horrible until it ends, and then the silence is worse: Nothing more quiet than predators.

A machine starts up somewhere, and I realise I've been dozing. Resilient, Dain's always called me, and I thought he meant stupid.

The doors to the outside are closing. I can smell the smoke of engines straining at their work. Dawn's coming another day, and the Master's not returned, and I've not had a visit from Madigan since that first.

There's trouble.

Trouble I'm not the cause of, not at least direct like.

And then, I see it, on the foot of my bed. A slip of paper marked in a spiral. The Hunter's spiral. And I'm gripped with the deepest of terrors. Things are creeping, tonight. They will come tonight, and I have it, a horrible rising certainty. I need to get out of here.

I open the door wider. Step onto the balcony, something hurls itself into the sky, and I bite back a yell. It's just a bird, but my heart's pounding. I look to the road and the great doors closing. I know I shouldn't. I swore I wouldn't. But that terror's rising. And I realise it's been there all along, building.

Some of my kind have taken to calling you the Feast. If I run, I could make it. I might. I grab my bedsheet, tie one end to the edge of the balcony and then clamber down, letting myself drop when the sheet runs out. I land a bit funny, twist my ankle a little, but I can still run—sort of. There's a low fence and I'm over it.

Carriages pass me by, three of them, crashing down the road towards the heart of the City, but I'm headed the other way. I'm safer in the light.

The Gates of Dawn are three feet thick, all steel and mechanics, gears as big as houses, big enough to set the Mountain ticking. And they're closing fast.

I'm running.

"Oi!" someone yells. But I keep my feet banging hard against the concrete road.

I bolt through the doorway just as they're shutting, tons of metal drawing towards me, bearing down on me, threatening.

Could be squashed flat, but there's no turning back, and when someone yells at me again, I ignore them. Dark shapes thrash past, the last of the bats.

A leathery smack to the face, and another, doesn't even slow me, not one bit.

I make it, the door closing behind me. I'm locked out, in the Red City. In the light of a red dawn. Smoke and dust and diesel. Parrots are calling, fires are burning, and I stand with my world behind me, locked away in the Mountain's rock and iron.

"Here he is," someone yells. "Here he is, the Day Boy." I think he says *the*; it might just as well be *a*.

How do they know?

Well. What else would I be?

Tennyson and the Poisoned World

Twitcher is just that. All twitches and worries. He shuffles, he runs. And when he's alone, he smiles. I don't know him enough, but I know he's smarter than he puts out, less frightened. There's an anger to him, a sharp edge all its own. And you see it with his story. Here it comes out, and when he's done with its telling, he always seems surprised, as though he's just been reminded of something. Something that he should never forget. That's Twitcher: He sneaks, but he's clever about it. Makes it look like something else.

> *You know how it is with poison. Dangerous, the sort of thing that can get out of hand, that can rise up and swallow you, like the sea does to the Masters, if they get too close—Tennyson says that's because the sea and the salt never quite changed the way*

everything else did. It remembers, and it will always remember with hatred.

Tennyson was a chemist. He made play with all that bittery sweet stuff. He was good at it. Some he helped, some he killed. He liked the killing. In secret.

The war was still on, but we were already losing it. The world was closing in, and they were at the edges, the Masters and the other monsters. No one quite got that the Masters were our last best hope, keeping the worst things at bay. But who would know that? Who would even suspect it?

Government thought Tennyson might find some cure.

He never wanted to. Why would he want to? He could see the poetry in it. Says it was splendid, those last days. Like a sunset. Like a sky flaring its last great light upon itself.

The beautiful fury in the dying of beautiful things.

And while all of them looked out, looked at what was coming, he looked in. He looked so deep within the heart of things. Where everything is muddy, everything a possibility, no matter how outlandish. Some singularity had been met, and now, it was shifting everything. The world weren't dying, it weren't even sick. It was dead. But it might rise again.

He opened doors. He found out secrets.

Nothing is set in stone, says my Tennyson. Nothing is still. And everything might be or might not. And what he saw, with all those magics of the past time, was a shifting of the hinges. Worlds changed forever.

There was a war on, but everyone, everyone, was fighting themselves. He found a way to bring us all onto the one path, to sort wheat from chaff. He flooded the world with his elixirs, and those that died thanked him. Those that rose up thanked him, too. Death is a gift that he gave out willingly. He made them all see Death's beauty.

There's a half-dozen of them. Some of the biggest men I've ever seen. Like that damn Hunter, but none's knifed up. They're confident in their strength, that's to my advantage. At least I've got that blade in my boot, though cutting's likely to end with broken bones; cutting's close work. And I reckon I can run faster than any of them if I've room, if I've a chance.

I puff up my chest. "What of it?" I say, and gesture at the lightening sky. "It's day, isn't it?"

Someone laughs. "You know what we mean."

There's the train tracks nearby. And narrow streets, running up the mountainside, and houses, plenty of houses. And I can smell bread baking somewhere, and the smell of the sun rising and baking the land. The ground's hard beneath my feet, and there's not a hint of green anywhere, no grass, no trees. It's a wilderness of buildings and people; sets my heart pounding so hard, it's hurting in my chest.

The biggest of them, a man with a black beard down to his chest, comes walking towards me. He don't need to puff his chest, he's as broad as I am long; kinda fella whose walking by blocks out the sun.

I look up and up at him. He looks down at me, thumbs in his belt. And the rest of them stand back.

"How'd you grow so tall?" I ask.

"We're made big in the Red City," he says. "Who's your Master?"

"What's that?" I ask.

The fella laughs. Me standing up to a giant with not so much as a slingshot to hand.

"You know what I mean."

"Never had no master." I crack my neck, left and right.

And he finds it offensive somehow; a storm knits itself together in those big dark brows of his. "You're coming with me, boy."

"Not coming with no one," I say, and I'm sprinting before I finish talking, kicking up red dust, and he swipes out at me, but I'm darting wide. Another tries to tackle me, but he's not nearly quick enough. I'm over those grasping hands, even manage a quick kick in his ribs, can't resist showing off. Don't take much comfort in his groaning. Too focused on the narrow road ahead.

They're faster than I thought, but I can keep myself in front. Just not far enough. So I start for where the street's all bends and angles. I take one turn, then another. But I don't know where I'm running to. All I've got is my speed.

There's a whistle on the rooftops. A cry and the banging of a bell. And I'm putting on more speed, lungs burning almost as bad as my legs.

A door opens to the right of me. A young face peers out.

"Here, in here," he cries. And because I can't think of anything else, I take the doorway. He shuts the door behind me.

"Who are you?" I demand when I've breath enough for talking.

He puts a finger to his lips.

Footfalls crashing down the street. Low cries. Men make ungainly predators. I feel some shame for my kind.

The boy stands there, ear against the door, not that he needs it, these blokes clod by all thump and crash and shouting.

"They're gone," he says, after a while.

"What did they want?"

There's laughter, lots of laughter, and I jerk around, quick, take in the room. It's dingy, crowded with chairs, and there's boys here, five of them, and they're all smiling at me.

"You," the door boy says.

One of the boys taps his skull. "They want what's in your head."

I can be slow some days, but the blood's pulsing. "Insurrectionists," I say.

"Some people might call 'em heroes," someone says.

Another laughs. "There's no heroes in this world. Just stupid men, and monsters."

I know these boys. I know their type. "You're Day Boys like me," I say.

The boy at the door bows. "We *were* Day Boys. Now we're the lost. The discarded. We're the ones the Masters let go. The softer ones anyway, the ones that couldn't quite bear to kill us. We was at the top of the heap, and now we're at the bottom." I look at him and he half-laughs.

"Memory's a goad and a bitterness, like you'd imagine."

"And those men?"

"Some of them were like us, it's how they know. Others not. All of them want the Masters gone. We hide until we get caught, or flee the City. Bit of dying in both of those. But all of us, though, we've done all right: We've collectivised."

I'm hardly hearing him.

"Dain would never leave me," I say. "Not here."

"We all thought that, but here we are, deserted or cast out or fled and not found." The door boy taps his chest. "I'm Grainer," he says, then waggles his thumbs at the others. "The tall one's Midas, that's Billow with the wispiest beard, Jack with the scar on his chin."

"Scrapper, I am," Jack says.

Grainer rolls his eyes. "That's Wes, with the long arms."

"Gets me outta trouble," Wes says, flexing his biceps. "And into it, sometimes."

"And the little one's Rat."

"I'll be a wolf one day," Rat says, and all of them laugh. Like they're playing at being men, and they are.

"How's it feel to be down here with us?" Grainer asks.

I pull the biggest smile I got, like that could pull the wall from behind me, like I don't care. "Pleasure to be with such fine gentlemen."

"Where you from?" Rat asks.

"Midfield."

"Country boy," Jack says. "Surprised you made it."

That gets my back up, like he knows anything. "Where you from?"

"Raised in these streets, and then the Academy when I was five, given to a Master when I was seven, and these streets again.

They have you, these streets. Even when you're gone, they know you're coming back to 'em. They're patient as the sky."

The Academy, I can't help but roll my eyes. Dougie's an Academy Boy too. He says it's the hardest school for the hardest Day Boys, outside of those Crèche-raised.

"You think that's funny," Jack says. "Serve our Masters to the best of our skill, work and work, never much rest. And now this, cast out like them angels. Our lives are bloody tragedies."

Grainer laughs. "But we're still breathing. And I chose this. Couldn't face the Change, and such a decision wasn't seen too kindly. Some gifts offered you have to take. So, here we are, not blooded or dead, bit sweeter than tragedy."

I'm still taking it all in. I've already set it in my skull that I'm not staying here long: This isn't my story. And it isn't near no tragedy.

Grainer must see a bit of that in my face because he smiles at me, but there's a hardness there. There's laughs and boasts in this room, but there's scarce a breath of warmth. I'd not wish a life with just Day Boys on anybody. I think I know why they end up getting caught. A lost boy can only stay a lost boy for so long. Lost boys end up found or dead boys. Don't know which I'm to be yet.

Then my stomach rumbles, and I realise I've not ate; that it's still just morning, and I'm in another world, and that my belly don't care.

"Hungry?" Wes asks. He reaches a long arm into a pocket and flicks me an apple lightning quick. I catch it—no drop for me in this crowd all hungry for failure—just a casual catch, like I've been catching things all my life, which I have.

"Break your fast," Grainer says—looking sort of impressed—he nods at the door. "We've work to do."

The city beyond the Mountain, outside the Gates of Dawn. The Red City. Dry as dust. The streets are narrow, the buildings' roofs touch—makes it harder to attack from above. Less space for the Masters to drop down from. And the edges of the gutters are barbed, which looks more effective than it probably is, or the Masters would have torn it down long ago.

"Always been folk like us Day Boys," Grainer's saying as he leads me through streets that curl, the low roofs above us admitting sharp fingers of hard light. I can smell my sweat and the sweat of all those other lives in the dry hot air. "Poor fellows, quick, but not quick enough for Mastery, and too wild for the other things. Cursed and blessed in one breath. Wasn't luck you found us. We're drawn to each other, all that turbulence of luck and dismay, it's like magnets for the body and the soul."

The Red City and the City in the Shadow of the Mountain wind around each other. The heart of domination—and resistance, such as it is. They say it's only left so the Masters have something to prey upon. Good for breeding Day Boys, too. The best Day Boys come from insurgent stock. Rebellion is energy, and it's that energy they desire. You've gotta stir the blood or it grows thick and sluggish, and Day Boys aren't cattle. We're help and trouble, and that's how they like us.

"You've gotta toughen up." He gives me a look part pity, part disgust. "May the Sun and Sea take them Masters that don't toughen up their boys. We've all done it, run this gauntlet."

Toughen up! I want to smack Grainer one in the mouth, but that'd prove nothing. He's not my enemy. He just don't know what I'm capable of.

"We've need of nails," he says, and parts his thumb and forefinger a good length, maybe ten centimetres. "At least this long. You'll see them, they're the ones daubed in red paint."

"How many?" I ask.

"As many as you can get, though ten should be enough; we take only what we need. And remember, they're after boys like us. You fail at this and you'll end up in the Cage House." He gestures across the city towards a tower: It's painted in the blue and white of the Constabulary. "They'll be watching you. You don't have the privilege of terror no more."

I don't know about that. I feel pretty terrified even though I know I can be cunning, and I can be quick. And just then I wish for Anne's calming voice. Thought of her sends a yearning for Midfield through me like a flooding river. I'd be at weeping, but this for sure isn't the time or place.

I can taste the dust; it's red, sticks to the back of the throat, all that iron. Dain said we're each and every one of us dust, and that's half the reason why the City exists.

I spit a spit at my feet. It comes out chalky and red: It bubbles.

"You ready to do this?" Grainer asks.

I nod. 'Course I'm not, but life don't hand us ready. Ready is an illusion. "Let's go."

Grainer grins, gestures down at the road. "Only you for this. Though there'll be distraction. Be ready when it comes."

I walk into the markets, clothes dirty, a smear of red mud down one cheek; clean'll stand out, Grainer had said, and here and now I can see the truth in it. No one looks like they've bathed in the past week. Just the dust for some.

The streets are narrow, the buildings high. I push my way through, everything tingling, more people here on this street than in all of Midfield, feels like. I take the next corner, and there's the shop. But before it, there's a butcher's. Wonder how old George is, back home. I push my face against the glass. I can smell blood. There's roo and venison hung, shocked of life by blade and gravity. Butcher catches me staring, shoos at me with a hand clenched round a cleaver.

Next door is where I'm headed. Hardware painted on a sign hanging out front. I walk past it once, plenty of people there for cover. I might just get away with this.

Somewhere behind me I hear whistling.

Sounds familiar, might as well be Dougie. Swells me, a mite, brings a tear to my eye, and I hurry back to the shop, to show that I haven't lost my nerve. The door jangles as I open it, eyes turn, but none linger. That's something.

The place reeks of steel and commerce, as Dain might say.

There's big round hessian bags, and the bags are filled with nails. There's even a bright yellow scoop for each, like these are sweets—which throws me right back to Mary's shop, and Anne, and I haven't got time for mooning on the past.

I flick a gaze towards the counter. A man with a hard face is working there, and he catches my eye, and I know at once that he knows what I'm up to. So I flash him a grin and half expect him to come over, but he just gives me dark look. Too busy or too lazy or too fed up with thieves.

I survey the bags, give them the once-over. There's the ones smudged with red paint, and I'm tempted just to reach in, snatch what I need and foot it, but I can feel eyes burning into my back.

I know predators, I know that prickle of a patient stare. You don't catch a thief before they steal, you wait and catch them as they're doing it. Proof incontrovertible, as Dain would say— although it never stopped him from jumping to conclusions.

If I had a watch, I'd be checking it right now. Good that I don't. There's a bang outside.

"Roof's coming down," someone cries. And heads are craning. I'm finding it hard enough to ignore myself.

Another bang, cursing and howling.

I slip my hand careful and quick into the nail bag, passing the scoop, and draw out ten of them red nails, then I'm through the door and running, stepping light over shattered tiles, and a man's on his arse looking stunned, head streaming with blood. No one cries and no one follows, and I take the turning streets, following those that rise up towards the Mountain.

Grainer slaps my back a block away. "Did you see our distraction?"

"Did you have to hit a man on the skull?"

Grainer shrugs. "Blood's the best theatre, my Master used to say when he was feeling playful. Fella's not dead. Barely clipped him."

"So how'd you do?"

I show him the ten, and he frowns. "I was hoping for twenty." You could bottle the disappointment dripping from his lips. This boy's trouble, and he's all that stands between me and the streets.

Twenty! I'll give him twenty.

The red-headed nails are long and hard and heavy. I slap them into his hand, and walk back. There'll be no distraction this time.

Twice in one day. I hover around the door, waiting for business, and when it comes, when those at the counter are distracted, I step lively to the nail bag. Ten, then twenty, then thirty.

I grab them, and turn to the door. "Thief! Thief!" comes the cry.

Hands grab at me, and I'm swinging out with a fist full of nails. I make it to the door and out, and I don't stop running for several blocks, until I'm somewhere utterly unfamiliar. But then this whole place is unfamiliar.

People look at me, then look away when they catch my eye.

I feel transparent, but there's no fear there.

"Hey!" someone cries, and I turn. Grainer. I come at him, my hand still tight around the nails. He takes a step back: He can see my rage, and the hurt in it.

"You always yell out thief the second time?"

Grainer raises his hands. "It's how we sort the wheat from the chaff. The crim from the dim."

I shove the thirty nails into his palm. "Don't you do that again."

Grainer lets the nails drop. I feel my jaw go with it.

"Never needed the nails," he says. "There's a baker's door across; you were the distraction. Come. Come home, there's bread for your belly."

And I can't help but laugh.

It's three days of thieving, and I get pretty good at it. Grainer's a teacher, and his lessons are sharp. But I get cocky. Cockier.

A bakery, noonday crowd, a fresh shelf of loaves. Me and Grainer. A hand closes tight around my wrist. "Don't think too highly of thieves around here."

Grainer's already gone, faster than smoke. Three loaves of bread missing, and the baker's shaking his head at the floury shadows on the shelf.

"Day Boy," I say. "I'm a Day Boy. My Master is Dain."

The baker's lips purse. "And your Master still wants ya? Don't look like you've too long left in ya."

I nod my head. "I swear it. I got lost, had to steal to survive."

"That story won't earn you much sympathy here, boy. Streets are a-plague with the likes of you." He folds his arms across his chest; there's flour all over them, they're the kind of arms that could beat out a sorry, and I'm not feeling too sorry. "I'm sending for the Constabulary, and they will get in touch with your Master. Let's see if ye've been replaced."

"He wants me, he does." I nod, looking contrite, looking desperate, and maybe I am.

The baker frowns, still considering, whether a beating's the more satisfactory option. Close thing. But he makes up his mind. "You better hope he does. Ain't much of pleasant that happens in the halls of the Constabulary."

The baker sends out the scowliest and smallest of his apprentices to find the cops. They're not long coming, and all that time the shopkeeper keeps his eyes on me, and the door locked. No escaping for me.

Four of them come, and they're big men, like those who waited at the gates, though better dressed and harder eyed. The biggest of them jerks a thumb at me.

"This the thief?"

The baker nods. "Says he's lost his Master."

"Has he now?" He crouches down before me, eye to eye. "We don't look too kind on thieves and liars."

"I'm not lying," I say.

"You better hope you're not," the constable says, and they take me from the shop, marching me in silence along the street, past Grainer who hardly gives me a look. There's strong hands closed around my arms, dragging me to the great tower of the Constabulary. Even if it's where I want to go, I can feel the heat of shame, hundreds of curious eyes studying me. But we're left alone, and by the time we reach the lock-up, I'm almost happy to go through its great brass doors. Swallowed up by the heart of the Law.

We pass some dire things on my way down the halls to the cells. The hardest sort of men breaking. Them that aren't broken make me realise just what sort of thing I play at, and that it's just a game. Nothing tough about me. I could be snapped in two and worse by these fellas. "You," they shout. "You. Come play. Come and play."

They grab at their crotches, they blow kisses from pursed lips and mouths with teeth all cracked. And some just stare with eyes dark and cold.

"Quiet, all of ya. Quiet!" The constable says, and it works on some, or maybe they're just done with their play. Still, quiet or not, I feel them staring.

And when we're past the worst of them, walking by men that hunch in their cells and sob, the constable lets go of my arm. "Men can be the worst monsters of all," he says with some kindness, shutting me in a cell by myself. "Here. You'll be out of harm here. I'll call your Master's university." He must see my confusion because he smiles a thin smile. "We've a line here, direct with the City. Not some backwards little town, we've working phones and all."

"Thank you," I say. "What's your name, sir?"

The constable shakes his head. "Ain't gettin' no name out of me. I was a Day Boy once," he says. "Now I'm this. Boys don't stay boys long." He smiles and gives me a long look. "You're old enough to know that; stupid enough to ignore it. Time's running down for you, either way. You've choices ahead that will need tending to if you are allowed them." He shakes his head. "Running. You should have never run. They look hard on it, 'specially those that decide to come back. There's a weakness to it. And you know what they think of weakness, even the good ones. Are you sure you want me to call your Master?"

"I'm sure," I say, and I sound it: even if he's lit a bit of doubt in me.

"Your Master's a good one, then," he says.

"Yes," I say.

I'm left alone in that cell. Hours go by, nothing to pass the time, so I spend it thinking of home: the way the streets are straight, none of this curving of the city. The curves are what surrounds us, the ridge of trees that runs behind the town, and the scrub that trails away behind it. And I think of the orchard, and Anne, and Mary, and the boys—those boys all strutting and laughing and mocking like they rule the world.

It's a long enough wait that I'm half certain this is it for me.

And then the shadow of a Master falls across the bars of my cell.

"So you have chosen to be found, eh, boy?"

I lift my head and Egan's hard gaze is upon me.

Egan can't stop smiling, and here I am in this cage.

"He says he belongs to a Master Dain," the constable says with a touch of tremor in his voice, and who wouldn't?

"I'm sure he does," Egan says. "And it is, shamefully, true; if not for long. I'd come to the City to find this one. I never quite expected he would find me."

I look at my shoes.

The constable clears his throat. "I have some small use for him, sir. Now that I know he's spoken true. We've troubles that he might know about."

"Look at me, boy," Egan says, and I do, because I have no choice. "Tell him whatever you know. And don't lie, I can tell when you're lying. The whole world can."

I do what I'm told. I tell him about Grainer and the other boys, and it stings a little. But what do I owe them? Grainer ran out on me.

When I'm done, to the constable's and Egan's satisfaction, Egan reaches into a pocket, pulls out a gold coin—Sun stamped— and presses it into the constable's palm. "For your trouble," he says.

"Ain't no trouble," the constable says, but he doesn't hand the coin back. "Not like some of them that come through here. Why, just the other d—. . ." His voice drops away, he's seen Egan's absence of interest. You never bore one of them, and that's a fact. "Ain't no trouble," he says, then glances to some papers, clears his throat. "I best . . ."

"Yes, yes," Egan says. "We have taken up enough of your time."

We all know whose time we've taken up.

I smile, and I get a glare from him that chills me to the marrow. "Come with me, boy," Egan says, and his voice is a cold blade. Of course, I follow him. I don't want to all of a sudden, but I do.

There's a carriage waiting for us, Egan gestures that I get in. And when I do, he follows, and there's not a hint of humour in his eyes. Perhaps I should have shut my mouth, and taken my punishment for the theft.

He taps the roof ceiling, and the carriage jolts forward.

"So. You know the scrambling life now," Egan says. "Didn't take you long to find your feet, however shakily. Dain taught you something at least, even if you have showered him in dishonour."

I look away, at the city passing by, those sodium lights. The haze of dust, the smell of diesel, coke and horses.

There's more silence. We pass through the gates, the City behind us, and ahead of us. All the light of that deep city and it illuminates Egan's displeasure.

"Master Dain, is he all right?"

"I am here, am I not?" Egan says. "We do not see eye to eye on much. But I used what influence I have to return here." Egan turns his gaze upon the City. "Dain was sent home. You ruined him, broke his heart. My Grove is looking after him. I was ready to hunt for you, and now—here we are. You and me."

"I am to go home?"

Egan nodded. "For a little while. No more than a year and probably less. You will train your replacement, a new boy due in a few weeks. But all this is nothing and nowhere yet. We've a sharper task ahead. You've been summoned by the first ones, the ones made on the sixth day of the world: the Council itself. They do not like it when boys run, it sets the wrong example. Surely you were aware of this. Dain did not keep you that ignorant, or perhaps he trusted you more than you deserved. We are to head there directly, and then home."

"The Council," I say. "The Council will eat me up."

And there's such regret mixed with my fear. Egan's right, I've brought trouble and shame to my Master, and he never deserved it.

Egan nods. "Perhaps, they have been known to do such things. Perhaps not. Now, I will give you what guidance I can. And I will accompany you." To find comfort in Egan's company is an oddity. But here he is all that is familiar. "You must listen to them," he says. "You must be honest. You cannot hide. They know all the hiding places in your skull, and the deeper you hide, the deeper they will dig."

We've gone down into the bowels of the city, down and around the Wide Circle Road with its face-worn statues—here a stony hand raised against the sun, here a head tilted in direct defiance of the killing light. And then we're hurtling towards the great Temple of the Sun, its light burning through the cracks in the carriage. At the foot of the temple, we disembark, and I've never seen Egan's face lit like this; there's a terrifying beauty in it. His skin as pale as cream and dark too, like it's both night and day. He slides glasses with smoked lenses over his eyes, and I'm left squinting.

In that awesome luminosity, Egan crouches down. "You must keep your mouth shut now, boy. I know how hard that is for you, but you must if you wish to live. And you must be brave. Fear and doubt could kill you here. You have never been in so much danger. Death has set his throne down within these halls, and even I might not be able to protect you."

The Council of Teeth. The frighteners. Not a Day Boy who isn't warned of them, isn't threatened with their scrutiny. We curse in their name if we're really crazy mad. Council this and Council that. Not that they hear us.

We walk beneath the Luminance towards a small door. A Master is waiting there. He looks at me, then Egan.

"So this is the one?"

Egan nods. And I do my best to keep my eyes cast at my feet.

The Master at the door considers me with smiling, deadly eyes. "Oh, I guess you believe that you've seen things. Hah!" He lays a cold hand gently on my head for a moment, then in a movement faster than I can see it, he's back at the door, swinging it open, gesturing that we might pass.

Egan grabs my hand, and we walk through the doorway, past its guardian. "Welcome. Welcome, Master Egan and little squeaking Day Boy."

The door shuts behind us, and we are in a room big and wide. It hums, with the hum of machines. If there's a stutter to my steps, Egan makes up for it. "If I had time," he says, "I'd have schooled you in this. But I do not. The Night Train runs late because of us. Because of you."

We walk across the room to another set of doors. They open at our approach, a small room—almost a cage—one side lined with buttons. Lots of buttons.

"This is a lift." Egan says. "You'd have read of them no doubt. You are not to be lifted, however. Not yet. We will descend before we rise again."

Egan presses the bottom button, and the lift drops. Down and down.

"This was once an installation. Military. It housed all the sciences of violence. The wickedness of man. But there were more wicked things in the world. And they were waiting. Are you frightened?" Egan asks.

And I nod, even as I am wrapped in the wonder of it; this falling box.

"Good. Fear'll keep you honest."

The doors open, and it's Egan who hesitates at the portal, and that fills me with a grander dread. There's a scream somewhere: There is laughter, and the hint of a low growl.

We enter a well-lit hall, narrow at first, that opens onto cages. I give the one nearest a good looking-at, and there's a still form in one corner. Just a lump of folded limbs, bent neck and misery. But as we approach, it stirs, and then it's hard against the bars. So fast it's less movement than magic, dark and swift. An incandescent gaze fixes on me like the North Star.

"Master Egan. Master Egan, a gift for me?" The voice is scarcely a whisper. "A tender little morsel?"

And I recognise him. "Dav," I say.

"Mark? Oh Mark, of course, it is. Been a good fella?" Dav stares at me, and I take a few steps towards him.

Egan's hand closes over my shoulder.

"Steady," he says. "Steady. He is but part-way done."

These are those that aren't discarded, and didn't run. These are Day Boys yet to become Masters. Shifting slowly from one form to another. And this is far worse than that lock-up. Here's a hunger that reaches inside of me. I can feel Dain, and Egan and all the others in these Masters-not-quite. I can feel the Change coming on them without the Mastery.

"Just a little," Dav croons in a thin voice that penetrates. "Just a little. Come here, Mark. I've new secrets to share."

And what was still becomes motion. Like a flock of pigeons that's seen the hawk, except I'm the prey, and a hundred cages are rattled and tested, filled with cries and moans, and *just a little*.

Egan squeezes my shoulder. "Move," he says. "Move. You're safe, these cages cannot bend to their will, but it does not do to linger."

It's a long walk down that hallway: the unbearable weight of all that hunger, all those eyes new to predation, rolling in their orbits, reflecting the light of the hall. The air's hot and dry, and there's the thin smell of old blood and rancid piss. And they beat their hands against the bars, and cast their shadows across the floor, whip-like and hungry.

"Just a little, Master Egan."

Hands reach through the bars. And I think of that other prison. The hunger's so different there, and yet I'd be dead and ruined just as quick.

"Not enough blood in this boy for the least of you. And what there is, is thin stuff," Egan says. "Not enough to fill you up."

"Just a little."

"No reason in them," Egan says. "Not yet. Just hunger. Walk, boy, walk. You are safe with me."

Takes forever that minute or two, but we reach the end of it. At last.

Another door opens and shuts, and we're at another hall, more metal walls, a short one ending in another door. No cages this time, no cries, nor sound, but for our footfalls, and the beating of my heart. I can feel a panic rising. "Deep, breathe deep. A thousand terrors could not prepare you for this place; better to trust in your breathing." The door is old and made of metal, but like timber, it looks as if it's swelled some, though I don't know how that can be. Rust stains the door, a deep flaking red towards the bottom. One corner's buckled a little.

"Prepare yourself," Egan says, and he presses a hand against the door and begins to open it.

———

It's always been blood, and human blood at that. Dain says that they can't subsist on anything but. Some have tried, and it may work for a while, but that way lies madness. Our blood is at once calming and exciting to them. Those new to Mastery—and thus not quite Masters, I suppose—will play with it. Or they'll deny their hungers and seek some substitute.

Never lasts. There comes a point when they succumb. And if they don't, they sink down, low and lower. Grow more monstrous, and that's the thing, they become worse than they ever feared.

Hunger's a nasty creature. We've all had our bellies empty, we know its pull. But they've a hunger beyond hunger. Cruel and vengeful.

Was a Master once who fed only on swans. Had a madness, before the madness. Killed a whole town. A Master such as that isn't a Master anymore, but something ill and wrong, something that must be destroyed.

They say it was the swans that killed him, a mighty flock of them descending. Wasn't nothing of the sort, Dain says.

It was the Council of Teeth.

The door opens stiff and slow and shrieking. Even with Egan's great strength it's a long time opening. And then before us is darkness. Such suffocating midnight. Egan's fingers close around my wrist so tight I can feel the bones moving. He drags me through, and it's like he's dragging himself.

The door closes and it's dark, darker than anything I have ever known, and it takes the breath from me: more than a punch. I am gasping and keening.

The sound of dripping water and something else, a dim rustling that grows louder. And all I can smell is blood; it chokes the air. Nothing old or dead about it, this is quick and new, and I can't help but prickle and fear at the sense of it.

There is a momentary flash of light, no more than a match lit, but it seems a brightness grander than the Sun. A light of revelation, a filler of cracks and crannies. And I see it all with such vivid and swift clarity. Maybe I die a little. Step from one world to another.

Beyond a shallow pool they stand, coffins of stone or petrified wood heaped and jumbled in broad pyramids.

No. That sounds too neat, sounds too much of man, and these aren't men. This is the Council of Teeth lounging in these caskets, so many of them, the coffins extending beyond my vision. Every eye is upon me. A driving, terrifying brightness. More powerful than any Master I have ever seen, but these aren't Masters either. They're lords beneath the Mountain. This is the true City in the Shadow of the Mountain, here where the dark dips deep, and down and down and down.

And I close my eyes, and I'm granted a vision. Of a midnight vehemence that unfurled from these deep roots of stone, that spread bleak crow wings to beat against the wind, to smother and to rule. It rose up, and fell again. And buried itself, patient and deep.

Then all is of pitch again, complete and smothering, dark but for flashes of light behind my eyes.

"Still," Egan says. "Be still." And I realise that I am fitting and jerking, my eyes rolling back, teeth clenching so tight they might crack beneath their own relentless pressure. "Still."

And I find the calm, his cold fingers tight around my wrist, his eyes staring into mine, and there's light in that gaze and a path for me to follow, and I am home in my skull, and the Sun is shining, and the world is settled into its familiar rhythms. "Come back from those shudders," he says. "Come back from the fear. Still. Be still."

"I'm here," I say.

"Good," Egan says. "Because you must."

"So this is the boy?" A voice rises from the dark. Deep and as old as the rocks of the Mountain, the air sings and sighs like the walls are covered in leaves or leathery wings, and there is nothing cooling in that breath; it smothers and burns. "You are here in the dark that reveals all. You are here in the heat that marks the wind's demise, where old stone folds and sinks into the fiery heart of the world. All the voices whisper here. Whisper and die."

"He is young," another voice says, "to be the source of so much trouble."

"He has a knack for it," Egan says.

There is a laugh that gives me goose bumps; I feel a little faint.

Egan's grip tightens, and a finger touches my face.

"What should we do with him?" The finger pulls away. "Boy? What should we do with you? I am sure you have an answer for that. If you haven't bitten off your own tongue."

"Let me go home," I say.

"Why should we?"

"So I can repair what I have done. The dishonour of running. The dismay of my Master. Let me finish my days in my home."

"We are not known for second chances. Gifts given are to be seized, not fled from. You were to study the ways of this world, and instead you ran. What right do you have of it now? What right of breath or heartbeat?"

I swallow, and I can taste my blood. "If I do not deserve this, then be done with me." If death is what is meant for me, then I would hurry to it with my blood quick in my heart. Hurry to it, and have it finish me at once. I don't want any lingering. That was my mistake when I saw the spiral: I should have stayed and faced whatever threat it represented. I want to speak of it, but, instead, Egan's grip tightens. And I know there is no room for excuses. "Be done with me," I say again.

There's a chattering laughter, a cricketing wave of it, that echoes in the dark halls. Laugh ignites laugh, which ignites more laughter. And I'm washed over by their humour, made to feel like nothing.

"You ran. You ran. And then, you have committed acts of theft, and lingered with insurgents. And then, you let yourself be caught. To run, and return. To be so meek . . ."

"He did what he did to survive," Egan says.

"And that is reason enough? A beast does that. Those new-born things in their cages, they could claim survival is at the heart of their madness, too, and it would be true. That is why we have cages; why we have punishments. We are the quiet after chaos, we are the reason of shadows. The Council of Teeth, not just the bite."

The dark is closing in, I can feel it almost as tight as Egan's grip. I'm a-sweat and a-shake, and I can't see them that would judge me. But I open my mouth.

"I've always been loyal," I say. "I've always served."

"And we would expect no less," comes that burrowing voice. "But have you served us well?"

There is a sudden quivering of wings, or limbs part insect, part warm flesh, where those things should not share a likeness. It sounds wrong, and it settles into me that wrong, settles and builds. A shrill hissing floods the air.

"Leave him with us. We will decide."

Egan lets go of my arm, and the door opens and shuts before my eyes can adjust to the shifting light, but I get an image of so many dark shapes. And I am alone, and in the dark with the Council of Teeth.

There's silence a while, just the sensation of eyes. Of being watched and my skin's crawling. Why do folks watch me so? But I stand there as quiet and casual as I can. This isn't much different from them lost boys. So I tell myself.

"Why should we not just kill you now?"

And I want to say that I am just now starting to live, that I'm missing home, missing Anne, and the hot rasp of the wind through the trees, that I'm missing the rising and setting sun, the great big blind eye of the moon. But I stand still, not shaking, even as hands touch my face again and again. Fingers cold and urgent like stones that have swallowed frost and forgotten to thaw, touch that hurts and numbs at the same time so you can't tell the difference.

"Speak to us."

"I have always served my Master to my best."

"Your best."

"Your best. We find that hard to believe. You have brought dishonour on him, and through him, us."

And here, I see what I should have seen long before. Dain is my Master, but he isn't his alone. Dain has his Masters, too, and they are ancient in their Mastery.

"So killing me will honour him? Will honour you?"

"Boy, do not argue. You've not the wit for it."

I lower my gaze to the dark at my feet, which is just as dark as the dark before me. Impenetrable and unknowable. There is no truth, unless it is the ultimate truths. The darkness that is the end of all things. But how am I to know that? All I am is a Day Boy; pulse aching in my throat.

"Boy, you speak our name too often in vain."

I try not to show my fear, but fear is all I am now. How could they know? They're just prodding and poking, all the whispering voices.

"You, Dougie. Yes, we know your names."

"The wind whispers them to us."

"And good Grove, of whom you'll be the ruin."

"We see disaster all around you."

"The last days of a Day Boy are a storm, spinning and wild."

"A battle of possibilities."

"Are you to be drawn here, or cast out?"

"Are you to be a Master or a servant?"

"Are you worthy?"

Don't argue, I'm thinking. Don't argue. Don't argue. I want to argue, I want to know what the wind says, and why is it so cruel? It can't speak to them all the time, the air is still a good bit of the time. What if I am only good when the sky is becalmed? Are they watching then? I want to know all these things. But I keep my lips zipped, and in truth, it's all I can do not to drop, shaking, on the ground and beg for mercy. Maybe that's what they want.

A hand, hard as sticks, rough as a shattered stone, closes around my arm. "You're such a little thing, not a thread of meat on you."

"Not a thread, but there's blood in my veins. And it is yours." I try not to have too much quaver in my voice, but it is there. The air chills, my skin gets prickled and bumped with the cold. I'm a nerve: busting and fearful. "All of it is yours."

And at this moment, it is. Is that what they want, an offering? I don't wish for the ruin of my Master. I'm not one to roll over and spill secrets at whispers in the dark, but I'd die for those I love. I tilt my neck. Not that they've need of such acquiescence.

The hand tightens, and then I am lifted up. Up through the dark, and all I can feel is cold breath, the beating of dark wings. And I'd piss myself here if there was piss in me, but I'm dry and cracked as the red earth outside. My lips are tight against my teeth. My balls have crawled halfway up my guts.

"I could split your skull," says a voice right in my ear. Skin's prickling now, that voice is loud, so close. I can hear the clattering of its teeth. Feel the working of its muscles, hard with exertion, but easy with it, too, like it was born to flight, not stone. "Split your skull and bleed the story from you. All your monkey words and your fear and pain."

"Let me fall," I quaver. "Let me fall."

And it does.

I flip twice through the air, darkness, darkness and down and down.

And then there's hands snatching me up again. And this time there might be a drop of piss in me! I'm human after all.

"Do not think you can tell us what to do. Down here we plan, listening to the wind, down here we are thought and

146

scheming, and you are part of that. All of you in the open sky. We are the Stewards of Blood, the Council of Teeth, and you are a child of sticks and bones and piss in your pants. We are those that rule—and we always have been. We're the shadows that come spilling from the cracks with evening time. We are the voice of reason and the despair that comes with it. Those we made still think they're closer to you than to us, but they aren't, even if you can make them think they are. For all their hungers, they've not got a thimbleful of beating blood within them. They've no pulse but for yours, and that is why they cling to you so. But here is where they will reside, one day, down in the dark, one by one. When we call them to us."

My feet thump onto the hard ground, and I land heavily and roll on my back into piles of rocks and old bones. It hurts, but I stand. The earth is brittle beneath my feet.

"Leave us," the voices say. "Leave us, and call in the Master." I walk back through the door. It is opened before me, by something fast and strong, another loud squeal, and into that lit hall I am almost pushed. Egan looks at me, and I'm blinking like a newborn thing.

"They want to talk to you," I manage, and cough up a little dust. Egan's lips thin. He straightens his jacket. Brushes at the shoulders, actually fusses a bit, and I can see some of the man he was, or even the boy.

"You wait here," he says, turning to me. "No matter how long. No running off."

I smile, sort of. "No run left in me," I say.

Egan grunts and walks back to the Council. And I'm alone. Nearby in the hall of cages, one of them howls like a mad dog, and someone laughs. And I realise that the heart of the Masters' world is all rage and madness. The heart of the world that I live in is a beast cruel and sick.

I drop onto the ground, and push my palms into my eyes; my head is throbbing. I want to be sick, but I won't throw up here.

"You did good," comes a whisper: Dav. And it sounds like the Dav of old, the one who taught me to fight, to hold my tears, to be brave. "I can feel their satisfaction."

I don't move my hands from my face. "I did nothing."

But there's no answer.

———

Egan isn't that long, and when he comes back, he is quiet, a little broken in a way I can't understand. And I can only guess at what he's seen. Because he can see in the dark: He has its measure, and it's terrified him.

"What did they say?" And I ask it gentle, no arrogance at all. For a moment I think he's going to say nothing. He just looks at me, and then he smiles as if at some passing fancy.

"That if I were to kill you, now would be the best time. Perhaps the only time."

"So will you kill me?" I'm too tired to fight, even if I could.

Egan shakes his head. "Time to go home," he says.

We don't speak as we walk back past them cages of madness. But this time there's no reaching arms or cries. The Masters-in-waiting are silent, subdued. I don't see Dav, even though I look hard. Maybe he's hiding. Maybe he's ashamed. But he is what he is now. And the madness will pass, because it must.

I raise my hand in farewell, and then those lift doors open, and Egan's shuffling me through.

We take the lift with not a hint of conversation, up, slow and steady, though I'm remembering that dark flight, and it feels to me that this lift could stop, pause, and plummet at any change of heart in them below.

The Master at the door seems disappointed to see us pass, but we barely acknowledge him.

Egan opens the door to our carriage. "Hurry, boy," he says. "The Night Train waits for no one long."

But that night it waits for us.

———

I was too young to remember the insurrection, but the consequences . . . Dain says it was the last gasp. Most of the town's adults up in arms. Killed two of Dain's closest allies, wounded another, so he had to be put down. But that wasn't enough.

The ringleaders, when they were caught, were forced to Change. When they were mad with hunger, their families were fed to them, and when that was done, they were caged, dragged to the center of the town to await the judgment of the Sun.

And it found them wanting, as Dain might say. I heard it tore strips from them and boiled away their flesh like the Sun burns away a mist. Only a mist don't go the way they went, crooning and calling, pleading to the Sun, calling to the town to join them.

And then, finally, screaming. Cruel, monstrous.

Necessary, Dain said.

I guess I'm running my mind over it the whole way home—picking at it like it's some sort of ache and a puzzle wrapped in one. Egan doesn't talk, just me and him in silence, and this time there's no books. So what can you do but pick at what's there and what's been said. Two fools from the country, and the wreckage I've made of my life. I could have had more of these days of working, but all I did was cut back the share I had. I knew that Dougie and Grove had their times extended, but I'd never thought it could really happen for me. Now I've gone and ruined it.

I sit and stare at the dark. Nothing to see but the dim lights of distant homesteads, and I wonder at the lives of those who live there in that middle-of-nowhere grim. How do you measure out such a life?

We stop near midnight in the center of town, Mr. Stevens there at attention, must've been expecting us: His beard's trimmed, and even though I'm still all thought and fear—*There's a new boy coming, a new boy*—home brings out the grins. The sweat of it, the heat, the smells. This is my home, and I can't help but feel a little heroic. I've survived the City in the Shadow of the Mountain, I faced the Council of Teeth, I stole the red nails. Who wouldn't be proud? Midfield seems a little smaller!

Egan smacks me sharp on the back of the head. "This isn't an occasion for swagger, boy."

And he is right. Dain! What will Dain think of me? Such a thought was a mere abstraction on the train, now it's an impending terror.

Egan can see it on my face. Masters can see everything. "You know your own way home. Can I trust you to make it there?"

"Yes, sir," I say.

"Good." And then he's gone, and it's just me and my dread and my shame.

I'm almost creeping when I reach the house, but it doesn't matter. He will be aware of my presence.

"Home," I whisper as I open the door. I step through and the world tilts, and he's there, dropping from the ceiling, darkness coalescing. A form both familiar and like nothing I have ever seen before. His gaze swallows me whole. Studies me. Looking for wounds, looking for the story of my week past.

"I'm sorry," I say, and that sets him off.

"Sorry?" Dain rushes at me, like a storm made man-like, but shorn of none of its rage. The whole house quakes and bends, draws in, and I am certain to be crushed in his rage. I feel my own bones move in their joints. But I have met the fury of the Council of Teeth, no matter my shame, I cannot submit. I tilt my head, let him come at me.

Then it is gone, that terrible pressure, and it is only Dain staring at me, and I can't tell what he is feeling. But it is more full, darker, furious and smaller.

"Sorry," he says, and I cannot tell if it is a question or an accusation or an apology.

He shakes like a child—but I am the child, not him—I want to reach out and comfort him, or run away and never come back.

Then he looks at me one more time and flees the room.

There's the river rushing, quickening around the bend, sun's hot, but it's a lessening thing, grown to its limits and already retreating. Summer's passing is a slow slide down and then a drop. Few weeks from now, we'll see our first frosts. The trees are already turning, shifting to the ambers and the reds. And the road here is shaded in that colour on either side of the bank, and Anne's standing beside me. All the colours I could ever want.

"How was it?" Anne asks. We shouldn't be here, but we are. And there's a sweetness that shouldn't be, that is sweeter than any other, but I keep it bound up. I keep it where she can't see it: the foolish smile that I'm hoping doesn't mark my face. I am happy and terrified at once. I haven't seen her in so long. How can she put a deeper fear in me than any Master? I've faced that Council, I've had troubles find me that I'd never expected and seen them off, and yet, here, in front of her, it doesn't mean a thing.

I look at her steady as I can. "It wasn't so bad."

"The City of Monsters? Really? Heard you ran. Panicked and ran, out into the Red City. Even I know that is a bad thing to do." She says that last bit as though I'm stupid.

Maybe I am.

We're spitting off Handly Bridge, down on a log that's got caught in the bridge, half-submerged. I'm thinking it's a crocodile, and why not? Come all the way down from up north, where they grow big as logs, and I mean big logs. Grey and grinning, and rising from the murk to bring down water buffalo, or roos, or a man. Masters aren't the only predators.

"That was just ill circumstance," I say.

"Master Dain talking to you yet?"

"A little."

"You should have seen him when he thought you lost. He came to see my ma. Such a sadness."

I feel my heart clench.

"I thought it might even be the death of him."

"And you?"

Anne gives me a sly smile. "I knew you'd be back." She spits out across the shimmering air. "So a person can live there?"

"Yes, but why you'd want to is beyond me. All those folks dressed up, all them Masters crowding out the living."

Anne laughs. "All that city politicking, Ma says it drives the Masters to distraction. Chasing their tails with their teeth, and filling the air with schemes and machinations."

I hock another spit. "There was some of that, I reckon, yes."

"So what's it like in the City in the Shadow of the Mountain?"

"Dry and dark," I say. "No river like this." I close my eyes, feel the sun on my face, smell the muddy smells of our muddy river—no dust. Then I remember that place deep below, and the shallow ponds that stand before the stone coffins. I wonder if they really are shallow. Perhaps they run deep, deeper than this river, down into the hollow places of the earth. Perhaps they are the true death of the winds, the drowning of them once they have given up their secrets.

"Were you scared?" Anne asks, and there's a weight of mockery in her voice. Maybe I'm showing too much.

I puff out my chest. "Scared to hell sometimes, but I handled myself OK. I'm still breathing, and I saw the heart of that city, I saw the spaces beneath their great brass Luminance." And it still haunts my sleep, that bright dark, those endless pools, the hands that closed around my throat. And where they touched still stings.

Anne folds her hands across her chest. "You saw the young Masters' cages, too?"

I give her a good look. "You know about them cages?"

Anne snorts. "And you didn't? Whispers drift both ways."

"Of course I knew about them."

I think about those mad things, their howls and their cries. "It was a dreadful sight. And I have seen many dreadful things."

Anne snorts again, spits again into that brown surge beneath. "You ever think about going in them?"

"That's not my decision."

"Don't be a fool," Anne snaps. "It's always your decision. That's the grand decision, and it's not one that'll be offered to me. Damn boys club, with your boys rules. I hear over east they don't just have Day Boys, but Girls as well."

"You think you'd be a good Day Girl?"

Anne shakes her head. "I'd be better than that. Put the lot of you to shame," she says, and then with a smirk—and Dain's right, smiles have a sting to them—she's jumped off the bridge. I feel my mouth gape as I watch her drop down into that brown. And all I can think about is that log, and it hitting her, or hurting her. I've no choice but to follow. She might strike her head, she might drown or be lost, and I'd be the one that would get the trouble of it. And I would likely die myself, and I'd want it, too. Like I'd pushed her. Like I could ever push her. Why is it that I'm always following? But I do. I jump and I hit the cold water, breath knocked out of me, and I scramble-swim up, feeling out for her. Like she'd be near me anyway, the current's not moving that way.

Anne's already at the shore by the time I surface, lying flat against the river sand, and I swim to her, mouth snarling. The water's cool against my body, but the swimming's a strain: I'm out of practice. I feel a rising panic that for all I've seen and done, it'll be this river that'll have me. I breathe faster, and faster. But there's a calm I can find if I want it, if I'm lucky enough: And I find it. Current's taken me a ways, but I start for the bank. I take it slow and reach the shore, quite a way from where Anne is lying.

I get out of that water, gasping and spitting, and make the slow walk towards her, passing beneath the bridge, looking around in case of trolls. Nothing, of course, but it'd be just my luck if there was. I push through tall grass, and she's there, stretched on the sand. And I think about how beautiful she is, just lying there, and something pulls in my throat like an ache, like a cry, like a silence more full than any sound. And I put a finger to my lips as if to catch it, but you can't catch that.

I'm about to speak when Anne laughs.

"I thought I was going to have to jump in and rescue you there," she says.

"Just a stitch."

Anne's eyes widen, all a-mock. "A stitch you say. And you a Day Boy and all."

"Yes and it—"

"You're a good friend," Anne says.

"The best," I say, and she looks at me with those eyes of hers, full of quick thought and cutting edges when she wants them to be, but now they're sad.

"I'm frightened for you, Mark."

"Nothing to be frightened of," I say. But we know it's a lie. We know there's plenty to be scared of in this world, and not all of it is my Master's kind.

The winds are cool now, no more of those furnace breaths— these have shivers in them. And the sky is so clear, just the leanest streaks of cloud amongst all the blue.

"Don't you change," Anne says. Her lips touch mine. Just the scantest of kisses. There's a rattling roar in my head, and when it's gone, so is she, and all I can hear is her laughter, and the river finding rocks around the bend. I don't give chase, I'm too shocked by it. I drop to the sand, my feet pointing at the brown water, and my eyes to that autumn-blue sky. The kiss still a heat on my lips. It floored me far worse than anything Dougie ever threw.

But how come I'm smiling?

Then I think about the music. I forgot to tell her about the music.

When I'm mostly dry, I find the Culverts' place, and mark the door with the circle and seven. And there's yard work to be done, and I'm quick to doing it in the cooling afternoon. Rake the leaves, straighten the back fence.

Dain's stirring when I come in, but he doesn't call for me. He moves through the house, a presence obvious, a pressure in the air. But he keeps from me, and I keep from him.

Dinner's over with quick, and the cleaning of the kitchen, and I really have no idea what time it is. My head's full of a different sort of rhythm.

"This damn book, this endless book," Dain shouts, and I smile until he calls me into his study. He has one hand over a sheaf of papers, ink staining his fingers. And I feel like it's the us of old.

"You'll finish it," I say, almost like I believe it.

Dain laughs. "There are those that scribble more furiously than me, writing words that no one sees. In these everlasting selves we've become, we've lost the wit, the inclination to produce work enduring, instead we are that work entire. We are the Imperatives, and it seems that is enough." He pauses from his pontificating. "Boy. You smell of the river and you smell of that girl. Must you always disappoint me?"

I open my mouth to speak, but he silences me with a gesture.

"I'm not angry, not tonight," he says. "You came up against two unstoppable forces, rivers and girls. I've no answers for that, other than to express my disappointment; you know my and Mary's wishes on the matter. Must you always make things so difficult for yourself, Mark?"

I hang my head. I've no answer in me, though I wish I did.

And all I can think of is that kiss.

"Boy," Dain says. "You disappointed me. I went to the City to plead for your position, and to keep you on here for another year. Instead, you brought shame to me. Instead of continuity, there is to be a new Day Boy within the week."

And that hits me almost as hard as that kiss. "Egan said I was to train him."

Dain nods. "His name is Thom. You will have a few months and then your tenure will be done. Dav had longer, but you were younger, and untrained, not like those Crèche boys. And I had more influence even back then."

"I will not let you down," I say.

"Of course you won't." That he sounds like he means it brings a tear to my eye. I wipe it away, before I start snuffling properly.

"I saw Dav when I visited the Council," I say. "Dav half-changed in the belly of the Mountain."

"I know," Dain says. "I am sorry you were a witness to that. I am sorry for all that happened. But it is done. The path to Mastery demands a long time in the Wilderness of Hunger, a long dark time. You don't make steel with a gentle touch. But it is a hard thing to see."

When I look up, he's gone. Out into the night. And the pages are scattered on the table. That book that doesn't want to be written; that book he's been writing since I've known him. I pick up the pages and read, but there's little about them, to pull me in. Mainly dates and figures.

1988, Inception.
1997, the Glaring (A rigorous intercept).
2002, the Great Crash.

I can't make anything of it.
The last page I put upon the table, and on it is written:
Don't read my things, boy.
So I don't.

They all have their yearnings. *Their artistries. Their obsessions. Egan's tall house with its deep basement has a yard full of sculptures, half-finished. Curious beasts, expressions empty, that make him yell in frustration. Kast has a garden that he tends, but anything that grows in it is the Parson boys' doing. "He don't have the touch," they say. Tennyson's equations cover a great blackboard in his house that stretches along the rear walls. Twitch says he works and works at it, but his proofs are proof of sense. And Sobel, I don't know what he does, but he keeps it hidden. Sobel doesn't like mockery.*

They've all the time in the world for their passions, and have found themselves at passion's end.

Maybe the blood is all that truly fascinates them now.

Maybe all those Masters are fooling themselves, playing at Great Works, when they've no great work in them.

Sobel the Good Soldier that Went Bad.

Dougie tells this story like it was a book or a play. There's noises and motions, crashing and fire. He's one that isn't given to pride except when it's his Master. There's more of Dougie in this story than you would you think, or less. I know he thinks himself a soldier. But he don't have it in him, not really. There's a weakness in his heart. He's covered it with cunning, but he'd turn and run. Sobel wouldn't pick a boy other than one like that. He knows a soldier is a service and a threat, and Sobel doesn't want any threats.

There was great battles in those Before days.

All them engines of war. Turning, grinding down, and it don't matter which way they face, there was plenty to do the dying for them. Always was in those last days before these calmer ones.

Trenches laid out ragged across the ruined earth. Forces directed this way and that, but there was no forward motion, only a quickening retreat. The world was shrinking, in all ways. There were jets and rockets, and secret stations in the sky. But they fell into the wells of gravity like stars. The heavens broke them, and new monsters walked the earth. New, or so old and forgotten they might as well have been new. Everything old is new again, they say. So it doesn't matter which you side with.

There were protocols.

And when the engines fail, there is always the soldiers. Men and women (yes, the women fought, too, don't be so shocked). Bodies to hurl against the dark frenzy of a world given over to change.

And there he was, in those trenches. He fought with the best of them. He saved many lives, before he was swayed, before he started taking them. Says there's a certain heroism in giving in. Sobel was always too big for the resistance. He fought when it could fit him, and when it couldn't anymore, he shed it like a skin. Oh, they say there was none like him.

Weren't no cages then, just the open spaces of the battlefield and a quick shifting of loyalties, a following of new Imperatives. You know how it is. When he became . . . what he is, he returned to the headquarters.

Gave his final briefing. That's what he did: And it was written in their blood.

There was no resistance after that; in truth there scarcely was before.

Soldiers finish things that they never get to start. He knew that, he has that deepest in him, that finishing drive.

Sobel was a soldier. And he finished them. And now he is here.

Some soldiers are let to pasture because they deserve it. Some soldiers are let to pasture because they are feared. You can decide which my Master was.

Dain's left me a note. *Certain has need of you.*

Certain's farm is just out of town, down past the river and over Handly Bridge. I cross that thinking of Anne. She'd be in school, I guess. I been there once—on Master's business—looks to be a boring place, all that laying of pencil to paper, all those maps. I prefer Dain's telling of the world. He says I get to see it as it is, that the school's story isn't right. Blinkered, is the way he puts it.

Certain's pottering in his shed when I reach it. His dog, Petri, runs out to greet me—she's a blue heeler.

He comes out of that shed, favouring his good leg, and wiping dirt from his face. "You ready to work hard?"

I nod, and he smiles. "Well, you think you are."

And that's what we do beneath that autumn sun, and there's no let up in either. There's fences need fixing to keep out the deer and the roos, cattle to tend, and Certain teaches me patiently. He's gentle with the beasts when he needs to be, firm when that's needed, too, and Petri's always there, alert.

"You get a good dog," Certain says, "and the world runs easier. First few years, when I tried my hand at this, I tried it alone, and I tried it awful." He wipes his face with his sleeve, gives me a long look, and it's judgmental and generous at once. "It's a hard thing, leaving them. A lot don't make it. A lot feel the guilt, or the power lacking behind them, and it makes them cruel. Or weird, and those don't last long: They walk out of town, and they never come back. Some fear the night. Lie in bed waiting, and it's worse for them because they've never known just what that's like."

"What about you?"

Certain gestures at the land about us. "I work my acres, I live as good a life as I can, and I feel all that stuff, too, but I try to forget it. Put the past where it belongs."

He shows me how to fix a fence, how to put the posts in true, and return tension to a wire.

And we talk of simple things, not the Council or the Masters, not the other Day Boys, but ordinary town gossip. Certain's got his heart set on Mary, I can see it, the way he talks of her. I don't talk about Anne, but he manages to make me blush when he mentions her, and I know I don't need to.

Not just the town we talk about, but the land. It's got its severities, but it can give up splendours. The north field's black earth, nearly dark as my fingers, is fertile and good for growing wheat. The southern field's red earth, clay and hardworking, needs constant correction: We're at it with gypsum to break it down a bit. He's got a few head of cattle, a couple dozen sheep. And all of them demand different things depending on the time of the year.

Most of the time, though, we work in silence, and it's comfortable. There's no need to fill it with myself. There's no need for boasts or anger. The work is its own talk. And I like it.

"You could come work with me," he says at last, when we're packing up. "Dain says he can clear it with the Council. I can spare you a lot of the big mistakes," he grimaces. "And the drink, too."

I feel my belly drop. "I guess this means Dain's made up his mind," I say. "About me."

Certain sighs. "Dain'll change his resolution a half-dozen times between now and then. It's no gift, what he'd give you is pain—you seen them cages didn't you, boy? In the belly of the Mountain. I saw them once myself. It's slow and it's painful, for those chosen ones, and not all of them that enter come out right.

"There was a madness to those first ones, and they've contained it somewhat, but it's still there. Think long upon it, if you're ever offered that. I seen it, what it can do. A mate of mine—Day Boy like you are, and I was—he got the Change, grabbed it with both hands and all, and it drove him to such madness that they had to put him down like a dog." Certain scratches Petri's head. "But not before he came back into town, all rolling eyes and screams, strong with the blood and the hunger. Took three of them to hold him down.

"I was there when he died in his cage, watching as the sun split the horizon. He didn't scream, he laughed, he caught my eye and he laughed, and flesh burned from his bones, and he laughed."

Certain shakes his head, takes a long draught of his water.

"Why'd he come back?"

"We'd been mates. Close. He'd wanted to share. Them Masters are sentimental folk. Drink your drink, boy, you've a long ride home." He scratches his head, and for a moment he isn't staring at his land, but some moment long past and painful.

He takes a breath, and smiles at me, eyes crinkling. "You think about it. My offer."

"I will," I say.

Certain leaps down the steps and onto the path, and I drink the last of that cider and I get my bike.

I'll think on it, but there's a while to go yet.

I take a detour. Ride to the edge of town, where the road turns ragged, boiling with grass, all rising crusts of tar and concrete, and the old signs sag and sing in the wind. *You're Leaving Midfield,* says one.

I wonder what that might be like, to leave and not come back.

There's plenty out there, towns and the like, and other cities (maybe), but there's haunts and ghouls, too, and cold children, and all sorts of damned things. I shiver a little, then I turn my bike around and ride back into town, and then take the winding path home.

Said I'd think about it, but I already have an answer.

I **dream of** the City and it's burning. I dream of the Red City and I'm running down those ruddy narrow streets, the drunken Hunter behind me. I come to the door of them lost boys, and I bang a fist hard against it. Grainer opens it, but he doesn't let me pass—there's a light in his eye. I try to push through, and he slaps me to the ground.

"We're all burning tonight," he says, and I can feel the heat on my back. Sweat stings my eyes. "You best come tomorrow when we're all dead."

Door shuts.

And I turn to face my Hunter, and there's nothing there. "Gotcha," the Dark says, and there's a knife in my chest, stuck and unmoving, and all I am is the dying.

I wake with a yell, scrambling up against the headboard, cracking the back of my skull against the wall.

"Nightmare?" Dain asks, and he's standing over my bed, hand reached out to my face. Well, that doesn't help! Lucky I don't tend to a weak bladder.

I sit up. Nod. For some the nightmare would start now,

with a Master waking them. They only wake you when they want to scare or if they're polite and enjoy conversation, like Dain. They feed mostly without anyone ever knowing. Fast and silent, in and out.

"You've been having bad dreams a lot lately," he says. I don't bother lying, just nod.

"I remember what it was like to have bad dreams, and good ones."

"You ever miss them?" I ask. My back's prickly with sweat.

Dain's sitting at the foot of my bed.

"No. No, I don't." He stands, lips part grinnish. "It's good you're awake, means I don't have to wake you."

I look to the window, can't be later than 2 a.m. Might not even be midnight for all I know.

"What needs doing?"

"There's a lost girl."

Anne.

Dain sees; shakes his head. "No, not Anne. It's the Dalton girl."

"Sally?"

"Yes, Sally. She is missing."

I look at him hard, and he shakes his head again. "No, no. It is not one of ours. We do not hide what we do. This is our town, we are its Masters. People do not lose themselves without our permission."

"Then where is she?"

"I don't know." Dain says. "Get dressed, and be out the front in five minutes."

I dress as fast as I can, socks mismatched, and am still sleepy-eyed and blinking when we leave the house. Dain doesn't run ahead or disappear, but walks by my side. And I've a memory of a cold hand closed around mine, a handkerchief dabbing at my snotty nose, and the tears that filled my eyes.

Been a while since we walked together. Be quite pleasant weren't a girl gone missing now.

The moon's rising, and the sky's streaked with clouds. I can smell smoke greasy with wet wood. There's lit torches everywhere, working their way through the dark. And I wonder why we were so late on the scene.

"Thought she'd be found by now," Dain says. "Kids have a habit of running out, once or twice. But I was wrong. There's something wrong about the whole thing."

The whole town is up and in the square, and to one side are the Day Boys and their Masters. Sobel glares at me, but it's more a matter of habit than true ire. The rest don't even spare me a glance.

Dougie gives me a little bow, and Sobel clips his head. Grove grins, and Egan whispers something in his ear; the smile dies on the vine of his lips.

There's a tension here, and something that borders on anger.

It's Dain that walks to the middle of the square. He raises his hands, and all chatter stops.

"We're to take the east and the south sides of the town," he says. "There's plenty enough people in the woods."

Like there can ever be enough people in a search. How much space does a young girl take up? How easy would it be to miss her? To walk by whether she's hiding, or dead still?

Far too easy, of course.

"Where do you want me looking?" I ask Dain.

"Under the houses, down Esbeth Street, across to Main."

That's eight blocks, but I can do it. He passes me a lantern.

And it should be some sort of magical night with that moon and those clouds, and the whole town out, like some sort of fairy carnival, but it's loud and desperate, and we search the town, and I hope it's just Sally walked off in a huff somewhere. But from the look of her parents, both quiet, eyes wide, I know that's not so. This isn't a running, but a snatching and stealing. Another rogue Hunter maybe, though why they'd take a girl instead of one of us boys don't make no sense.

The air's smoky with lit torches.

And a wind comes up, and it's another hint of summer's failing, like the borders of some ancient empire's been ceded up, and the troops are falling back to the next stronghold, sliding up north, sorrowful but no less certain in their march.

I scramble under house after house, calling her out. And I don't find nothing but growling dogs, and cats, and dust, and more spiders than I can bear. But I keep looking, covered in webs by the time I'm done. Just walking back to the center of town, night growing later. When I hear the call.

And I start running.

Sometimes the stories don't work out like you want them to. I never found Sally Dalton. That was Dougie, and he wailed into the night, and came back with eyes wide, and he didn't say how she looked, and I never wanted to know. I could see the raw of it in his eyes, and that was too much.

World's an awful cruel place.

I saw Anne held tight in Mary's arms, and Mary, laughing, mocking Mary, glares at me when I come close.

So I walk home, alone, and Dain is waiting for me in the kitchen, already a cup of tea there, steaming, and I fold my hands around it.

"Nothing we could have done," he says.

"And who did this?"

"The trail leads into the wilderness. If they're half bright, they're already miles away from here. Doesn't matter. We'll find them. Justice will be done."

"Justice won't do much for Sally."

Dain sighs. "No, it won't. Sometimes all we have is the strength to make sure something doesn't happen again. And even then . . . Mark, this is a dark world, it's always been a dark world, and it is all too quick and casual to remind us of that. There's storms and fire and flood, and the hungers of the mad. And this thing is rare, it has always been rare, but it is even rarer now. We protect our own, even if that isn't enough. He will be brought to justice."

And I leave it at that.

Two days later, a man's body is left in the square, arms bound with wire, throat cut. No one I know, no one the town knows. Don't look like evil. Just looks dead.

Dougie and I, we poke it with a stick on a dare. But there's not a hint of pleasure in it. The body just lies there. And we're left standing like fools, or worse, like we've done something that mocks Sally. And I know she was sweet on me. That she didn't deserve such a death.

The body's burnt. The ashes cast into the river by a priest of the Sun, and that's all that's said on that strange fella dead.

"Did he do it?" I ask Grove. "Do you think he really did it?"

"Of course he did," Grove says all definitive. "Otherwise they wouldn't have killed him."

Sally's buried in the cemetery on the hill, under a tree that flowers white. You can look down on Midfield from there; watch everything that's going on. Prettiest places are always kept for the dead, not that they care anymore. People who visit them up on that gorgeous hill might, but who visits the dead? Who sits there mourning and admiring the view? Doesn't make a whole lot of sense.

When I'm gone, I'm telling you, just chuck my quiet bones by the road, it's what they've known all these years, and I'm not one for ceremony. Ceremony's too close to what them Masters have.

There's crying and sadness, and that night, the five Masters visit her grave, and lay night flowers upon it, and a symbol of the Sun. None of which brings her back of course. She's lost. Dougie found her, but she's lost forever. Tears, flowers and suns don't do nothing for that. We're all lost eventually, I guess. We've all cried a little bit, but I don't remember tears like for poor Sally Dalton.

Part Three

A Gunshot, Aimed at Birth

The World Thought Otherwise
Like It Always Does.

Nine years old, that's pretty much all I know.

The train pulls in, and Thom steps lightly to the platform, his papers checked by the Ticket Master, who pats his head and grins at me. "He's all yours, boy."

I flick the Master a coin. "For your trouble," I say, and the smile slips. But he takes the coin, and the train gets going again. I look around me. Half-expected some of the other boys to be here, but no. And that's a good thing.

Mr. Stevens gives me a nod, as he heads back to the line. It's just me and the new boy.

"Well, let me look at you," I say.

He's a small one, all right. I could carry him above my head like a bag of leaves.

"I am what I am," Thom says. He grips a small suitcase in one hand so tight I can see the whites of his knuckles. It's heavy, I can see him struggling, but I don't make no offer of help. A Day Boy's got his pride.

"Yep, you are at that. Strong westerly could blow you over the ridge. We've miles to go before you sleep and all."

Thom heaves a little sigh.

And I give him a grin almost as wide as our Master's, and twice as true. "Oh, woe is us and misery."

Thom drops the suitcase and bunches his fists, and it's a struggle not to laugh.

"Don't mind me," I say. "I'm at mock, we all are here, but you'll get used to it. Don't waste a fist on a foolish smile. You and me, we're allies—as close as—and I'll be teaching you the traps. So don't start with the fighting."

Thom scowls, lifts his heavy bag, and we walk home.

Dain is waiting for us. He nods at me. "Thank you, Mark," he says.

I give him a little bow.

"Though you would do well to not annoy the Ticket Master so."

My face grows hot and red, and I catch a little grin on that young Thom's face.

"There is a lot you will learn from Mark, Thom, and some things you should not. You are a Day Boy, but that doesn't mean the rules and proprieties do not apply to you."

Thom nods his head, and Dain reaches out a hand. "It is a pleasure to meet you at last."

Thom takes it, and it's a good shake. He almost doesn't look scared.

"Mark will show you to your room."

"Our room," I say, magnanimous—I put the new bed in a couple of days back, carried it piece by piece up from the cellar.

"Do as Mark says," Dain says. "He will teach you the ways of this town. He knows it like few others." He nods his head, then is gone. And it's just me and Thom.

He drags his case after me, and pushes it onto the end of the bed. "You got a lot of stuff in there?" I ask.

Thom shrugs.

There's not much in his case to be sure, even for such a young one. A pair of heavy boots, jeans, shirts; one which has a yellowing oval picture of a bat on it. He's a few heavy books, too—they were the weight of that case—and I look at them with interest until Thom closes the case and slides it back under the bed. Maybe I pried too close.

"We've plenty of books here," I say. "You like books?" Thom shrugs again.

"Good." I look at my hands; rough and sore with the day's work. "You tired?"

He nods.

"I'm tired, too," I say. "Bone tired. There's work in the morning."

But I don't sleep much and some time late in the night, late enough that morning can't be too far off, I hear something I've not heard for a long time. I hear a young boy crying.

It's all right, I want to say, but I keep my mouth shut. You don't take away a Day Boy's pride. You don't tell them it's all right to cry into the dark.

You just let them do it.

———

We're up early, and there's a list of chores. Such a list like I've never seen, but it's all simple stuff—a door to be marked with the circle and seven, goods to be bought, yard work—that'll take us around the town. I get Dain's logic. The boy needs to know his home and quick. Besides, we have an extra mouth to feed.

You don't know a place by staying indoors, you know it by walking and riding. I've got a bike for Thom. But today we walk. He pulls on a vest, near enough new and a flat brown cap more stylish than what I'm used to. Dressed up. I give him the look up and down.

"Working clothes," he says.

I'm feeling a bit threadbare against them. Nicest working clothes I've seen. I can't quit staring.

"What do you wear here?"

Shake my head. "What we're given."

Thom looks down at himself. "This is what I was given."

"Then it'll do," I say.

Out in the sun and the clear blue sky, Thom's skin is pale as dry silt. He blinks in the light and takes a deep breath, like it's his first.

"You'll get used to it," I say.

Thom nods.

Dougie is sitting in the shade under the awning at the tanner's, picking his teeth with a twiggy bit of stick, pretending he does that all day. He gets to his feet, slow, and sets his gaze on Thom. Doesn't seem too impressed. "So this dandy-hat the new one?"

"This is Thom," I say.

Dougie reaches out a hand. "Douglas," he says, and yanks his hand away as Thom reaches for it. "Gonna need to be faster than that."

Thom sweeps out a foot so casual it's like it didn't happen, and Dougie lands hard on his arse, breath whoomphing from him.

"That fast?" Thom asks.

"That fast," I say, and we walk on, leaving Dougie with his legs out straight and dust on his pants, wondering just how he got there. Could offer the bastard a hand up, but I know he wouldn't take it.

Thom's all pleased with himself, for sure, even chuckles a bit. So, as soon as we're out of sight, I give him a clip under the ear, make certain he's not expecting it—because I saw how quick he was, too—but I nearly miss anyway. Get the feeling he expects most things, even before I know to give them to him.

He skips ahead, light on his feet, flashing a big grin back at me. "What?"

"You so desperate to make enemies?"

Thom gives me a look of genuine surprise. "I did what I had to. In the Crèche . . ."

"This isn't the City," I say.

"I know," Thom says. "I know."

I laugh. "You surprised him, yep . . . I'll give you that. What you've done is confuse him, but he'll want some sort of payback, bloody or otherwise. I want to hear about this Crèche of yours."

"I'll tell you one day I guess," Thom says.

"You two," Grove shouts. "Slow it down."

Grove catches us as we walk onto Main, takes a while because we don't really slow down that much. Puts a hand out to Thom.

"You must be Thom."

Thom gives that hand a good old shake.

"And you're Grove."

"Yes indeed," he says, pleased as punch that someone's spoken of him. "Like your cap, by the way."

Thom smiles. "I've another exactly like it at home. This one's yours."

He takes off the cap, fiddles with it, makes it somehow bigger, and passes it to Grove. Three movements fast enough that Grove is still blinking, not sure what to say.

"Nah, I couldn't—"

"Got another just like it," Thom says. "I won't take that back. It's yours."

Grove looks at me, and I nod. "How do I look?"

"OK, I guess." They'll all be wearing caps in a week or two from now. Not me, of course. On principle. Though Grove does look fine in it, the bugger.

"Hear you might be working Certain's farm. After your time," he says.

"Might at that," I say.

Grove nods, and slaps my back. And I know he's genuine. "Was worried after your time in the City. Thought they might cast you out. But this is good news."

"Yes," I say.

"Was going to miss you. Now I won't have to!"

Only until you go to the City. Only until they groom you for those cages. But I don't say it. Just smile back at his smiling face.

"Nice cap, Grove," Mary says.

"Better put in an order for a dozen of them," I say. Mary puts a note in her big book. Something like order caps, I reckon—she closes the book with a loud clap before I can get a view.

"And this is Thom," I say. "My replacement."

Mary frowns.

"Don't pretend you didn't know," I say.

"Mark, why would I pretend that? Why would I even need to pretend that? Heard you'll be working out at Certain's farm; can't get rid of the likes of you. Now where's your list? I'm guessing it'll be a big one this time."

I pass it to her, and it's generous all right.

"Lucky there's two of you," Mary says.

I don't think it's lucky at all.

"She seemed nice," Thom says as we lug all that stuff back home. Soap and flour and milk and meat and a good bag full of food headed for the coolroom. "And, I'll give you this, that Grove is a fine fella. Doesn't have a drop of betrayal in him."

"He doesn't at that," I say.

"It's sad," Thom says. "World's going to eat him entire. Or you will."

What nine-year-old thinks these thoughts, let alone says them? A kid of the Crèche, so it seems.

"Shut your fool mouth," I say.

Thom repositions the bag on his shoulders, settles it there, dripping at the edges. "Truths said or not are still true."

Give him another clip under the ear, and this time he's not ready at all for it. Never felt more satisfied.

But it's a brief thing, that joy, because I know he's right.

"Storm's coming," shouts Twitch, his bike crashing past our place, wheels twin blurs, joy and panic in his eyes. He brakes and slides, gets off, face beady, wiping at his brow, straightens his new cap on his skull. I give him a look, and he doesn't even notice. "Was up on Cravin Peak, clouds coming in all ways," he says, words all bunched together. "Gonna be a wild thing."

Other bikes are converging like those thunderous clouds, and I'm wondering why we weren't called up to the lookout. Dougie rides right next to me. I look around for Grove, but he's not there.

"Now that looks better," Dougie says gesturing at the newly mown front lawn. "Was a disgrace."

Storm's been coming all day, as much under our skin as in the sky, feels like. The sky blue as a sky can be, and unseasonably hot. And me taking Thom all over the town, letting him draw the circle and seven. Showing him the place where I was cut by the Hunter: seemed to think it was all my fault. Would've hit him, but there's truth enough in that. This day was an itch you can't scratch: electric and flat all at once. Been building to this. That smudge of dark on the horizon. And that smudge is a spreading stain, and a tension that pulls down low and to the top of your skull.

"Gonna hit before sunset," I say.

"Long before," Dougie says, scratching his scalp.

"And it's going to be wild," Twitcher repeats.

The others nod. We're going to need to see to the safety of our Masters.

There's a couple of roofs that need tending to, so we go in groups and start working. Hammers and nails. A riot of industry, as Dain might say.

And then in she rolls. Sudden massive thunder. Lightning forking, rain coming in sheets.

The storm's raging when I see a girl on the road that fronts our place. I run out and see it's Anne. I drag her in, Thom waiting at the door for us.

"What ya doing? Out in this damn storm," I say, once I get her a towel.

"Came faster than I thought it would." She gestures at her bag, bulging with this and that. "Was out doing deliveries."

The house is creaking. Lightning cracking and beating the earth outside, like the world's raking its dazzling fingers across the town.

"Well, you're just going to have to wait it out," I say.

"We'll look after you, miss," says Thom, and he's standing so straight it makes my heart ache.

"Don't need no looking after," Anne says. "Just need cover."

"I've the stove burning," I say. "Tea's on."

She nods at that. And we're soon drinking that tea, dark and sweet, and feeling the house shake.

"They say the storms are getting fiercer." She takes another sip of her tea, stirs in some more sugar. "Like the world's trying to rid itself of us. And them."

"Need worse storms than this," I say.

And there's a burst of thunder that makes me jump, and a crash of something heavy that doesn't help with the jitters either. Thom laughs, and I give him a look, but I can see that he's as spooked as I am.

A girl coming out of the storm, even if it's a girl we know, seems awful suggestive of odd things to come. And Anne, if I'm true about it, scares me more than anything. Even if it's the sweetest sort of fear.

"Storms bring monsters," Anne says.

"The monsters are already here," Dain says, making us jump. He likes an entrance. "Miss Anne, I am sorry, but it's true. The monsters have been here for quite some time. This is just a storm. Now, you may stay the night. If there is no mischief."

Anne blushes at that; there's some heat in my cheeks, too. "Or I can accompany you home through this storm. Don't worry, you will be quite safe."

"Will I now," Anne says.

Dain's face shifts in ways I'm not sure I've ever seen it shape. He folds his arms across his chest: all careful and considered. Protecting himself, or her, or both of them.

"Your mother and I have an agreement." His voice is soft. "And I am a man of my word."

Anne looks at me over her teacup. "Well, you raised him proper. And that goes in your favour," she says, and I realise that these two had scarcely ever said a word to each other. And that that goes for most of the town. What they're used to, and what I am, are such different things we might be in different towns. "I'll spend the night here, thank you. But if you would let my mother know? I know you'll be out in this, all of you will."

Dain nods his head. I can see the storm in his eyes, his pupils wide. The Masters are men of moods and heights emotional. And he stands there, body electric with the wild air.

"There's a piano in the living room," Dain says, as though she doesn't already know it. "If you would do us the honour."

Anne smiles. "The honour would be mine."

I'm glad now I've kept it dusted. Not that Dain would allow anything else.

Anne plays a few dancing notes, then looks up at Dain. "You keep this well-tuned."

"I tune it myself," Dain says, and there's more than a hint of pride in his words.

"So it's true what they say about you?"

"We hear the notes, perfect, yes."

She plays, music I've heard, and music I haven't. It's a beautiful sound. Dain seems to relax; more than relax, he's transported. But it's Thom that surprises: He has the biggest, purest smile I've ever seen on his face. After nearly an hour, she stops. Dain's eyes have less of the storm in them. He is still as stone. Anne looks at me, as if to ask if that's what he's always like.

I shake my head. Takes a lot to drive the storm out of a man like him. And all too little to draw it back.

"My mother will be worried, Master Dain."

"Yes, yes she will," Dain says like he's just woke from a dream, and I guess he has. His pupils expand, and his head swings towards the door. It's calling him again.

Thom clears his throat. "I'm to bed," he says.

I raise my eyebrow; get the arch good, I can feel it.

"You'll be sleeping on the lounge, I guess," Thom says.

Dain looks at me with those storm-lit eyes, lightning and thunder, the threat and the echo of it, and I feel myself wilt, my eyes wander.

"Yes, 'course I am," I say.

So it's decided, Thom to his bed and Anne to have mine.

Dain's there till the others are abed, and me dragging stale cushions from the linen cupboard to place on the three-seater. He watches me make up the couch good and proper. "You will be a gentleman," he says.

"'Course I will," I says. "When am I not?"

Dain snorts. "Then I best give Mary a visit."

I can see he wants to be in the middle of that storm, that he wants to run with it.

"You best," I say.

He's already gone.

And I spend the night a-toss and a-roll on that damn lounge, leather stuffed with bricks, I reckon. My head on cushions smelling of dust and age; it seems to have shrunk some because I can't get myself to sleep. And I'm thinking of Anne and Thom in the other room.

I wake early, it's still dark, but I must've got some sleep: Dain's staring over me. The storm is quietening, but for the rain's soft breath and fall.

I sit straight up, blinking, confused: Is it day, is he up in the day?

Dain raises his hand, gestures for me to lie back down. He's soaked to the bone, his eyes glowing, but he looks like the night's done for him well. He looks restful, calm almost, if any of his kind were capable of calm.

"No need for you to rise just yet," he says. "There'll be work for you to do in the morning."

"I was a gentleman," I mumble ruefully.

"You always are," Dain says with a chuckle. "You always have been. Now sleep, long day ahead."

I'm up first light and the rain's still falling, lighter soaking rain, got coffee brewed, and I'm sitting on the verandah, watching the rain fall. Smelling the damp in the air. Sometimes all I want is for nothing to change, but those regular shifts of season, the heat into cold, the cold into heat. I want to stop time and step out of everything, and watch the world around me, as I am. But all I get is these quiet and brief times. Me, and this dark brew, and the lightening of the day, and the ache that runs through my body, like tears and laughter mixed together. I'm a young bloke, but I can't help feeling that time is running down, that it's slipping from me. There's nothing for it but to take some pleasure from the cup in my hands, from the world and its silence.

I'm sitting there, maudlin and watching the rain.

Hear laughter behind me.

"There you are," Anne says, and she smiles at me. And I'm happy to see her, and angry at once, cause my quiet sadness is broken, and even that ache is fragile, and I'm jealous—there, I admit it.

"He's always up early," Thom says.

"Fella can have too much sleep," I say, and I take my cup and brew them some more coffee, and we all sit there looking out at the rain, silent, everything silent but for the hiss of it. And

Anne's hand touches mine, and there is a rushing wild as any storm within me, but I sit still. Until her hand lifts, and it's like it never happened, and maybe it didn't. We stare out into the lifting gloom. And maybe I do want things to change.

Trees are down, and the light picks the wounds from the shadows one by one. Eucalypts that have fallen, bottlebrushes that have split, green apples dropped. Got axe work ahead.

"Tell me when you want to go home," I say to Anne.

"Soon," Anne says. "Mary'll be waiting."

I look to Thom.

"Get some umbrellas," I say.

We walk through the wet. Thom splashing through puddles, Anne and I walking close.

"He adores you, you know," she says. "You keep him safe."

"Much as I can," I say. "Ain't much safe in this world."

"We all know that," she says.

Mary's standing at the door when we arrive.

"Ma'am," I say.

She frowns at me. "You been a gentleman?"

I nod, even manage it without a smirk. Because I have been, haven't I?

"He saved me from the storm and all," Anne says.

"Don't know why you were out that way," Mary says.

And I feel a little heat again. Mary pays a bit of attention to that, but lets it pass, both of us too good at reading faces. "Thank you for bringing her home."

"Pleasure," I say.

"I brought her home, too," Thom says.

Mary smiles. "'Course you did. Now, I've bacon cooking. You all hungry? There'll be work for you boys, no doubt."

No doubt of that at all.

So we eat at Mary's, and by the time we're done, the rain's fading down, following the storm into the east, and the sun's up, and the sky looks as though it's been scrubbed, and we get to home and work with full bellies. Trees need breaking down and carting off. Axe and saw work, the sort that a full belly's good for.

We cut through wood, we jump from centipedes and scorpions. And we do it in silence, mostly.

"She's quite the girl," Thom says.

"She is at that," I say. "And don't you get no designs."

Thom don't say nothing. Best not to, I'm the one with the axe.

———

They like the sea, they worship the Sun, and music is their third love, as Dain says. Not blood, they never count it as love, it's a base sort of thing, that desire. Music for them is a door to quiet. Music is almost as perfect as their forms. And they can sing, and they can dance—I've seen both—maybe play a fiddle or a flute to some jauntiness. But music, great music, is something only we can give them. That's why the great Orchestral Hall is near the heart of the City in the Shadow of the Mountain.

Music is close to their hearts.

And it's in our blood. That makes us the sweetest of musicians.

Autumn's the season beset with pasts and futures. Memories hazy of both. Summer bleeds into it, then winter rears out. The first frost comes not long after that storm. I like them changes. I like the cold, until I'm sick of it. And the river that seemed inviting takes on a somber sort of air, and grows misty as though it's knitted itself some sort of gown.

There's apples that need wrapping up and putting away, and fences that need mending. Storm has left its raggedy thumbprint upon the earth, and brought us a new weariness to contend with.

I don't know how I did without Thom. I managed, I guess. Just like he'll manage without me. But past and futures bleed.

I let him mark the doors of those my Master visits. And I watch. Soon I'll be out of town, working the farm. Switching one labour for another.

Already I can see that Thom's got Mastery in him even though he's just a lad. It's in his walk, the steadiness of his gaze.

There's nothing ill-fitting about him. He's as blessed as Grove in his way, but he knows it, expects it even. Might set a bit of jealousy in me, but I'm too busy for jealousy.

———

Dougie calls a meeting. There's a swift scratch of chalk across the door, midway, to tell us roughly when. I rub it away with a thumb.

"Keep your wits about you," I tell Thom.

He sighs, the reproach of the underestimated.

We reach the cave around midday. I don't come here that often, there's too much of Dougie in it. This is his kingdom. Could have been Grove's, but he's never wanted it. He leads from a distance, way out front, and mostly none of us can see him. Dougie isn't like that. He's cunning in his thick-headed way. He sits and talks and gets down with us boys—even if it's just to give a clobbering. Won't see Grove doing that.

We've a few lanterns burning: gold light, thin smoke. Place smells of smoke, and boys: a musty kind of stink. Bad odors and bad feelings; it's why I don't come here much. Isn't a bit of the town more hostile. And this is my bit.

There's a small stack of books in one corner, even a tattered comic or two, colours thin, fellas and ladies in the pages, gods almost, leaping and doing the sorts of things that gods do in godly cities. None of that ever made sense to me, but Twitch likes them. There's a chair that someone dragged up in another corner, looking about as beat and threadbare as something can be and still own the name furniture.

We're all of us there when Dougie gets up on that chair and clears his throat.

"Good to see you boys," he says, face growing proprietorial. "My boys, in these times of cold and turbulence, the change of them seasons has sent a new colleague to us. And set itself to cast out an old."

I tense up, and he gestures calmly at me. "Now, dear Thom. You know us all, but we know little of you."

Thom nods at that, and looks to me.

I shrug. "What do you want to know?"

"You were Crèche-raised, weren't ya?"

"Yes."

"What's it like in that belly of the Mountain? What's it like being of the Crèche and all? I was Academy-raised myself."

Thom can't help himself, he snorts, gestures to Dougie to button his lip, and I see a little more of what the grown-up Thom might be like.

"Life in the Crèche isn't like anything you have ever seen," Thom says. "There was my ma, once, just the memory of light, of being taken. But since then, just the dark, and the lessons, and the lessons, and the dark. Masters everywhere, whispering, more Masters than you'd have ever seen in this town. We were raised in the dark, they said, because their words was the illumination, their eyes the truth. That's what the Crèche is like."

And all them Day Boys are standing there, wide-eyed. Even me, because I could never draw him on it. We all heard of the Crèche, but never known someone who is from there before he came along.

"In the Crèche, we aren't just raised to be Day Boys, but Masters, too. They tell us we're being raised to be Changed. It's classes in oratory and history, and fighting and living in the dark. And the Council sees over us."

I don't say nothing. I've seen that Council, I know the truth of it. Just nod my head a little, and Grove gives me a look. Knows me too well to let that slide.

"Why you nodding there?" he asks.

"I seen the Council," I say. "I spoke with them."

Dougie laughs, they all do. "You're the biggest liar of us all."

"Ask your Masters if you don't believe me," I say, then shrug.

"Continue with your story, Mr. Thom," Dougie says.

"We was raised next to the Council," Thom says. "Heard the screams and the laughter of those cages where the new-made folk are unmade and set upon the righteous path. Saw the music halls, too, where the Masters line the walls and listen to them that can play. They've a hunger in that dark place for all the things that they can't make." I give him a look; this is the most I've ever heard him speak at once.

"You talking this up?" Dougie asks.

Thom's voice goes soft. "You think I need to?"

"I don't know what you need," Dougie says, and it's Grove's turn to give a good old snort. "Maybe a fist. I'm ready for you this time."

"Quiet," I say, and Dougie glares at me. Thom, too.

"Come here then," Thom says.

"You come here."

And he does, light as a knife. Slips a foot behind Dougie's ankle and while he's swinging his fists out, Thom's already flipped him on his bum. You'd think after the first time Dougie'd be anticipating such a move, but he isn't. He whoomphs, and sits there looking stupid. I tense, ready for the possibility of a fight. But Dougie just laughs, and gets swift to his feet like it was nothing, not even a slight. He grabs his hat from his head and waves it in the air like some gentleman of old.

"Continue, continue, my good man," Dougie says. And we're all laughing.

"I'm like all of you. Just know that dark place better, is all." He gestures to the deeper part of the cave, where there's no light, just an encroaching shadow, a breath of the depths. We've all followed that cave down, deep where it narrows and widens, and grows a sullen sort of watchfulness. The cave mouth Dougie's made his own, but his grip loosens with every step out of the circle of meagre light.

Sometimes, at night, I swear I've heard that dark whispering my name.

"You ever have friends?" Grove asks.

"Some. But they're dangerous. Can't never trust them." He looks at me, and I nod. We both know the truth in that, and it's like he's warning me, which I guess he is. We all know our natures, even if they can surprise us sometimes, but we can never really know others. Never. Dain says that we fight our natures, which is what makes us human.

"You ever betray anyone?" I ask Thom, and he smiles.

"You got some tips?" Grove asks.

"Never do it obvious." Thom says it like it's a recitation, a lesson taught in some crueler classroom than I've ever known. "Make them think it's good for them, even if it's not. And never be caught holding the knife. You drop it if you have to; bury it all the better. We betray people all the time, but we're good at justifying it, and there isn't a better justification than a hidden hurt, a betrayal not realised."

I know Thom, but I hardly know him at all.

"Thanks for that, boy," Dougie says, and I can't see his eyes beneath his hat. "You're one of us, that's the truth, but we've done nothing official."

I get a little cold at those words, a shudder pinches me close. "No need for anything official," I say, starting to rise.

Dougie sighs. "Mark, you haven't got a say in this. Your time's comin' to an end and all." Damn fella keeps saying that, like I don't know. "And now to the meat of this meeting," he says, chuckling a bit.

He whistles once, and hands are grabbing me. I look to Grove, and I can see things fighting in his expression. Was he in on it? Whatever it is. I give him a stare, and he squeezes his hands to fists.

"This ain't right," Grove says, and he stands, a good couple of inches taller than the tallest of us. "This ain't right."

"Should have known you'd have no taste for this. But here you are." Dougie says, and casually punches Grove in the face, unexpected and swift. I see the lights go out of him, and it's almost impossible not to laugh. Poor Grove drops.

"Run," I say to Thom, but it's already too late.

The Parson twins are hitting him. I shake an arm loose. "Not your fight," Dougie says, and there's a flash of a knife, polished to such a sheen that I can see my face in it. And something strikes me from behind.

I **come to** on the stony floor, rubbing my head, groggy. Someone is standing by me. I can see their boots, a bit of mud on the left one, splash of blood on the other.

"That you, Grove?"

"Yep. You OK?"

Thom is there, and his nose is bloody, one of his eyes is black, and his lip is split.

Grove's standing over him, rubbing his stubbly jaw. "Never thought it was made of glass," he says.

"I'm sorry," I say. The words come thick and muddy.

"Gave as good as," he says.

My arm is sore. I look at it, and on the meat of my biceps, a shape is carved. Bloody as all hell, but I can make it out. I blink at it. A letter G.

"What's that for?" Thom asks.

"Ghost," I say.

It's a lurching, slow way home.

Dain don't say nothing when he sees us both. He knows the ways of boys, but he looks at that G, and his eyes darken.

"Get some antiseptic on that now," he says.

That G is deep, and it's going to hurt in the healing. Hurts a hell of a lot now. Hurts enough that I know I'm no ghost.

I'm lying in bed feeling sorry for myself when I notice it. "Hey, you're not crying," I say.

"Been a while," Thom says, and I think back on it, and yes, he's right. I can't remember the last time I heard him, at least a week. "You tell anyone about those tears, and I'll cut you worse than any G."

"Fair enough."

Next day, my arm sore and red, we see a lot of the boys out, and most of them are bruised. But like always, talk of it is done. But for the blazing cut to my arm, but for those bruises that speak of deeper truths, it's all done.

I'm talking to Thom when I feel it slide over me, some kind of faint.

I wake up all sweat and shudders; my arm's on fire.

Dain's looking over me, grim as all grim.

"The wound's gone septic. Didn't I tell you to put something on that? Do I have to teach you all about hygiene?"

"Next ta bloody godliness," I say.

Dain's jaw juts. "I'm getting help."

Thom's in the room, too, and he looks scared. "I'm fine," I say. "Fine as."

But they're already fading from me. The room fuzzy at the edges, like something's taking a bite out of it.

"Why's it getting dark?" I ask, or something, or maybe I don't say nothing.

—

Next time I wake, the fever's broken. There's a cold cloth against my head. Sheets are damp.

"You had us worried," Mary says, and frowns. "As close to dead as I've ever seen."

"But I'm still here?"

"Yes, you are."

I get the shivers then. "Mary," I say. "Tell me something."

"What?"

"Anything. Anything. I'm cold, I'm—just talk to me."

And she starts a chat, one-sided, mostly cause I'm drifting in and out. About the weather, about Anne's deliveries, about the puppies that the Mitchells' dog had, and the comet in the sky that I missed. Burned out the stars it did, but it's already dimming. And she tells me about Anne's da, and the way he left the world, and she tells it without bitterness, just the way it went.

And she holds my hand gentle, and I let her, and I slip down again, but her voice makes that dark a better place. And I sleep.

"You're looking stronger." Thom lifts the cold cloth from my head, squeezes it, wets it some more, and then down again on my boiling brow. Fever's risen a bit.

"You learn that in the Crèche?"

"Eh?"

"How to look after someone, not just kill them?"

Thom nods.

"Rounded education, then." I try and sit up, don't make it too far. I'm feeling frail all right. "How long have I been abed?"

"Nearly a week," Thom says. "You should have seen Dain, he was frantic. I think he might have Changed you. T'was Mary that stopped him, told him he was being a fool, that in that state all he'd raise would be madness and hunger, and did he want that for you?

"Dain snapped at her, thought he might bite her through. Said he didn't want that for anyone. Not anyone."

"So I was nearly one of them?"

"You was nearly one of them, but it would have been a struggle for you, even then."

I know. They don't take to the new, all that much. They don't like it. And I'd seen those cages. I'd have been locked away in my own madness for an age.

"Dougie's right," Thom said. "I didn't believe it, but I seen it. Dain hates himself, and he hates his kind. That's a dangerous thing." His voice lowers to a whisper, and there's a horror in his eyes. "It'll kill us all."

I want to slap him, but I manage a scowl.

Thom laughs mocking. "Be brave, little man. That's all we got, isn't it?"

And I think of him, and those years raised in the dark. And I feel a bit sorry. He never had what I had. He's just a little boy.

When I get up from bed, just to do a piss, it's a shaky rise, and I can tell the truth of my illness. I can feel bones pushing against flesh. My cheeks are hard against my skin, like I was eaten from the inside out. And every bit of me is aching.

I look at me in the bathroom mirror, this Mark-ish skeleton. I give it a grin, and I stare at the red scar that was once a G.

More truth to that ghost than I want to admit. Death hasn't left. He's just waiting. Death is always waiting, and I'd forgotten it like the fool I am. No matter, Death's always waiting to re-mind you.

"You'll fill out," Dain says when I leave the toilet, making it sting even more. That he can see it, that he feels he has to say it.

———

I get my visitors. Certain comes a few times, even brings Petri. And that dog licks my face, tail banging on the floor, like she's never been happier to see me. Missing the farm, I am.

"It'll be there when you're better," Certain says, and I think he might even be missing me.

All them Masters come one by one to visit me in my sick bed. Not for me, of course, but for Dain. Not a-one of them, I reckon, would care if I carked it, and some would be all gleeful. Old Sobel stands at the foot of my bed and stares at me with nasty beady eyes until Dain calls him away.

Tennyson just pokes his head around the door, gives me a grin with more cheek in it than my near-death deserves. But that's Tennyson. Kast is there when I wake up, and I don't know if he's decided to eat me or what. The room is cold, the window wide open.

"Freezin'," I say. "Give a sick man the comfort of a closed window."

He shakes his head, and leaves me (through that window, shutting it after himself with a click, like the snapping of an angry dog's teeth) to troubled sleep.

It's only Egan that bothers to talk to me.

He comes in by the door, Thom trailing him.

"Out, out, little one," he says, gesturing back the way he

came, and Thom does what he is told. This isn't our Master, not even a chance to argue anything away.

"One always gets what they deserve," he says. "That is a truth that all these long years have taught me. You brought this down on yourself, boy. You're like this damn town and there will be a reckoning."

"Say hello to Grove for me would you, Master Egan?"

Egan looks at me like I am the worst of smells. "Not dead though. Not dead at that."

No, I'm not.

None of their boys come, and I don't know if they're afraid of me or Dain. He speaks of them now, not dismissively, but with jaw clenched.

———

I'm well enough to get about a little, though Thom spares me most of the work, so I'm bored and sick, with too much time on my hands. Sometimes I go to Anne's place. Lurking, Dain calls it, but I'm just listening, no lurk in the attention I pay. She plays that piano, all furious. She's a talent all right. You hear it, and you hear sadness and joy. Anne's going places, who knows where, but she's chasing those pure and angry notes.

When she plays, I'm not the only one who listens. I never know what it is she's playing, and the names wash off me to forgetfulness when she tells me, but I know the beauty that is the perfect expression of nature's gifts and effort, and I hear it in her playing, and that's enough.

I'm bruised and sore, but still I'm there, listening tonight.

"How was it?" Anne calls out into the dark.

I stand there still.

"Mark, you tell me. How was it?" Her voice has an edge to it.

"Good," I call back.

"Just good?" Now it's sharper still, and I'm wincing; there's worse hurts than the flesh.

"It was near as perfect as a thing might be."

Anne laughs. "I've missed you," she says. "Now, home with you. Before trouble comes and gets you for good."

It already has, I reckon. Found my heart, and given it a serious squeeze. I'm too full of feeling to be a ghost.

Almost run straight into Twitch as I walk onto the road.

"Mark," he says, seeming all casual.

"What you doing, Twitch?"

"Nothing," he says, looking at his feet.

"What, you lurking or something?"

"I'd never," he says, but I can see his face glowing even now.

"You be on your way," I say. "You be on your way."

And he runs out into the dark, and I can hear Anne laughing.

It takes a good three weeks before I feel like I am not skin and bone, and that my muscles have more than a memory of their strength, and by then winter's here, pressing cold fingers against the edge of the earth.

But cold don't matter so much when you're working hard, and I'm sweating over firewood. Thom can't lift this axe—some weight you can't finesse, no matter how hard-raised you are—so I don't have no choice. The wound's pulling on my arm, and there's an ache in my chest, and the taste of snot in my throat. But I don't mind, labour has its pleasure; just wish I could breathe easier. I take a big hocking spit.

"Delightful," says Anne from behind me and I turn, trying not to stumble beneath the down-earth-weight of the axe. Anne's bundled up. And standing still I can feel the cold, too, feel it starting to slip in, like it always does this time of year. But there's another heat at the heart of me.

"This is sweating, spitting work," I say, and lean a bit heavier on the handle of that axe, feel it sink into the earth, and try to hide my heavy breathing.

"Looks like it," Anne says.

Slow breaths. Deep and slow breaths. "Why are you here?"

"Mary said to invite you and your Master over for dinner. And Mister Thom, of course." He dips his cap.

"I'll pass on the invite. Once he's awake and all." The sky's already heading towards dim, the little sun's tracking its way into the west. A grey cloud passes over it, and things get a bit colder. No more sensitive a season than winter. Always ready to pull a shift on you.

"It's tonight," she says.

"Short notice, but I'll pass it on. Can't be tapping on his coffin and all, they don't like that." I'm leaning harder on that axe, and the cold is filling me, gonna be shivering soon. Hate that I look so weak in front of her.

"Best get back to that wood," Anne says, and leaves me to it. I swing the axe over my head, glad I can lift it. Was a time, not more than two weeks back, when I thought I'd never be able to lift it again.

"You could've told me she was there," I say.

Thom just grins.

I swing and split another log. Thom sets another one down, and I swing and split that too.

"How many more have we got? Can't you at least tell me that, *Mister* Thom?"

Thom shrugs, and smiles.

There's nothing gentle for a sick man in this town, not even amongst his own kind.

Dain must be curious. Because he dips his head when I give him the invite, then gestures at me and Thom. Hardly a second's thought to it. Though I can see a bit of disappointment. I suppose he wanted to work on his book tonight. Books exert their own pressure, it seems.

"Best draw yourselves a bath," Dain says, "and get your Sunday best. If we're going out for dinner tonight, I want no scruffiness."

"You really want to?" I ask, half not-believing it. Just as I'm excited to be seeing Anne.

"And why shouldn't I?"

"At least we'll get one night of good eating," Thom says.

I swing at his head, but he's already out of the way. Too quick by far, that smug bugger.

The damn collar's prickling me. Sunday best doesn't get much of an airing even on Sundays.

Clothes as stiff and starched as possible. Can't blame anyone but myself for that, though Dain could have taught me better, I suppose. Thom looks like he was born to good clothes, barely scratches at his neck, seems capable of breathing. Twice Dain slaps my hand away from fiddling with my collar and tie.

"You're done, boy," he says. "You're presentable, so don't mess it up."

Thom smirks at me from beneath that neat part in his hair. My hair's a state, won't straighten, sticks up in the back like I've just gotten out of bed. He was the one that knotted my tie, and he pulled it too tight. Got a knot in my gut, too.

Dain looks at his watch.

"We are late."

We pass Egan on the way to Mary's.

"Gentlemen," he says. Eyes like embers.

"Egan," says Dain.

I want to smirk at him, to do a little dance. Get what I deserved, I'm getting a nice meal, a walk in the dark.

"And where are you going on this fine night?"

"None of you—" Dain slaps the back of my head.

"Mary Harris has requested our company this evening."

Egan dips his head, glares at me. "Please give Ms. Harris my regards will you, boy?"

There's nothing nice in those regards. He stares at me like the wolf in whatever fairy story you'd like, take your pick, charming as a knife in the belly.

"I will, sir," I say after a pause that's awkward enough, I reckon.

"See that you do."

He nods at the three of us, then strolls into the dark.

"Man looked hungry," I said.

"You know he was," Dain says, sharp. "Winter's settled in. We're all a little hungrier."

Dain once said that winter pulls the hunger through their hearts. Night growing, the sky clear. Winter's the secret time of them.

A wind picks up and follows us through the streets, puffs up our shadows, thins the crescent moon to a cutting edge. Dain's eyes are brighter than the moon, and twice as sharp. Thom whistles a little melody, clear in that cool night, but Dain hushes him.

We're almost somber by the time we reach Mary's house.

It's lit up, and warm, and Anne greets us at the door. Light and the smell of good things cooking rushing out through that door at us. Her gaze flicks from Dain to me and Thom, and she smiles—I can see the mock in it if no one else does.

"Welcome, fine folk," she says, and curtseys.

"May we have the pleasure of the house?" Dain asks. Say what you will of me, but my Master knows formalities.

"You may," says Anne, and we pass in. Me at the rear, and I get a hard kick from Anne.

"You look like all kinds of awkward," she says, her voice low. "Well-dressed awkward, but definitely awkward."

"Did you say something?" Dain asks.

"Said how nice you all are."

"The boys scrub up well," Dain says. "Now, where is your ma?"

"In the kitchen," Mary yells. "No meal I've ever known cooks itself. You get to the parlour. I'll be along."

So we sit in the parlour. There's a piano in one corner.

"How's your playin' goin'?" I ask.

"All right," Anne says.

Dain smiles at her. "Would you play for us now?"

Anne's dressed in her finest, too. She rubs her nose. "If you'd like, I can."

"I would like that very much."

And she plays that beautiful sound. "The Cat and the Fiddle Dance," I think, or maybe the "Slow Maiden's Grief," and then some of the Oldest Music. She plays and her face is calm, like she isn't breaking a sweat, like this is easy and she looks . . . she looks transported. Skill and happiness and delight, that's what I'm hearing. And I get a little sad; I'll never be worthy of this, not one bit.

Mary joins us partway through, and she listens and we listen, and when Anne is finished, and the world is just the world again, and my neck's back to itching in that collar, all of us clap.

"Very good, Miss Harris," Dain says. "Thank you."

Anne looks flushed, a little flustered, nothing like the music that she's just played, she's back with us now, back and vulnerable. "You're welcome," she says.

"My girl's a talent, all right," Mary says, and then she shoos us into the dining room, our feet creaking and clattering on the wooden floors.

"There's plenty of food," she says. "Hope you boys are hungry."

And there is meat, and potatoes and peas and pumpkin. And a thick gravy. "Nice to have someone cook for a change, don't you say, boys?" Dain asks.

"Nice don't even begin to—"

"Don't talk with your mouth full," Dain says.

Anne coughs into her hand, to hide what is an obvious laugh.

"I'm an easy guest," says Dain. "I don't eat."

Mary tilts her head. "Oh, I've catered for you."

Dain raises his hand, but still bares his teeth. "Later, perhaps."

Anne don't say nothing at that, but I see her grip her knife tighter than she needs to. Dain's more often gentle than most, but that don't mean anything for those times he's not. And these cold months where the night is long and the day threaded with weakness, he and the others are wilder than ever.

When we're done with second helpings, and dessert and second helpings of that, we're back in the parlour, plump and worn out from eating.

Mary looks to me and Thom. "Now, boys, would you mind taking a slow walk of the block? And you, too, Anne."

Anne hesitates.

"I've things of a private nature to discuss with your Master here."

"We won't be long," Dain says.

So that is how we end up back in the cold, walking with Anne. We take Main Street, and reach the park. There's old metal swings in here, and Anne sits down in one of those seats, her legs dangling. I'm rubbing my full belly. Thom is looking up at the stars.

"You can certainly play the piano," Thom says. "They prize that sort of thing in the City."

"Do they now?" Anne says tilting her head, giving him all her attention. And I can see the soft mockery in that gaze, but it makes me jealous, nonetheless. Why can't I enjoy the sight of her, the lines and fierceness of her eyes when they're not set on me? I'm a fool, that's why.

Thom nods, all earnest. "Music is the highest of human endeavours."

"And why's that?" I ask.

"It's pure emotion. The Masters like to be reminded they can feel."

Anne laughs, clear into the sky.

Thom looks at her. "Why is that funny? I don't understand."

"You will," she says. "One day you will."

"Why can't you tell me now?"

"Because the world thinks otherwise."

The moon's slinging into the west, and a dog starts howling.

"Maybe we should get back," Anne says.

Mary's wearing a scarf when we return, and she's paler than ever. Dain's eyes are dark and narrow, though his skin is flushed with new life. He looks at me, then Anne. There's something sad and furtive in that look, something almost ashamed.

"We must be going," he says. And we bid our farewells.

Dain walks us to the front gate. Something cries out into the dark, loud, and on the edge of town, there's a sharp whistle, and Dain turns his head towards the sound, then back to us.

"I expect you to head straight home. The linen needs cleaning tomorrow, and the blankets," he says, then he is gone into the dark. No writing for him tonight.

Never any rest for the wicked.

———

The Masters rule the town, no doubt, but they aren't the town, and they know it, and what kind of kingdom is that, when most of the world's sleeping? Their times of weakness and strength are the reverse of our own. They rule our waking world, but from a distance. Some folks say that they don't rule nothing but the dark, and we've never wanted that.

That's a dangerous sort of thinking.

Night is always coming.

It is another cold night deeper into winter when I wake up Thom. He blinks at me, and I feel a little poor for him. Been a busy day cleaning the Sewills' yard—we'd marked the door the day earlier—and that's always hard labour. They let us do the work. Those Sewills are getting on, about the oldest couple in this town. Both of us are sore and weary. But this evening's not one for sleep, it's a night for other things. The moon's where it should be, and I can feel it.

Thom raises a feeble hand, like he's never been woken before; almost makes me feel sorry for him.

"You best get used to waking in the middle of the night," I say.

His lips curl solemn, and he gives me a sort of look that's all hardness. "I'm used to it." And he's up and on the edge of the bed. "What needs doing?"

I shake my head. "Not what needs doing, but seeing. Dress warm."

I'm all ready to go. Which is mean of me, I guess. It's so I can glower and mutter at his slow dressing, but we've plenty of time.

We open the door onto the night, and it draws us out, like a true night will, as though we're nothing but dust lifted on the wind.

It's bitter cold, and a sky so clear that the stars burn. Breath steams from us, and no matter that we're dressed warm, it's still a shock, like jumping into water that's colder than you expected. The moon's a sliver in the sky, but everything is so clear. Land looms around us, blue and hulking, drawing in and receding, and you suddenly get a sense of how big everything is and how little you are, but it's still wonderful because small and brief, you're still here and breathing plumes in the dark: defiant and proud. And there is no one more defiant than us.

I can't help it: Despite everything, I start humming. I shouldn't, but I do. Not everything is a should: Some things are a must.

"Why you so cheerful?" Thom asks.

"It's night. It's night and we're alive!"

"You're crazy," Thom says, but I can hear the joy in his voice, and I know he understands; a night like this you can't help but.

We leave our yard, by the back way, jumping the fence and following a path marked by roos, and strengthened by the boys that have followed it, boots hardening the earth. It runs up into the ridge. But we're not heading that way.

We walk in the dark, but it's not so dark when your eyes adjust. Something crashes away through the undergrowth; roo or razorback, though they stink to high hell and this don't smell of anything, and the cold air's too clear, and a boar's usually too smart to come this close to a town.

About half an hour of walking, and I turn to Thom. "Now, you must be quiet," I say.

Thom starts to say something, and I shush him good.

"Silence and we live. Noise and . . . we may not."

Thom looks at me. And I wave my hand in the dark. "But what a night to die!" I say.

A little further on, we start to hear it. At first it's nothing more than a faint low sound, but it's the thread that we follow, and it thickens as we approach.

Singing.

Pure and wild song.

A couple of the other boys are in sight, Dougie and Twitcher, and I nod to them.

We clamber over a rise, and then another.

And there's light as well as song, and I'm gesturing to Thom to get on his belly. That last rise we crawl up. And there they are.

The fire's burning. A bonfire bright and huge, and they're throwing logs into it, stuff the size of big tree trunks, and tossing them with an ease that only the Masters possess. And they're singing to the fire. Singing in some language I don't understand.

The song is sad and pure in the cold air. It's everything I feel whenever I stare up at that clear starlit sky.

All of them are there below.

Building the fire, dancing around it. And when the ash rises, they let it fall where it will, no matter how it burns their flesh.

And in this light I can see Thom's face, see the curl of his lip. And then the understanding; well, the first crack of it.

They're singing to the Sun. They're mourning it. They're yearning for it. But all they have is the night, and the flame—which could kill them just as proper. And now, and here, they're not being the Masters, but folk bereft. Folk who've given up their past for something else.

There's weakness and sadness here. There's all the things that the Masters hide. And it makes your eyes well, you feel something rare towards them, and it's pity.

Poor lost men. Poor yearning men, with just their stars and moon while we have everything, all of it spread out across the night and day. Some things don't have a substitute. Some doors closed can't be opened anymore, because in their closing, they become walls.

I can see the pity in Thom's face, too. But we're not done yet. I can feel it coming close. The song bunching up, filling the dark, and then there is a moment of silence.

They bring in the man. Dain does it, leaving the fire for the shadows, and leading him back in. The man stumbles, and Dain is gentle in his handling. He whispers something like you might at a frightened horse. There's no cruelty in this, that's for later.

The man is short, not much taller than me. But he stands there steady, still some strength in him. I can see he's frightened, but he's like the mouse that the cats catch and play with. There's no chance for him, and he knows it.

Egan's the first, and I see it because I know where to look. His mouth widens, and with sudden movement, he's by the fire, metres crossed so swift it's like they weren't metres, like the world made a mistake of measurement and is cruelly readjusting. Then he's biting the man's neck. The man howls, and the rest are at him, too, all those distances corrected. And there's no singing, just the sounds of feeding. The slaughterhouse sounds of bone cracking and muscle being ripped apart.

"Close your eyes," I whisper.

But Thom doesn't, and I'd think less of him if he did.

I didn't either when I came here, dragged awake by Dav, who showed me this, because we need to understand.

It's not pretty, but it's the truth of them.

There's another victim, and another.

I don't recognise any of them, but that doesn't make it any easier. We watch those two, and then Thom's tugging at my hand. And I understand, and we leave the Masters to their feasting. Dougie and Twitch coming with us, grinning like loons.

Thom's crying. And I let him cry. I don't feel all that good either. But some things must be done.

"Shut up," Dougie says. "Shut up, little cry baby."

And I'm ready to backhand him when there's a distant detonation, and another.

In the heart of Midfield, a bell starts ringing.

Dougie and I look at each other, then down into the town where the noise has come from, and there's a flare blooming in the dark. Bright enough that we can see each other's faces clearly.

"The Night Train," we say, both at once.

And we're, all of us, running into the night, towards fire and doom.

When I see the ball of fire, rolling up into the sky, I can almost feel the heat of it. I cover my eyes to shield them from the light, but it passes.

Others are with us, more boys. Thom's by my side, panting from his run. There's confusion everywhere, it's not just us. Unsettled men failing to settle their horses, a few guns visible, but no one with any idea where to point them. Constable Mick's there, too. Looking at that fire on the horizon.

"What's been done here?" Dougie stands next to me, brings one hand to his slack mouth. He shakes his head, like that will tug loose the image from reality. "What's been done here?" he says again, and there's another great bang.

We have our ideas, but still we run and run, and we get to those tracks and the bridge over the river, only it isn't a bridge, but a twisted wreck dropping into the brown water, a scattering of debris, and there's the flaming ruin of the Night Train.

"Look," Dougie says, finger pointing at the river. Black forms are floating there, shapes moving in the river, and the river itself on fire. Smoke rising, mingling with the river's mist, then the wind tears it open a crack. And I get a glimpse of a world's ending. Death I've known, but not so much of it, not all at once.

There are screams. Dark shapes lifting, lit and blazing, along the bank.

Me and Thom stand there, both of us steady and stupid.

But we can't stay here long.

We turn a bend in the tracks, crawl a little more, and then we run, back into town: the light behind us. To the thin screams of people dying.

The Masters are there, coming down out of the hill. Swift and silent. And they stop when they see us. Dain gives me a hard look, a suspicious look. He doesn't say anything.

"The Night Train," I say. "Blown up on the bridge."

Egan looks to us. "All of you boys. Home with you all. This is not work for you."

"Home, the two of you, home," Dain says, straight in my ear, and he's gone before I can even say yes, or tell him to be careful.

And then they're all gone and going, rushing past me like an ill wind, so fast I hardly see them.

And there are other boys coming.

"Back to bed, we've been told," I say. "Back to bed."

"What does it mean?" one of the boys asks.

"Insurrection," I say, not knowing anything, not knowing anything at all. The night is lit with that fire. People already rising, the rest of the town coming to life. Shocked awake, and hurrying to the river.

"What do we do?" Grove asks.

"Nothing to be done. We've been sent home," I say. "Let them find out for themselves."

Dain is late coming back, almost with the dawn. His lids are heavy, his lips droop. He smells of smoke and ash, and there's blood beneath his nails that he's quick to wash away in the sink, as though he's embarrassed.

I wait for him to speak. Watch him work at scrubbing his nails and brushing the ash from his hair. He cleans his face, but half-adequate. This night's had its taxing of him.

"Didn't save a single one," he says soft and low. "That river, that fire, and we on the other side of it."

"What does it mean?" I ask.

Dain just shakes his head.

He leaves me then to go to his rest, and Thom and I do something we've not thought to do, nor ever considered needing to. We make sure our knives are close at hand, and we guard our Master's house.

And in the brief times that I let myself drop into sleep, all I can see is those flames, and the dark shapes rising, and all I can hear is the echo of those screaming voices.

No one comes that day. Nor the next. But that's the way of change, I reckon. You think you see it when it's coming, but you don't until it's done. Maybe not even till long after.

As it is, two nights later, there's a shifting and roaring to the west—the sound of engines and energies, and I wake, and Dain is standing over me.

"Stay here, boy," he says. "Do not dare to leave this house until the morning."

His eyes allow no space for insubordination.

Next morning we're all at the river, and there it is. A new-built bridge, entirely. So much for rebellion or whatever it was. The night after that, the Night Train comes through, and it's like it never happened at all.

But it did.

It's coming on late, but a few days after the bridge grew itself anew, twilight near enough, there's a knock on my door, and I know it's no one that I know. Small enough town, and you can recognise any knock. Most of them sound the same: a little hesitant, a little forced. But this was confident, even threatening. Don't ask me how I can tell, but I just can.

I nod to Thom, and he's got his knife clear and so do I. Uncertain times, and it don't hurt to be too careful.

I'm the one who answers the door, and there's a man with a beard down to his chest—like some bushranger of old—and he flashes a smile that makes me even more wary.

He's holding his hat in one hand, gripping it tight with hard fingers and scarred knuckles. The hat's about as beat-up a thing as I've seen, patched and re-patched. His face isn't much better.

"You Thom or Mark?" he asks.

"What do you reckon?"

That ugly smile only gets wider; he aims a spit back onto the ground. "Mark, may I enter?"

I don't move, and he lifts the chain around his neck. A gold

Sun: there's a Sun tattooed on his wrist as well. "I'm one of them that serves," he says. "I'd speak with your Master."

"You know he's not up yet."

"I know, but I'm not waiting out here when there's in there. Neither's Sarah."

"Don't intend on it," comes a warm voice from behind him. I look past him to a woman in shirt and pants stained with dirt. Sarah smiles at me from beneath a brimmed hat.

"Hello, Mark," she says.

"Who are you?"

"We're servants, like Rob said. Auditors. The ones that keep the wheels turnin'," Sarah says. "We're just like you."

"But you're a girl."

Thom snorts at me like I don't know anything. "Women can be servants," he says.

Sarah's grin turns a bit wry. "The Masters aren't as particular when they need things done," she says. "Now, let us enter."

Still I stand there, knife in one hand.

"Let them in," Dain says from behind me. His eyes are wide with first evening, hazy even, but they narrow when they focus on me. "Hurry to it, boy."

So I do, but I don't lower my knife. The bearded one looks like he might pat my head, but he reconsiders at the last minute, and it saves him a finger. Sarah stops when she gets to me, and gives me a steady, studying sort of look.

I can't help it. I feel myself blushing. "I wouldn'ta let me in either," she says, and her eyes are flashing with humour.

"Then you've not changed," Dain says.

"Oh, I've changed all right," Sarah says. "Not in them fundamentals. But I've seen a thing or two."

221

"Good," Dain says. And that's where the conversation stops.

He turns to me. "Get them dinner," he says.

It's the weirdest supper I've ever had. Thom and I sharing our table, a little out of practice.

Rob sits there eating in silence, Sarah talks of the long roads, and how they're longer now. How they once chased a man to the gates of Death, and how he wasn't a man anymore. And once, they were stalked by a tiger, or something like it down the Namoi way. She knows the stories we boys like. She has a scar that runs from her wrist to her elbow on her right arm, and she catches me looking at it, and gives me a wink.

"Tough job we have." She runs a finger along the scar. "The road's long and full of them sort of things that would kill you, and not just insurgents. Be dead but for Rob. He could say the same for me."

"We've scars, all of us. Ain't that right, boy?" Rob says.

"Got my share," I say.

"I bet ya do." Rob gives Thom a long pale stare. "You don't look like you'd scar easy." Thom just eats his supper. Not one for eating and talking. I'm not either, to be honest.

"How long can we expect your company?" Dain asks.

"Till we're done," Rob says. "There's a host of unhappiness beneath the Mountain. You don't blow up train tracks and leave skipping for joy." And he gives me a look that says he knows that I know what he's talking about, like I'm the cause of it all somehow, which seems strange and unfair. Then he's gazing up at Dain. "Don't worry 'tall, you'll hardly know we're here."

After supper, I'm making up the spare rooms.

Rob helps with the sheets, and looks into Dain's room. "So he don't sleep down beneath the earth?"

I'm noncommittal, and Rob laughs.

"No need for that. You ain't responsible for the choices of them that lord above us, no matter how peculiar. Not the safest of things for one such as him, though, is it?"

"There's nothing safe in this world," I say, thinking to the time I told Anne just that. "Anyone thinks so is a fool."

"Amen to that," says Sarah, all of a sudden, leaning on the door. "Amen to that, I say. There's nothing safe, and no one. We're all monsters lurking under someone's bed."

I offer to make up the other room, and Sarah shakes her head.

"Just one bed for the both of us," she says, and I'm all at blushing again. "Now, to sleep with you. Rob and I can take care of ourselves."

"And then some," Rob says, and he gives Sarah such a look that I just have to be gone and out.

I don't sleep so well that night. Tossing and turning, thinking of scars and miles, and those long dangerous roads Sarah spoke about. Thinking of her smile and her wink.

If Thom has similar trouble, he don't show it.

Late I hear the Master come in, and then talk. Low and a little heated, but it don't last long.

Later I find some sleep. Just as the night's shifting, and there's colour edging its way up the ridge, driving the shadows before it, and pulling the new day behind.

Seems a moment later when Rob's knocking at the door. "Up," he says, and I know my sleeping's done.

I'm tired, leading them around the town, Rob catching me yawning twice, making Sarah laugh at his mock of it.

They talk to all us boys, talk to the men and women in town. Rob has me take him out to Certain's farm alone, and while Certain gets me at choring—and there's always an endless lot of them, and can't he see I'm damn well knackered—he shares a smoke with Rob. And when I'm done with finding eggs in the henhouse, and fixing a gap in a fence, they're sitting in the verandah, hands cupped around their ciggies, an old tin full of the ash of those they've already had.

Rob's laughing and so is Certain. But there's an air of formality to it, of pretend. And something I don't understand. Like they'd much rather be putting away their smokes and their banter, and punching each other. But they don't because they know they can't. Maybe because I'm there?

"Took up a lot of your time," Rob says. "You still need the boy?"

"I'll send him along after you," Certain says.

Rob straightens his hat, and saunters to the gate, looking

back just once, to nod at me as though Certain's not there beside me.

"He's looking for someone to hang," Certain says. "You be
careful around him."

"He's friendly enough," I say.

"He's friendly enough, but there's a venom in him. Was a
time I wanted what he got, was a time I was ready to fight him
for it."

"What happened?"

Certain looks down at his hands, and rubs a thumb over the
scar above his knee, like it's bothering him. "Bloodied noses, and
me finding that I didn't want it. Still not sure if he made me see
it, or I came to my senses. Either way, it was the right decision.
You be careful like you've never been careful in all your life."

"I am the very bloody model of circumspection in all
things," I say as correctly as I am able. Certain gives me a clip
under the ear, affectionate, even if I'm dazed.

"And watch your swearing." He looks to the back of Rob,
and sighs. "What a world this is to make men like him and boys
like you. Thought I'd seen the last of him, and here he is, back
like a ghost."

"You know Sarah, too?"

"Sarah's here?" Something passes cross Certain's face, I don't
know what it is, but he looks all of a sudden like a man who
might be given to drinking tonight.

"You better be away," Certain says.

And I know enough not to say anything.

"And keep to your caution. Round him, and round her.
Don't want you on the end of no rope, not until the western
fence line's finished."

I give him a bit of a face.

He doesn't even smile. Just looks down at his hands as he rolls another smoke, careful, as if he's never done it before.

When they're done with their questions, they pack their horses, and ride with the dawn. The sun at their backs, like they're chasing their shadows. But they're back early that afternoon, air beginning to chill, with a man tied up and walking behind them.

Mr. Stevens. It's Mr. Stevens, the signalman. He's been crying, his eyes are red, his nose running.

"Get the other boys," Rob says.

And I do.

Certain's right. Rob is gonna get his hanging. Not until Mr. Stevens is bloody and toothless, though. Sarah's there, too, and while she don't join in, she don't stop him. Rob hits that man hard and harder. He don't heed his cries. Pulls him close to listen a few times, but he's not satisfied with whatever the man says.

His fists find their way past his raised hands, and only when he's done, and Mr. Stevens is panting and breathing like he's broken inside does he rope the man's neck from the tree in the centre of town, and yank him up slow and long. Mr. Stevens' feet shivering in the air. Not going to forget that. I've seen worse, we all have, but still.

We're all there to watch because those we represent can't. Doesn't pass much for entertainment. But we're called, and it's done that afternoon so the Masters have no say in it.

"This is what you can expect," Rob says, just loud enough to hear. But he doesn't need to speak any louder, every ear is straining. He taps Mr. Stevens' leg, still dangling and twitching. "Ain't no mercy for insurrectionists. Just death, brutal and quick."

Not quick enough, I think, but I must be learning a little something because I don't say it. I don't say nothing.

Rob cuts the rope, lets the body fall. Walks over to me, face so blank it might as well be stone.

"We're done here," he says. "Well. Not quite."

Rob turns to Mick the constable. Rob's shorter than him by a handspan, but he don't look it now. It's like Mick's shrunk in his shoes.

"I've half a mind to put you up there, Mr. Constable," he says. "More than. We come back here for some other reason, some other darkening plan hatching, and you *will* hang. Should never have happened; when we come, we come too late."

Rob spits at the constable's feet, and turns nice and slow, and I can see that Mick is battling the urge to hit him. Hard. But sense prevails, I guess, or fear, which is just another sort of sense. I can almost respect that. Strike an auditor, and you might as well strike Death herself.

Rob winks at me. "C'mon, boy," he says. "We need to talk, you and I."

I walk, and Thom follows until Rob raises his hand. "Ain't a talk for you, Mr. Thom. This is just between me, and him."

Thom doesn't look happy about that; he kind of hovers there, looking at me.

"I'll see you at home," I say.

Thom nods, and starts on his way back.

"A man don't need a second shadow," Rob says. I nod my head. And we walk a while in quiet. Heading back to the Master's house, down these familiar roads made strange because of the fella I'm walking with.

"Don't like this town," Rob says. "A fella like Stevens killing all those folk. Don't excuse what I done, mind. That was right and proper cruel, ain't proud of a bit of it."

"But you did it."

"Do it again if I had to, you can't have people getting thoughts. This is the world we live in now," Rob says. "That man killed three dozen people. He destroyed the train line. He got his due. But it leaves a ruinous taste, for sure. Taste a man might need to drink away. Not here, won't let none of these bastards catch that." He stops, and I can see the tears on the edge of his eyes. "You think I didn't start all nice? He could have spoken then; he chose not to." He sniffs once, long and loud, and spits again, in the direction of the tree. "But I ain't walking with you for forgiveness." He looks at me, then gestures west to the end of town. "Not everything begins and ends here. What do you say? You want to come with us, boy? I've the authority to offer such a boon. I know the measure of things. I can read a boy and see what he will become."

"And what will I become?"

"A dead set killer, if you don't get yourself killed. You stay here, and what have ya got? Just fences to fix, and monsters to feed, and the boredom, that cold crushing boredom. You know what I'm talking about. You look to the sky and yearn. Them like us do. We ain't ever going to become like your Master, but that don't mean we can't find something better."

He gestures at the sky. "You ride with me and Sarah, and you'll see the heavens dance at night in the far south, all colour and movement. You'll come to broke-down cities filled with haunts and haunted, and seas as dark as that beneath the

City in the Shadow of the Mountain. Ain't a long life, and it's hard, but it's good and beautiful. You'll see the great wide land."

I look at him. Not even sure what to say. But I can feel the pull of it. Rob hesitates a little, then the words spill from him.

"Don't know much of the world yonder. Just the sea, and the odd island or two near enough that a boat might make the crossing. That's a vast border, an unwalkable one. The world curls away from us in all directions. And it's gotten bigger, like it shrugged it shoulders, got itself a spurt of growth and wildness. The storms are madder even than when I was a kid. The dark's darker. We didn't need the Masters when the world was small, but by crikey we need them now."

"I hardly even know what an auditor does," I say.

"We'll teach you just what we are." Rob says. "We're the thread that binds the land together. We're tenuous, and frail, frailer even than that Night Train. But without us, without the line, and the Law, we're not a country, just a bunch of towns, sliding into each other, drowning in their own meaninglessness, waiting to be devoured by monsters."

"Monsters enough in this town," I say.

"Not like this, not like you'd believe. Once saw a thing, big as a train. Smoke pluming from its great toothy face, saw it streak across the sky as if it was hunting for something. I hid. Couldn't have been hunting me; something so small? But I hid anyway, fear so deep within me that it ate at me like a sickness. And the next town I came to was torn apart. Devoured. Even the Masters dead, like it had hunted them first, dug them out, like an echidna digging out white ants.

"Only ever seen such a thing once. Far south and west of here. But you don't forget something like that."

"What you trying to do, scare the boy?" Sarah's caught us up, just outside of Dain's house.

"I don't scare too easy," I say.

"No, you don't," Rob says. "But you should. There's dark times coming for you, hungry and wicked."

I give my chest a puff. "Got my own wickedness to match."

Rob scratches his beard, then pats my arm and walks inside.

Sarah chuckles. "He's a poet, can't you tell?"

"He don't like me," I say.

"He does," Sarah says, voice low. "He likes whatever Certain does. You come with us, you'll break that man's heart."

And she says it like it's a fact, not good nor bad, just something lying there for me to either pick up or discard.

"What about you?"

"I made my choices. Ain't for love, that's sure. Hearts break, they're about the most fragile thing we've got." She shrugs. "I made my choices, and so did Certain. Don't let anyone tell you choices are easy. But what Rob says is true. It's a wild, beautiful world out there. You get in your heart to travel, you find us out if you can. Ain't no life like it." She gives the town a longish look. "Sometimes it'd be nice to—" She shakes her head. "No, it wouldn't. Sleepy towns are for sleepers."

"Not too sleepy," I say, "when there's a fella set on blowing up the tracks."

"Sometimes sleep is troubled," Sarah says. "Don't mistake it for nothing else."

"I know restlessness, and I know sleep. This town's stirring," I say, and it is, I can feel it, even in this winter cold. And it scares me a little.

She reaches out, grabs my face with her rough hands, and looks me deep in the eyes. I can't help but turn away. "Maybe. Or maybe it's just you, kid."

That stings a little: I'm no kid. But her laughter softens it.

There's generosity, not mock. My face burns.

———

Rob and Sarah leave without me. I can hear Sarah's laughter on the wind, the warmest sound in the winter air. Rob gives me one last hard look, but he accepts my decision.

"So what are you going to do?" Thom asks.

"Do what I'm supposed to do," I say, and head off to Certain's place to help out.

He nods at me when I arrive.

That's all he needs to do. And we work at the fence by the creek, rewiring it—the damn thing broke, all his cattle finding their way to green and dangerous pastures; getting them to come back into Certain's land is the hard part. But it's good work, turning thoughts from miseries to the actions of the hands, and the back, the joy of work met and accomplished. We finish it by late afternoon. All stock accounted for.

Certain swings the eastern paddock gate shut, resting his elbows on it, staring at the field below, and the mist that's rising as the sun falls. "Glad you made your choice," he says.

"For now," I say.

"Every choice is only ever for now. You start thinking anything's permanent, you're in trouble. Nothing's permanent about life but death." He flashes me a grin. "And that's coming from a fella named Certain."

231

Thom looks at me, up from the thing he's whittling. A stake—taipan curled around it. He puts his carving down, keeps a hand knuckled around the knife, and listens. Singing. Wind's howling, so it could be that. Shouldn't be able to hear much of nothing anyway; we had a snowfall about a week back, last huff of winter as spring starts to spring. But there's that windblown song, carried to us from the edge of town. Persistent and sweet.

"It's the cold children," I say.

His face does a little sort of skip, his eyes widen a bit. "You're lying. No cold children around here."

"No, not often. But they come. There's cold children everywhere." I tap my chest. "We've a truce and everything."

"You got a truce with them?"

I consider. "More of an agreement."

The singing's getting louder. It grabs you by the short hairs, faint then loud, then faint again. It gets in your blood, and plays with the rhythm of your heart.

"How'd you sleep with them singing like that?"

"Best to ignore it," I say.

"Where's Dain?"

"Out on business, they all are. Said he might be gone all night."

Which is why, I reckon, they've chosen to come here now.

The Masters are away. It's a time for children. "Best we stay indoors," I say.

I grab my coat.

Thom's still holding his knife, a little thing scarcely good for grazing anything but soft supple wood. And the cold children are hard. "I'm not going out there."

"Suit yourself," I say. I don't blame him; last time I took him into the night, he saw the truth of our Masters, plain and simple. This isn't much safer; might be the opposite.

But he comes when I open the door. Scarf around his neck, shrugging into his coat.

Dougie's walking down our street, whistling.

"You gonna see the cold children," I say.

He smiles, gives an expansive sort of wave. "Got an agreement, don't we?" His eyes are shining. I reckon mine are, too.

So it's the three of us that walk along the cold dirt road heading out of town. Why just us, not Grove or the others? I couldn't tell you. And the singing gets louder and quieter, and louder, but gradually the quieter is shorter and the louder longer.

Past the end of town near the bridge, there's a clearing edged to the west with trees. Old ones, pines as high as anything out of the City beneath the Mountain. We stand there, and the singing swells and fills our blood.

I don't know the words, but there's hunger in them, and something of the stars and the darkness between. There's a weariness, too. I feel all weepy just standing there, and I catch

Dougie rubbing at his eyes with a handkerchief, and I wonder why I didn't bring one; my nose is streaming in the cold. And a wind's got up, so loud and fierce it almost drowns out the singing, until it gives way.

And then, in the dark, the singing stops. And it's silent.

Thom grabs my hand.

"No need fer that," I say, then I realise that it isn't Thom. The fingers have snatched the heat from me, my teeth are chattering. A girl with bright eyes, moon-bright, dead-light-bright, looks up at me and smiles.

Her teeth are sharp as killing blades, her smile is cold and cutting, and about as beautiful and dangerous a thing as you might see.

"Hello, Mark," she says, all sing-song and radiance.

"Mol," I say.

"You remember me?" Mol asks.

Of course I do. I remember when she wasn't so cold. When she used to pull my hair, when I was younger than her. But now she's younger than me and more ancient—there's the timeless weight of star-shine to her.

I blink. "I remember our agreement."

"Agreements are odd things, Mark. Tenuous. Light as the wind, and as swift to shifting."

I clear my throat. "We're bound to them, by Law."

"No lawyers in the woods. Just trees and the air and us."

And there, in the woods, I feel my throat catch. She's got that sharpest of grins out, the widest of eyes.

"Where's Thom?"

"Safe."

"Safe? Master would kill me if I—"

"Dain is far away, far, far away. And I am here." She touches my throat with a fingertip. Mol's eyes are bright as glass beads.

"Yes, you are."

"Yes, I am. Shall I sing for you?"

"I think you already have," I say.

"Shall I sing some more?"

I nod.

And she does, and I remember those days before she was cold. I remember the sadness of it, the death that wasn't a death, but a mistake, a bit of the Change that got in her and spread. Masters have a dread of ending those they make—unless they're born of punishment, like those insurgents marked for a cruel death beneath the Sun. Such mistakes are hard admitted, and feared, too, feared almost as much as anything.

Most of the cold children do die in time, of their own accord. But those that don't, they call to each other. Like lonely birds or wolves or something mournful and beautiful. And they gather, and they sing.

Sometimes they hunt.

But we have an agreement.

She's singing, they're all singing, her kindred gathering around, glowing all fairy-like, dancing, too. And it's a sound sweet as it is terrifying. It's a hook that can land you, lance you so deep.

She touches me once and hesitates. "Your agreement is sound, my sweet little boy. But we can still play."

I blink and there's Thom, and there's Dougie. And they're looking at me eyes so wide it'd be funny if we weren't piss-ourselves scared.

"Run," a little voice whispers.

"Run," I say. And the others are already running, and things are coming out of the dark: all teeth and claw and leering grin. And that forest seems awful big, all at once, and we're awful small and racing. Snot and tears frozen to our faces, lungs as raw as the winter-hard earth. Trees slapping us, branches snapping and grabbing. Wind a screaming pressure at our backs, only to flip—*light as the wind and as swift to turning*—and whip our faces like we're the ones running in circles, and maybe we are, to that sound of children that aren't children singing.

We run, and we run.

I don't know when I fall, but I do, and something grabs me, and lifts me as though I'm feather light, and I struggle. Like a tiny bird might struggle in the hands of a giant. Cold hands. Hands colder than you could imagine grip me.

"My, you're all grown up, aren't you?"

And she laughs, and it's the sweetest, most terrible sound.

I wake in my bed, my chin bloody, my body a length of bruise given arms and legs and a voice to squeak. Out of the sheets I jump, and they're tight around me. I struggle free. There's a boot still on one foot, and muddy footprints leading to my bed. The room's cold, the window's open, and first light is shining through.

I check on Thom. He's all right, too. Sleeping, thumb in his mouth. Doesn't even stir, but he's breathing. There's specks of blood on his pillow. I know we lost a little blood. But that's all right.

I've half-convinced myself it's a dream when I go downstairs. Dain's left me a note.

You should know better than to play with children, it says.

Thom's lessons are going well. He's settled in, knows the people who like their lawn mown just how, and who will be surly, and who is lazy, and just how much nonsense Mary can stand in her shop—and it's always more from him. And I'm trusting him to doing things by himself. Why, I'm almost a man of leisure with time to amble.

Leisure can be a dangerous thing.

I'm near Main Street when something grabs me by the leg. I almost tumble, but as tackles go, it's weak. I'm yanking my leg free, and he's shushing me with an urgent hiss.

"You," I say, and feel like a half-wit.

Grainer looks at me. Wild-eyed, desperate, but still with teeth to his grin. Even this far from home, he's the old Day Boy let loose. He's still my unwelcome future come to meet me.

"Me," he says. "All the way from the City."

"You shouldn't be here."

"No, I shouldn't, but after you was caught, they got us all. Broke in, and chased us out and worse. I was lucky to get away. Skill too a'course, on the roof and off, but luck mostly. Now I'm here."

"You been travelling all this time?"

He nods, gestures out towards the main road. "It ain't good out there, but the train line's easy enough to follow, even if it's dangerous." Another hint of the old swagger. "Things wait along that line that even fire don't scare none-too-much. Creatures all tooth and cruel-eyed. Some of them men." He wipes at his brow. He's half a finger missing, the little one, its end an angry raw stump. "I need you to put me up."

"I can't," I say, but it don't sound all that convincing to me. "I can't."

"But you're home and still got your Master. You're someone of consequence and matter." He looks so down, fumbles with his hat—where he got it out there or whom he got it from, I don't know—there's a bit of act to the clumsy and the humble. This isn't Grainer, not as I remember him. It is as well, though.

Must be too quiet for too long because he looks up at me.

"My time's almost up, our house is too full," I say, "and my Master would know, soon as he opened his eyes. He'd smell you. He'd smell the red dirt on you. He'd gobble you up." I know he most probably wouldn't, but I like a little drama, and I don't want him too cocky.

His head dips lower.

And I take a deep breath. Don't like what's coming, but I say it anyway. "I know where you might be able to stay."

"You do?"

Certain looks him up and down. Shakes his head, but I can tell it's for show.

"You done much yard work?" he asks. "Speak truthful now."

Grainer shakes his head. "Been a Day Boy, been a scrambler, don't know much about yards."

"You'll learn quick enough. There's chooks that need feeding over yonder." Certain points to the pen. "Fill that bucket hanging from the fence with the seed you'll find in the box in the pen. Then scatter it across the pen, handfuls. The birds ain't fussy. Do you think you can do that?"

Grainer nods. Certain frowns, grabs Grainer's hand, studies that bloody stump of a finger. "We'll see to the proper cleaning of this, first."

"I'm right with it," Grainer says.

Certain shakes his head. "You'll be right with it until your hand drops right off."

He treats the boy and cleans the wound, and it's a painful business. But when it's done, and Grainer's got his colour back, he says his thanks, and gets to work.

"What you doing putting this on me?" Certain demands, but he don't sound too angry.

"He's a good boy," I say. "Got me out of trouble in the Red City." Got me into trouble more like, but I don't say it. Me being caught ended up far worse for him and his boys. I owe him a debt as I see it. I pay them when I can.

Certain considers him, working his way clumsily in the yard, but working nonetheless. "You know I ain't an orphanage."

"He takes me as boy who knows how to work," I say.

"What about you?" Certain studies my face, and I try to look like it's nothing. "You know what you're giving up? Only one spare room in this house. Think what you're doing here. Even if I'd consider it, they won't let that many of our kind work together."

I know it, and I don't need him to say it. "Some choices you just have to make because they're right. Not because they're right for you."

Certain squints at me. Measures my words like I'm a man, not a boy, like I've earned that.

"He can stay then," Certain says. "You go and tell him the good news."

Certain don't look at me after that as he walks inside.

"You're staying here," I tell Grainer, and the Old Boy nods. "Certain will work you hard, but it's good work."

"This your place?" Grainer asks. "This your out?"

"You going to work harder than you ever worked."

"Yes," Grainer says.

I nod. "You better go in."

And he does, and I look at that house like it's the last time I'll ever see it. And, in a way, it is.

―――

Dain wakes me in the middle of the night, no gentleness, cold hands to slap the dreams from you. I hear him sniffing at the air. "You've dust on you boy. You smell of the Red City."

"Had a visitor today," I tell him, yawn, rolling back on my side, all slumbrous.

"Out with it," he says, pulling me up. "Make yourself some tea, you look ill."

"A fella does when he's snatched from sleep."

"Enough complaints. Tea, then talk."

I'm drinking that tea, and telling him about Grainer. When I'm done, I can see he is at once angry and proud.

"Sometimes you please me well," he says. "But this is no good for you."

"I'll be all right."

Dain's brows furrow a bit. "Him showing up now, I don't like it; the time's all wrong. Or too right."

"Nah, he's just showed up. Like them cold children," I say it casual, but I'm still embarrassed. "Like the winter winds. Some things happen because they happen."

"Winter winds don't just come and snatch away your hopes."

"They do at that," I say. And whose hopes is he talking about, his or mine?

"I could talk to him. Draw out the truth." He could, too, just like drawing out blood. I don't know what truth it would be that he might find, and I don't know just how deep he would need to go, but I sense that there might be death in it, accidental or deliberate. And I won't have that.

I shake my head. "Draw what out of him? The long miles, the dark things what he saw? I could see all that in his eyes. I could see the truth. He found me out because he knew I would help him, like he helped me in that city. I'm not going to fail someone that's made the effort of all that road."

Dain laughs. "What are you going to be, boy? What are you going to become?"

"What everyone who lives long enough becomes. Have to grow up some time."

Dain rests his chin upon a hand, looks down at me. "Perhaps I've judged you wrong. Your flight in the City turned my head against it . . . but still, perhaps, you might rise to Mastery."

I feel my eyes grow wide. "You think?"

"I'm not one to speak lightly of such things."

There's all sorts of light and heaviness vying for supremacy in my guts. I never thought this might be a path to which I walked. And now it's laid up ahead, grey stones bedded, stretched to a horizon beneath the sun. But do I want it? Do I want that cage? Do I want that hunger?

"Think on it," Dain says.

Think on it! It's all I can think on. A pup spinning after its tail. Yes and no. To feed or to feed?

A few days later, I visit Certain. Just a social thing, Certain don't need me, and we don't play at it. We're both straight-up kind of men.

Sit in the shade of his verandah, spring's settling in. Winter's slipping away, there's already a bit of heat to the sun. Just the suggestion of summer, but that's the weight of the land now; it's where we're heading, no doubt at all. I'm wondering where I'll be come summer. Seemed so long away, and now it isn't.

We're sitting there. Not as man and boy, but two men. Well, that's how I'm feeling it. Not much need to talk, I've a cider in one hand, just drinking it, enjoying the cold against the pale heat.

"He working out?" Grainer's in the yard, seeing to a fence that I'd meant to fix a week ago, and he looks like he knows what he's doing. I can tell he knows we're watching, that he's not quite as relaxed as he could be, or ought to be. But who's to blame him?

"Yeah. You weren't wrong."

"Fella that can walk here from the Red City all on his own has depths," I say.

Certain laughs. "Like you don't?"

Nah, if I had depths, I'd know what I was becoming. I'd know how to choose between monster and man.

"So who are you inviting to the dance?" Grove asks.

Now I look at him, I can see he's had a growth spurt, there's more than a sprinkling of stubble on his chin, and he's awful proud of it. He's rubbing that hair like it's some sort of lucky charm. Me, I'm a long ways off beards and I can feel it. I never liked him looking down on me, and now it's from higher up. But Grove don't have a cruel bone in his body, and I'm not going to punish him for nature's endowments. Hard work being so magnanimous, though.

"Didn't know I had to invite anyone," I say. And to be honest, my mind is still too full of that dance with the cold children to ponder long on the subject.

"I'm gonna ask Anne," says Grove.

And all of a sudden I'm interested. Thom's cocking his eye. "You don't want to do that," I say.

Grove frowns, and I can't quite believe that we've ever been friends, not close ones, anyway. "Too late," he says, the knot of wrinkles still fair in the middle of his forehead. "I've already asked her, and she said yes."

Don't know if I've ever felt so cold in my guts. "She said yes?" Grove nods his head.

"Good fer you," I say. "I don't intend on asking anyone."

And I don't. Doesn't mean that the week before isn't a misery. Days getting longer means more time for worry. What's Anne doing, saying yes to the likes of Grove? I know what she's doing. I rub at my smooth chin. Doesn't help that the town's all at fretting, too, getting ready for the dance and the visitors that it brings. The central cellars are cleared out, the great, safe sleeping places for visiting Masters are set up. There's banners and bunting, and all that get-up for a festival that lasts but a night.

And Dain works us hard. We're scrubbing floors, cleaning windows and walls, hunting out dust, and it's a fine thing for hiding. Not a spiderweb in the house, not a speck of dust. Our hands are raw with our labours, cracked as the ground in a big dry.

The night before, the Night Train stops at the station, and the Masters come out. The big ones, the lords of greater towns, and even some from the City itself, tall and small, shuffling and stepping proud, dressed as fine as the night, suits and canes and the latest fashions. Madigan's there. He gives me a look with a bit of judgment to it, but I ignore him.

Dain and all the others are there to greet them. Mayor Aldridge makes a speech short enough to get through without too much mumbling.

Me and Thom are dressed in our best, better than our best, for Dain received a package a few days before. Two suits and hats, proper fedoras, in big round boxes. We're looking right dapper, and even though mine's a bit big, Dain says I'll grow into it. Even Thom seems satisfied.

Dain don't say much, looks at me, and says something about this being my last dance as a Day Boy, and that a man needs a suit.

One thing I don't do is visit Anne. Don't go to listen to her music, don't hear her laughter. And there's an ache to that stubbornness that goes right down to my gut. But I'm not bending.

They're all there: No one in the town would miss this. Certain's in a jacket an inch short at the arms, his pants fresh pressed. He picks at the collar of his shirt like he's still a boy. I'm picking at mine, feeling too hot in this damn thing. It's a glove that never fit and has decided, all of a sudden, to tighten. Grainer's absent though, and I can understand why. Cast-outs don't always want to be found.

Anne's arm in arm with Grove, in a dress I've not seen before. It makes her look . . . something I can't describe except if someone was to bump me, I'd burst. She's with him, but my face is burning.

But she's not there for dancing: Grove leads her to the piano, and there, in front of dignitaries and Masters, she plays.

She starts off casual and simple, something for toe-tapping, there's a beat, a tension, a sort of low melody, almost like a growl of thunder that is never really small, because it has intentions. It swells, makes the skin prickle, and there's nothing in that hall but her and her music.

She never sounded like this before. Not in all the times I've sneaked a listen, all these years. Even that time at the dinner where she played for us, or the time before during the storm— now it seems like she was only practising. Like all this crowd lifts her, like she's found some place beyond her skill—even hers—and the right time to use it. It's like she's grabbed my heart and squeezed it hard.

Music is like that. Good music, good song, and this is the best. This is the choir in the City in the Shadow of the Mountain. This is pure and wild all at once.

And then she is done. There is applause, loud and long, and every Master is looking at her. Madigan is writing something in his notebook. Sobel's nodding his head slowly, and then he turns and looks at me, and smiles, and it is the sort of smile that makes you question just how many hours you might have left of your life. And I get a sense of something terrible coming.

And after all the congratulations and such, the bowing and curtseys and what not, when the band starts up, she smiles at Grove and leaves him, his face twisted in confusion (enough that I feel a twinge of pity), and comes over to me, and that pity fades pretty quick when she smiles. How could two smiles be so different? But I think either of them could kill me.

"That was for you," she says.

"Thank you," I say.

"To say goodbye."

Can't say nothing, my jaw's dropped. My shoulders sink as though there's a weight in my gut drawing me in.

"You—"

"They've called me to the City," she says. "I'm to play for the Masters."

"No."

But I can see it in her eyes.

"I don't want to hear it," I say.

"Hear it or not, it's true. I'll be gone tomorrow night."

Anne touches my arm, and I don't pull away. "Tomorrow,"

she says. "See me by the Summer Tree tomorrow. We'll talk about it then."

I grunt something and turn. Leave her to Grove.

Thom's nowhere to be seen, and Dain is talking to Madigan. So I stomp home, and throw myself at the bed.

An hour later, Dain's knocking on my door, looking mad as all hell. Holding a piece of fine paper in his hand. I don't even get a chance to ask him about Madigan—in fact I don't care to. And besides, he doesn't wait, just starts on like I already know what he's about to say.

"They're taking Thom back to the City," Dain says. "I'm to get a Day Boy from the Academy in January." He looks at me with a not-quite smile. "So we have each other for a couple of months more."

Don't know how things could get any worse.

Thom comes home late as I'm drifting off. I sit up straight in bed and jab a finger at him.

"You're leaving."

He gives a little shrug. "They called me back to the Mountain. They say I'm not suitable here. It's too dangerous, they say. I'd be wasted."

"They're doing this to punish me," I say.

"What?" Thom shakes his head. "It's not about you. They think it's too dangerous to have me out here. After the Night Train." He looks to Dain, who's sitting there silent; maybe he's been there all along, but it gives me a jump. "I'm sorry, Master Dain."

Dain shakes his head. "Isn't your fault." He looks at me. "And it isn't your fault either, Mark. That's always been the risk of having a boy from the Crèche."

"And what do you want?" I ask.

Thom looks at me like I'm the youngster. "Doesn't matter what I want. Tomorrow night when the train arrives, I'll go back to the Crèche. We're just Day Boys. We go where we're told."

Wasn't sure I even wanted to come here, but I do. Of course I do. How can I not?

When a girl asks you to the Summer Tree, you can't help but feel your nerves rise up. I've never been asked before, and it makes a fella bilious, this change in things. This not-having-been to having-been. And it's Anne who's asked me. Anne who's soon to go away and leave me. So much is churning in my brain and my belly. Anne; Thom, too. I should have been the one called to the City. My time's done. I'm over with this place, or it's over with me. And now, I don't know what to think. But she asked me here. My Anne. She told me when and where, and she is the one who cannot be denied.

Anne makes me wait, no surprise there. Maybe she's standing in the dense wood beyond, maybe she's watching.

I take my leisure, nervous as it is, beneath the shadow of that old tree, looking at the red flowers about to bloom. They'll light the clearing up like fire, and then with the first big storm, they'll fall and cover the ground in sweet clots. This tree's been doing that since whenever and back, and it will be long after I'm gone.

Bees are busy at their work, the trees loud with them, the sky streaked with their passage, east and west and north. Good dozen or so hives around here. George keeps them. That honey will taste of the Summer Tree. That honey's the sweetest of all. I'll want none of it this year, and no one can talk me into thinking otherwise.

I catch a movement to the left of me. Not her. Just a deer that looks at me with eyes too big and full of the world, then crashes off, a tawny blur, into the undergrowth, like it knows it's almost time to be frightened.

Going to be the hunt around here, in a couple of days. The woods are full of deer, and they'll be moving up into the High Land with the turning of the tree. And if we don't keep their numbers down, they'll eat this woodland bare, and start coming into the crops. Another reason, too, in that killing, Dain says. They let the hunt continue, year in and out, because it reminds folk that we're like them. That there's predation in us all. Even the trees eat the sun, he says. Can't see how that's true. Seems like a fare too thin for something so big.

I run a hand over the tree's rough bark, grown out of the sun. Twigs snap behind me.

"You set your fancy on the tree?" There's a bit of laughter, penetrating, almost like the laughter of those cold children.

Anne's standing there, smiling, and it fills me with a kind of joy and an ache all at once. But I'm not crying, I've already decided that.

"And what's wrong with that? Man can fall in love with the moon or the sun, why not a tree as beautiful as this?"

"Oh, those things are dull and clockwork. Predictable. You'd be bored quicker than a crow to carrion. You need the change that is folk."

"I've found some steadiness these last months. Haven't you seen it?"

"Yes," Anne says.

I smile at her. "Growing up, Dain says."

"Why didn't you ask me to the dance?"

"Didn't think—"

Anne's lips thin. "You never do."

"We're always dancing," I say. "Even now. Just no music."

"Enough of those twisting words," Anne says. "Stop with that and answer me."

"What good would it have done? You're going away, and you knew that you were going away, and you never told me. Didn't even hint at it. Made like it was furthest from your mind."

"You never asked."

"Why would I even suspect?"

And, all of a sudden, she looks tired. "Mark, I've played that piano. I've played and practised and played. I played because I love it, because it's what I am, but I was calling, too, calling into the dark. Calling them out because I don't want to live here. I don't love this place like you love this place. I'm no Day Boy, and I'm damned if I'm going to let them have my blood. They can feed on my music, and it'll be mine to give. Not have taken just because I live and bleed."

I reach out and hold her hand. And it is warm, and she doesn't pull away. She looks into my eyes, and I think I might drown in hers. There's a silence that reaches into forever and is as quick as a single beat of my stuttering heart.

"When they took Da away," Anne says, "I was little. But I knew they would come for me. Not for Da's crimes or my ma's, but because that's the way of things now."

I keep a hold on her hand, but it's only because she lets me hold it. Her fingers stick to mine, joined by our sweat. They twist and twitch with little shivers, and I can feel the music in them and the strength.

"They're coming for us all," she says. "In the end, that's their plan. It's the only reason that makes sense. Question is, do we fight it? What if fighting it'll only make it all the faster?"

I don't know. I've never really fought anything. None of the spits and spats have been true fights. I've just lived and raged and laughed, and tried to live a little longer. "There's a pleasure in all that fast and wild."

"There's no pleasure in that for us. You've lived the rich life. You've had the right to fight, to mark your ground. We've not had that ever: A moment's defiance is a death in the sun, or a death in the shadows. We hang on the comings and goings of the Night Train like flies spun on a web.

"The world changes," Anne says. "You know that. It doesn't stay the same. Was a time when I cried in the dark, but I don't do that now."

"I don't want you to go," I say.

"When has this ever been about what we want, boy?" Anne says, and she pulls her hand gently from mine, and folds my fingers closed. "It's never been about what we want. I don't even know what it is that I want half the time, for all my plans. How silly is that?"

But I do. Well, I think I do, and it's not this. I don't want to lose this. I can't. I'd set my heart on this want without even thinking on it, just knowing.

She grabs my other hand and stares at me, like she is trying to remember everything. I'm doing that, too; forcing a pin through this horrible moment, trying to capture the sweet along with all that bitter.

Day's already moving along. Night's coming, and when it does, the engines of the Night Train will be stoked. Whistles will be blown, and the train will shudder and roll, and build up speed until it is across the new-built bridge, until it is out of sight. And she will be gone.

She kisses me gentle on the cheek, pulls her hand free of mine. And I want to turn and tilt her head to mine, and taste those lips again. But I don't, I can't. So my cheek burns and my eyes sting with a grief I've been denying. "I have to go, Mark. My mum is waiting for me. I have to say goodbye to all my friends. You, you I wanted to give this explanation to. Because—"

"Yeah, I know why," I say. Standing there, not sure where to put my hands now that she has freed them.

"I better go," she says.

"You better."

She looks at me once, and runs back towards town.

And I'm left there, in the shade of the Summer Tree.

Not my finest hour. But you don't have too many of those.

Thom's mostly packed when I get home. He's left his books out.

"For you," he says.

I look at them, and feel my tears welling, but I don't give way; I don't know if I'd be able to stop. There's a heaviness in my joints and in my flesh, such a weight as could bend me low. I flash a grin, even though it hurts quite fierce.

"Sorry. This should have never happened," Thom says, and he looks suddenly old and hollowed out, and not like the boy I know. "I should have seen it coming, but that's the way of the world, and none of us are ever going to stop its turning. Thanks for taking me under your wing like you did. Thank you for that. I won't forget it."

"You keep an eye on my Anne," I say.

Thom puts his suitcase on the floor. "I will, I promise. I thought you two were . . . that you'd have each other always. But the world thought otherwise. Like the world always does." He closes his bag; he's taking less than he came with. "She'll be looked after. She will be respected and cared for. You know how they are in the City? How they love the musicians above all? She will be honoured. And she knows how to look after herself. I will do my best to make sure that no harm comes to her, but there is very little harm for a woman like Anne. Her virtues are understood."

Makes me sick again to hear her spoken of this way, of things I'm still too raw to be missing. "You packed?"

"Yes," Thom says.

"Then we're going fishing," I say.

It's a fine way to see the day to its end, plenty of laughter, and not a single fish caught. Think back to the time Thom tripped up Dougie. There's not a chance of revenge for the poor lad now.

———

I help Thom with his bags, Dain walking beside us.

"You be careful, Mr. Thom," Dain says, with a formality that surprises me. But then, Thom's not Dain's anymore.

"I will be, I promise," Thom says.

"It's not just the Crèche that you'll need to worry about. I've enemies for sure, and I fear my presence will have tainted you."

"I'll be careful, Master Dain."

"Trust no one," Dain says.

"I don't."

Dain pats his arm. "Good boy."

Then Dain's tapping my arm. "Give me those bags, Mark. I'll see to them. There's a person you might want to be talking to."

Anne's standing yonder, with Mary. And Mary's as stone-faced as I've seen her, and I can sense her resolution not to cry, same as me. Peas in a pod of grief, us two. Mary glares at me, but there's no heat to it, and then whispers something into Anne's ear. She nods, and Mary hugs her tight, and then is walking away from the waiting train and into town.

We don't say nothing, her and I, as she passes. We don't need to.

And then I'm running to Anne, and I'm holding her for the first and last time. "You and me . . ."

"I know," she says.

"There's not time for all that I want to say. Not ever enough time or space in the world for that."

"I know."

And that cools my heart despite the heat.

Anne laughs. "You're a fool."

I am a fool.

I kiss her once. Not long. Nothing more than a brush of lips, and she's pulling away, and I'm on five types of fire. There's a whistle blowing. She grabs her bags, just two—how can they contain a life, but they do. The Ticket Master leads her onboard. And I stand there trembling.

"It's all right," Thom says. "You'll be all right."

The Master's already back out, and looking down at Thom. "Are you ready, Mr. Thom?"

Thom looks at me, all awkward, not enough words or time for us either. Never is at the end. "I have to go."

So I give him a hug, too, and he hugs me back, all bony arms.

"Be careful," I say, stepping back to see him one last time.

And he's just a boy, going home.

"You know I will be," he says.

And then he's on that train, too.

The last whistles blow. The doors crack shut. The train jolts forward, lurches, steadies, quickens. And I stand on the station, watching it go. Faster and faster away from me. The Night Train's speeding up, and Anne's on it, Thom, too. I can't see them. But there's a chance I can still catch them. I run, not even knowing what I'm doing, pick up speed, even as the train jerks and slows, its front end hitting the turn across the river. I reach out, almost touch the last carriage, but then there's cold hands wrapping around me, lifting me up. A colder voice in my ear.

"Don't be a fool."

I struggle, but Dain doesn't let me go. "They're in there!"

"And there isn't anything you or I can do to change it."

I know it. I know it, but it doesn't stop me from hating him then and there, his easy strength, the way that this doesn't hurt him, the way that he shifts so that my own struggles don't injure me. Fluid and as hard as stone. He isn't a man, and there's no point in hating, but in that moment, it's all I have.

"You get on that train and you're dead. I can't protect you, not the Sun or the moon could protect you from the weight of their inquiry." He still doesn't let me go, and the train is already over the river, running faster and faster, and the two people most precious to me are its cargo. My heart's aching, tearing. But he don't let me go.

"Thom can look after himself, you know that. And Anne will be cared for. She has a skill, a true mastery of beauty in her fingers. She will be rewarded, she will live well. You know that, too."

"And what about me?"

"You. You have a choice."

"Do I? Do I just?"

"You go on living, boy. Never know what tomorrow brings. Sometimes it's a slap or a boot or a kiss or a scream. You live even though your heart feels torn out. You go on, because that's what I've taught you, and some day you may not regret it or hate me. And, more importantly, you may not hate yourself."

And he must see some sort of stilling, because he lets me go.

The train's gone. There was no way I would have caught it.

"Home now," Dain says. "You've work on the morrow." There's that, at least. There's the work.

So I walk home, and it's Egan I see. Coming at me down West Street. He's smiling and full, with the fullness of hungers sated. Not that it ever is, not really with these folk. Looks like he's won, looks like he's been waiting for me, and I get a sense how petty these fellas are. How little are their pleasures in this little town, that he'd bother with me and my miseries. No misery too small if it means he might hurt Dain a little, too.

"Night, sir," I say.

"Night, young man," he responds, polite as ever. He stands still, not a bit of movement in him. But the motion is all around him, in the air, in the earth, in the animal juddering of my heart. "Lonely one for you."

"Yes," I say, and I don't bother hiding it, don't bother suppressing my pain, nor do I throw it out. If he's looking for a fight, he's found the wrong sort of stupid tonight.

"You've few friends around you, now," he says. "Think on that. This town is all the leaner of comforts for you now."

"Yes, sir," I say. "Good night, sir."

Egan looks at me like I am some sort of puzzle that he's failed to solve. At last he frowns. "Good night, indeed," he says.

And is gone, all at once, into it. As good as this night, as bleak and dark and terrible. And I'm alone. I'm alone.

But I feel like, just for a moment, I've won something. Knowing that winning now might be losing later. It's always that way, isn't it? Victories never last long. Hold them or let them go, they leave you anyway.

When I get home, bruised, and bitter, there's a small package on my bed, wrapped in brown paper. I tear it open.

And in that package is Thom's hat. It's wrapped around the stake he carved, the taipan's eyes coloured eggshell blue. I lift it in my hands, and I realise that he never made it for himself. It's weighted perfectly for me.

The next evening, after a day where I reckon I couldn't have done less if I tried, Dain calls me to his study, asks for two shots of his whisky. And when I bring it, I see such a look of contrition that I don't know whether to cower or laugh, and can't muster much for either.

I set the whisky down on his desk. He looks up at me from the book he's reading. An old, well-thumbed thing, the yellow jacket thinning to brown in places.

"Mark," he says, "there are some things you need to know. There's two reasons I went to the City. One, as you're aware, was to speak for you." He stands and puts the book down on his desk. "The other was to speak for Anne." He looks at me, perhaps to gauge my reaction, I can't help myself, my fingers curl to fists. But Dain's lips thin.

I take a deep breath. Then another; neither's deep enough.

"She will be safe there. She will be respected. She has a talent, and a will to use it. And she wanted this. Not just Mary, Anne wanted this." Dain takes a sip of his drink. "So, do you hate me, too?"

I pretty much do right now. But it comes out as a child's cry, not a man's. "Why does everyone go?"

"Because everyone does." He pats my arm. "Your time will come, boy. Sooner than we will credit it. That's the way of things. You will forgive me? And her?"

"In time," I say, and I don't sound like a child anymore.

"Time dulls every sting, believe me." Dain picks his book up again, and sighs. "I've read this book a dozen times. Nothing new since we came," he says. "No new stories. We put an end to them."

"Why don't you write some? Finish your book."

His eyes narrow at that, but he lets it pass.

"I keep trying," he says. "It's dead, if I'm honest. Withered in me. But I still try."

Perhaps that's all the Masters have left to them, an unchanging eternity, a dulling endless road. Perhaps that's why they hold to their old feuds; they've so very little left that even hatred is a treasure.

Been a year since I was hunted in the river and now the other hunt is on, the deer hunt. Guns are cracking, fools shooting at shadows with rifles banned but for this single day of the year. Whistles blowing, drums beating. Deer running for their lives.

Morning, and there's always a list left on the table.

And there always will be—except there won't. I still don't know what's coming after, and in truth, there's a panic in me. When I'm done, who's going to tell me what to do? Where will I be? This town doesn't have a place for me. I used to think it did; maybe that was true, but now it isn't. Not anymore. I have to push those thoughts away, and focus on this, on these. Still work for me; still purpose. And panic fades in the face of drudgery.

Lists and lists: I'm in a valley of them, all those words written neatly, piling up, do this, do that, get this, see to that. Here's some writing that he's finished! Though it's never-ending. I'm not in any mood for tasks, but I'm in less of a mood for a clip under the ear. World's got its challenges enough, and I'm done with pain. Done with looking after anyone but myself. Who else is there in this town?

I study that damn list. The doors to be marked, and the places where money's to be paid. Then the yard work. I'll see to these things in the order made out. Make my circuit of the town, close in on home. Good to have a plan. Seems like everyone else has.

There's a line scratched on the door. Dougie's called a meeting at twelve. I'm not going. He can come and drag me out of bed for all I care. I wipe the damn line off with my thumb. Easiest job of the day.

I go out and make payments with those Sun-stamped coins. Mary calls out to me across the street. I don't feel like talking, but I come anyway. Of course I do. It's Mary, she's all I have of Anne.

Into the shop I go, and she shuts the door behind me. Pours me a tea, gestures at a stool by the counter. "Sit."

I take a sip of that tea, and wait. And she doesn't sit with me, doesn't even pour herself a cup, and I look at mine suspiciously.

"You set to poisoning me?"

Mary almost smiles at that.

"I'm not Tennyson, but there's all manner of poisons, I suppose. Mark, I was the one that sent her away," Mary says. "A girl like that, like mine, this town's too small for her. This town would have killed her."

And I know what she means, I know she's talking about me. I don't know what to do. I don't know how to feel. I want to hit her, I want to put the world between forefinger and thumb and squeeze until it pops. But I don't. I just put that teacup down, gently. "You know what you done to me?"

Mary nods. "But don't you realise that this wasn't about you? This was about her. She's safe now."

"You didn't like me an' her," I say.

"No, I didn't. I like you, Mark. I love you, almost; as much as one can love one of your sort. But I love my daughter more, and I had to let her go."

"But she loved me."

Mary laughs and it's as thin and bitter as any poison. "You don't know nothing about love."

"You ever stop to think that you don't neither?"

Mary slaps me. Hard enough to loosen teeth. "Foolish boy. Foolish, foolish boy. All you know is chest-puffing and sentimentality. You think the world loves you for what you are? It hates you for what you do. You serve the monsters."

My eyes are wet, and I don't hide it. I let her look. "How am I supposed to be? Where am I supposed to go? I've lost it all, and I gave it all away. What else am I supposed to do?"

Mary's face softens some. "You'll learn that. And maybe survive it. My Anne is safe, and maybe you are, too."

"Nothing safe about this world," I say.

Mary nods. "And there never was. But you have to try. And your Master thought likewise."

Don't hear anything else. Because I'm slamming open the front door, running onto the street. Running away from her.

I'm feeling those tears. They're just welling up, and there isn't a thing I can do about them. Not a thing. I don't feel like paying any more bills, I don't feel like walking. I find myself a bit of gutter, and I sit in it, and I sob, knees pressed against my chest, face down.

"Eh," Grove says from behind me. "Eh, what's this about?"

I give him a fair bit of glare. "You know what this is about."

Grove settles down. "It's all right," he says. "What's done is done. You might see her again."

Might don't mean nothing, I want to shout, but I keep my teeth shut, stop my lip quivering. Squint through the rude light of midday at my friend. If he blames himself for Anne's leaving, I'll give him a serve of knuckles, I swear.

"Ain't the end of the world," Grove says, and laughs. But I don't laugh with him. "All she did was talk about you, you know."

Don't even crack a smile.

Grove winces. "Boy and girl in love. Nothing new there. You're not the first to find tragedy. Not the first who's been messed with by the world."

I look at him hard. Like this lad understands such things! Maybe Anne said no to him, maybe she was interested in me, but what does that amount to? World's never messed with him, not hard. It hasn't pushed the way it's done with me. He's made for this world, and it accommodates him.

"Now, enough of your moping. We're running late for that meeting of Dougie's."

"Not going," I say.

I'm yanked to my feet. Grove's eyes burning. I think he's going to hit me. Second round from those I count as friends. But he doesn't.

"You're a Day Boy," he says. "When a meeting is called, you go. Until you're not. We're late as it is. We'll have to cut past the Summer Tree."

Half the town's in the woods. Shooting at stuff. There's guns cracking, whistles blowing, and all them deer regretting the tradition, regretting that they're not already in the High Land. Isn't safe to be in these woods, but here we are. The Summer Tree, with its red flowers ready to drop in this heat.

I can't help pausing. Standing in front of it, clenching my fists, like I could strike out at the world and get in a good hit.

"You'll be all right," Grove says. His head swinging this way and that. "But we have to hurry."

A deer skitters in our path, stops dead still when it sees us. "Bugger me," Grove says.

A gun cracks nearby. We both jump, and laugh.

The deer stares at us both. Long and lingering. And then it does something peculiar. It walks up to Grove and sniffs his hand. Such a beauty, and here we are before the Summer Tree.

"Something's set their heart on ya," I say, and it's the first time I find a bit of light in the day. A wind starts blowing. Warm and from the west, and the deer doesn't move. Keeps its eyes on Grove.

Grove settles himself on his haunches. And extends his hand. He touches it gentle behind the ears. "World's too cruel for the likes you. Run, little thing. Run."

"We better, too," I say, and the deer comes to life, startled by my voice. It's all a flurry of legs, and fear, and it's racing west past the Summer Tree, back into the woods.

Grove gives me a look, irritated. "You scared it," he says.

There's a crack of gunshot, real close.

Grove grunts next to me. "I think—" he says, and that's all he says.

I scramble to him, and he's blinking at me. Gasping for air, and I'm holding his hands, and there's blood on them. And he's moving his mouth, but there's no words coming. His hands grip mine back. And I'm looking into his eyes.

He lifts his head a little.

"I'll get help. I'll get help." But I don't want to leave him. "I'll get help."

I hear myself start yelling. Then people coming. And Grove's there, and I'm holding him, and there's blood, and more blood, a lifetime's worth. And he's just looking at me.

"Sorry," I say. "So sorry."

I just want him to yell at me. To curse me and hurl a plague on my house like in that play, but he don't. Just looks at me with his frightened eyes.

He tries to lift his head again, squeezes my hand even tighter. So I lower mine. Can hear his breathing, frantic. But then it catches and slows.

"Don't—" he says—there's more blood in his words than sound. He shakes his head, and there's no hate in his eyes, just a calm rising up, as he falls into nothing. And his hands aren't holding me back anymore.

I'm howling, and Mick comes at us through the woods. He's holding his rifle, and he sees what he's done.

"You," I scream, still on my knees, and I lift my bloody hands. "You."

"All I saw was a deer. Big old stag. The boy, the boy, is he—" He shakes his head, his eyes are wide, never seen such horror in a man's eyes, not even Mr. Stevens' when he was hung. "All I saw was that deer. Not the—"

But he's already backing away, dropping the rifle, and running. And even then, on the sharp edge of my hatred, I know two people are dead because of that shot. Because of me.

"You," I say to his back, but he doesn't bother turning, and I'm already filling with pity for him. There's nowhere he can run, and Grove won't ever take another step.

There's others coming at me, eyes wide.

"He's dead," I scream. "Shot dead."

I'm holding him, and none of them come near. A circle that they can't seem to breach, too frightened, like those gentle-boned boys that watch us fight.

There's flies though, big fat bastards coming for my friend, and I'm brushing them away. Big fat flies so quick to find him, like they find all death. Not gonna have him yet.

"He's dead," I say, and my eyes burn, and I'm brushing away those bastard flies. And they're on my face, too, crawling over my tears. Flies aren't fussy. Flies will eat anything. And I can't brush them all away. So I do the best I can with my friend. I do the best I can.

It's Certain and Mary who come. Who push through that mute circle. Who pull him from my hands. How long have I been there? How long did people do nothing? He's cold in my grip, and I scream and swing, but Certain's got hold of me.

"Calm," he whispers. "Calm."

Then louder. "Dougie. Twitch. All of you. Grove needs seeing to."

Don't need seeing to. He's dead. Won't need seeing to again.

Dougie nods. Him and Twitch, they get their arms around Grove. The twins do, too. They lift him up gentle.

Dougie looks at me. "Egan's gonna kill you," he says. "He won't let this lie."

Right then, I don't care. In fact, I'd welcome it. I nod my head. And they carry him into town, away from the Summer Tree, and the deer running to the High Land, away from his blood.

"You'll be all right," Certain says, but there's a shake in his voice.

"No," I say. "No, I won't."

Certain doesn't say another thing, just squeezes my shoulder.

"God help us all," someone says. God sure as hell won't help me.

Certain's there with me when Dain wakes. He rises groggy, but is quick to see that the world isn't right. And I'm barely moving. Just sitting in the kitchen. Cup of tea in my hand that Certain must have given me, cold and undrunk.

"Grove's dead," Certain says. I have no talk in me, just an ache that fills my body, deep and dire. "Mark was with him when he died. You know how Egan gets. You know how this'll play."

Dain nods.

"Boy, my boy," Dain says, and he holds me. Just a quick embrace, but I am sobbing.

There's a great low moaning out in the dark that builds and echoes back from the mountains: a roaring wild sadness. Egan's woken, too, and his grief is tied to a great rage.

Dain nods. Looks to Certain.

"Stay with him," he says. "There's so much danger for him."

"I don't care about no danger," I say, cause I would let it wash over me this night. Drown me.

Dain dips his head towards me. "You should. I want you to. Grove would want you to."

"He's dead, he don't want nothing."

Dain strokes my face with his cold hands. "Oh, my boy."

He tilts his head, hears something I can't. His eyes narrow, his shoulders hunch, and he shows a little teeth.

"Keep him safe," he says to Certain. "You've ash on you?"

Certain nods.

"Good, keep it near."

Then he is gone.

I hear them in the darkness. The terrible noise of Masters at fight. Distant then near, shrill and low, and all the sounds that rip the fabric of the night. One time there's a bloody big crash, the earth shakes. Certain sits taller, but he doesn't leave my side. Bag of ash in one hand, axe in the other.

"What you going to do if he comes?" I ask.

Certain gives me a look, he isn't one to lie. "Nothing I could do. Master in full wake, and rage. But I can stop you walking out there. I can keep you from getting yourself killed. There'll be other Masters out tonight, looking for leverage, perhaps looking to curry favour with Egan. They might kill you just as easily."

"And what if I want to die?"

"You don't. Believe me when I say this, for I know," Certain says. "Even if it feels like you want death, you don't."

And maybe he's right. I stay in that kitchen, and I hear them Masters at fight. Not a bit of sleep I have. Or maybe I do, and that fight becomes part of it. Certain sits by me.

"I want to change it," I say. "I want to change it all back."

Certain sighs. "Only thing we can ever change is ourselves.

Even that's hard. Thing is, Mark, we never change as much as we want, and we always change more than we fear."

He rises when the door opens.

"Put down the axe, man. I'm not some wolf to be cut," Dain says, and he stands, unsteady, his clothes torn, flesh marked with all the violences of battle.

Certain drops his axe and his bag of ash. "What happened out there?"

Dain shivers a bit. "We filled the sky with our rage. The collision of Imperatives." He looks dazed. "With claw and fang, and all the dark sendings and snarls of my kind, we fought, brought down hail, and trees. And the others lurched and gyred around us, but they did not interfere. They knew better. Either of us could have killed them this night. He fought with all his strength, and it surprised him that I was his match." He blinks, and looks down at me. "Surprised myself. You need to sleep. You're safe for now."

"No one's ever safe," I say.

"Foolish, foolish boy, to say such a thing when the whole world has been bent to your welfare," he says, voice scarcely a whisper driven soft by the sun so near. "The worst is done. The worst is done."

He nods once to Certain. "You can go now, but I would appreciate an eye kept over the house."

"It'll be done," Certain says.

Then he is out the door.

Dain touches my shoulder with a hand that isn't cold, but feverish. "Sleep," he says, and he stumbles, almost falls. I'm on my feet, and he leans on me. I take him to his room, and pull low the shutters and the blinds.

"You keep out the light," Dain says. "You make me proud."

And then he is falling into his dream-stark sleep, and I shut the door behind me. And I start sobbing. Not for long, but it helps a little. Just a little.

There's a knock on the front door.

I open it. Grainer's standing there.

"I'll be standing guard today," he says. I nod, but I am hardly paying attention.

Half the trees around our place have fallen, snapped at the trunk, stripped of leaves. And by the stairs to the verandah is a deep, dark furrow three metres long at least—some scar of battle. And all of this for me. For my life's ending, for its salvation.

I am ready to drop to my knees, but I don't.

"Thank you," I say.

I shut the door, and, somehow, sleep finds me when Death couldn't.

There's a funeral. Ours don't go with no pomp and circumstance. One at night, just the next night over, the body buried deep. And all of us Day Boys gather.

I'm sniffling. "He died cause of me. He died cause of me." Dain strokes my back with hands not given to comfort.

Already his strength is returning, like last night's battle was nothing. And then I'm sobbing—worse than little Thom ever did—and I don't care who sees it.

"No," Dain says. "No. There's no fault to be found for you in this. None."

Egan comes over, his face is bearded-thick with blood I can only guess is Mick's or he'd not be so brazen in showing it.

There he is dressed to the nines, in the finery of Death, and the blood is the final touch. He reeks of it. Blood and anger.

"I will not forget this," he says, with a calm that runs eight leagues deep, a calm so cold it could kill me as I stand. I feel my heart slow. "Your time is coming to an end, boy. And I will be glad to see those hours run down, like I saw the running down of the Old World."

His eyes glow with their rings of flame, and my Master's eyes burn back.

"You will do no such thing," Dain says low and hard, and it looks like they might start again.

Me, I'd be happy to die right here. All that hurt and hate at myself thrown up anew. There's not much I have left. *Why not be at it and get to Death?* I tilt my head; show my neck clear. *Come finish me now.*

"Stop with the folly, boy," Dain says and pulls me back. "And you," he glares at Egan. "You should know better. We have our agreements."

"Yes," Egan bares his blood-rimmed teeth. "Agreements."

But there's a settling in the mood. Sobel walks between them, and he's puffed up, entire. You can see the savagery in him, near unchecked, from fingertip to fingertip. His eyes are all fire and rage.

He spreads his arms wide. "Gentlemen. Gentlemen. This is not the time, nor the place for such fractiousness. Did not the last night draw the wound? Come, aren't we all fellows here?

"This is a time for grief, not fire and fury. Find yourself calm. Find yourself peace."

And that's how I see, again, the love they hold for us, even wrapped as it is in their cruelty.

Dain to protect me, Egan to seek vengeance. I can see it would
be easy to hate me, but Dain's never done that, quite the opposite.
And just now I don't understand his love. But I accept it.

———

Dain: the Book

So there he was, writing this book. Even as the sky was falling.

*Trying to capture what was already passing. He hunted for
them. The right words, the right order, the placement of this fact after that. As ruthless a predator as any of them. He didn't chase any
moon, just the light of lines heading in the right direction. Words
are curly buggers, no good for pinning down. But he was meticulous, thorough in the way of thorough men. Says he was so intent
upon the words, he forgot what he was saying, he forgot what the
words had mapped.*

Did it matter? Did it really matter?

*He had a library, prodigious. And it served him well, when
all those libraries in the air failed. When he could no longer pluck
a word from the webs of them, he still walked those shelves, could
track the long aisles of them. When he started, there were many. It
was almost a race, a meticulous chasing of the source and the madness that beat upon the world. But one by one, those other blind
folk fell.*

*And he hardly noticed, until he was the last one, letting him-
self in with keys stolen. And finally, not leaving at all. It was too
dangerous outside then.*

*Wars had fallen into one war. The library had fallen into one
man.*

*They found him with his books, and he fought them. But
what does a bookish man have to win him such a fight? His wit,
his words.*

They made him one of them. And the Change was at once furor and placation.

And he thought for a while that would give him time. But time isn't just a gift.

Time is a curse. 'Course it is.

And he forgot what he was chasing. He forgot to hunt the words. He became them, and that is a very different thing.

Dain comes in before the dawn from his vigil on the front porch.

He's holding a letter all official-like—come in the dark by bird or bat or whatever thing they're using now. Don't get too many of them, regardless. The sight of it makes me catch my breath.

Been three days since the burial. Egan's circled this place every night, and I've not dared leave the house when the dark falls. Dain's looking hungry. Twice he's called for visitors, and only George has come, and he looked at me with sorrowful eyes—more than I deserved. The others are too scared of the dark, of what Egan might do. So am I.

Not much sleep I've been getting. I hear Egan whispering my name across the night; hear Dain calling back in refusal. That messes with your dreams.

He taps the letter against his ash-burnt wrist.

"So when's the new boy coming?" I knew it was too good a thing to have until January.

Dain looks at me, like it's first thing that I said in three days. It isn't, but there's a measure of civility to it that's been lacking between us.

"A week."

"I'm guessing I'm not training this one?"

Dain shakes his head. "You're to go the Mountain. To be trained for the Constabulary."

That makes my stomach drop—no Mastery for me—and I get a thrill through me, too. Anne's in the City. "No choice in the matter?"

"No. It is not how I would have it, but I've no say in this. I've tried as much as I can. But there are limits."

"I know all about limits," I say.

"Yes," Dain says. "Well, at least you will be far from Egan there. And your future is sorted. Keep this quiet boy, don't even whisper it. I feel trouble coming, should he find out."

"Trouble's always coming."

Dain says nothing for a while, holding that letter in his hands. Then: "You be the man you want to be. Not what I need; you be the best that you can be. Will you promise me that?"

"Of course." I puff up my chest. "Strong enough. You taught me that."

Dain laughs. "It isn't about strength. Well, not altogether. Strength is just another kind of emptiness. It takes, it makes a hunger. Give it up, give it out for what's right; to help others, not just yourself. I'm not one to teach you that. I can't be. And I'm sorry for that.

"You know, the pain goes away, and then it comes back, a day, a week or a month and it's back, and I'm wondering if it ever went away at all or if I just chose to ignore it. When the pain is there, it is as if it was always there. Funny, isn't it?" He sighs. "Sometimes I am sorry to have done this to you. You are not deserving of it. And, for all the comments I may have made otherwise, I am the one that failed you. Caught up in . . . pointless endeavour. Petty feuds. How can I judge the other Masters when I am so flawed?" He folds the letter up, slides it in a pocket. "Had I only been paying attention. I think that was my greatest failing, not to see what was coming. I believe you did, Mark, and that is to your credit."

I have no idea what he's talking about, but I let him talk.

"Remember to keep your eyes open, they have taught you better than I ever have. You are a good boy, a fine boy, and I regret that I will not see the man you will become. Please believe me when I say I only ever wished the best for you. And it is my folly that I could not provide it. Sometimes the most powerful are the weakest after all."

"You spend an awful long time being sorry," I say, and he's in my face snarling, and I can see the terrible strength of him. He could snap me, break me, easy as breathing, and I would be dead. But it's a strength in check; I can see the cords of his muscles shaking. All at once the rage is gone, just gone, and he seems to be listening to something. Some distant chords of a song I'm never going to know.

"I'll be back," I say. "You'll see the man I become."

And Dain nods. "Of course you will. Now, to bed with you. I am what I am. I am my nature. Boy, I once said there's a poetry in us; in the eternity that is us. But I was wrong. Poetry is brevity, the sweet and sour ending of things. When time stretches entire before you, it's stripped of urgency, and there is no poetry. Every crime, every mistake and hatred, is not released, but clung to. Enough time passes, and all we are is our sins. Hold the sweetness of these next days to you. Remember this town, please."

"I'll not forget it," I say.

"I know you won't. You're a good boy," Dain says. "Even at your worst." He walks to his door and the room where I've already pulled the blinds and curtains. He pauses, turns. "Don't forget those gutters need cleaning," he says.

"I hadn't." My face shows enough for him to tell I had.

"Don't forget."

"I won't."

Dain smiles and his hand closes around mine. Cold as it ever was that hand. "Good."

And I sleep. Deep, worn-out sleep.

And I don't hear Egan calling once.

I'm up with the sun and the house is all quiet; always is now, without Thom. I'm having breakfast, the milk's off so it's just an apple, and there's a note: *Get milk, I can smell it from my room. Boy, how do you live?*

Five days left here, and that's what I get. I can't help but grin. I get myself out of there.

Oh, the day's a beauty for all my work and mood, even if it's rubbing it in: The sun's just sitting and glaring warm and getting hotter. I'm puffing on a smoke, and stomping down the road, the big house behind me. Might be some storm this evening. I keep an interest though I'll be abed, listening for the whisperings of them corrugations, and the soft rustling movement of Dain out and about.

I hit Main Street about the same time as most of the other Day Boys. We nod, Dougie at the front, all the others deferring, couple of mocks are thrown, nothing too serious. There's no fighting now. Things are all unsettled in some ways; more certain than ever in others. We'd not put our Masters' backs to no new battles. Might as well cut our own throats.

My time is almost done, and Egan has a new boy coming soon. Dougie's senior, without question.

There's some girls coming out of Mary's, and I make eyes at them. Still have to keep up the show, even though it feels empty. No Anne.

There's a few giggles, mostly they're just staring back. These are newbies: The school's taking in students from towns to the south. I haven't seen them before, but they know me by my proud stomp. Day Boys, as Mary says, we're all of a type.

"Ladies," I say, dip my hat, too—finally wearing the one Thom gave me.

"Off with that hat in here, charmer," Mary says, and I'm quick to it. Think she's a bit annoyed that I never bought one of the ones she ordered. "What's the old man want?"

I place the list careful down onto her counter, and Mary squints at the spidery hand and sighs. It's a long list. "I'll have it ready by three."

I nod and duck out, not before I snatch a handful of sour sweets. "On the tab," I shout, but we both know that is talk, she just throws a curse word or two my way, all half-hearted. What else can she do? I'm a Day Boy for a few days more.

So, I'm back towards the house, and cleaning, picking up stuff, then onto the lawn and the push mower. Hard work and I'm breaking sweat by noon. Damn lawn.

Go in for a cider, all wet and hot, and stop right in the doorway. The place smells. Even I can catch it over my own sweat. A death-stench in the air, and I run up into the Master's room and . . .

There's a bloody great big light-welcoming hole in the ceiling.

I know he's dead. He's lying there half burnt up. But I run to him, and I grab the heaviest blanket I can find. And I throw it on his body, and I swear he's looking at me, through those dark eyes.

The blanket hits his body, and then it just sinks, and I know he's gone to dust.

And it's just me, in that light where it should be dark, in our ruined house. And I wipe at my eyes. But I don't have any tears. Just me.

I go all bitter, start looking out at the sky marking the hours. Don't have much time left.

I open the door, expect to see four chalk Suns, but there's nothing as yet. Come the night, they'll be hunting me. For the first time I am glad Grove is gone, and Thom, too.

"Fight or flight," Dain had said to me.

They'll hunt me down quick if I leave the town; they'll smell me out quicker if I stay. I might make it, but I am full of doubt. Both choices are death as I see it. Fight, and I could make the world bleed a little.

I daren't hope for more. There's a cold shard of a cruel and wild determination building in me. I go back inside, and grab that stake that Thom made me.

Day Boys don't run.

I'm not a Day Boy anymore, but I'm not running either.

Not much time left for me, so it's to Certain I go. On my bike, riding fast as I can.

Ah, he knows something's wrong soon as I show up, can see it in my eyes. He's off for a steadier, a bottle of rum from up north, hands it to me straight; it burns on the way down and I'm doubting my steadiness.

"Dead then?" he asks, and I blink at him knowing.

"Deader than a stone. Just dust." And I know I should be bawling, but there's a coldness in me and it's growing. Crying's for later, and as far as I see, there will be no later.

"Shit," he says.

He breathes a deep sort of breath. "Well, you've got some choice. Bolt or kill. You know how it goes."

I puff up my chest. "I'm not running."

Though it's dawning on me that vengeance is hard 'less you got a Master backing you up. Can't see none too good in the dark.

Certain nods. "Well, you haven't got long, and there's gonna be all hell. Sure you don't want to run?"

On the road I'm just as dead, and Certain knows it. Matter of time either way. The ones that did this won't let a Day Boy stand. There's too much fun to be had, not to mention paybacks. I'm thinking about the boys, thinking if any looked too smug, or avid at Grove's funeral. None who I can remember.

If they knew they'd won, they buried it deep inside.

Certain's been talking, and I had hardly paid it notice. ". . . you start this, and all of them—"

"I know."

I don't know where Grainer is. I don't bother asking, don't want him part of this.

Certain leaves the room, then comes back with a knife, one that means business, curved and meat-ready, and a bag of ash. I snatch them out of his hands before either of us loses our determination. Got killing to do.

Dougie's sitting on his porch, yard immaculate, and he sees me coming, swinging to a halt by the front fence, leaping it neatly.

"Eh," he says, and I nod. He don't seem fussed. And I don't have time to be questioning his confidence.

There's a grin on his face, but he's already rolling me a ciggie when I knife him, quick in the neck, and he looks at me knowing what I snatched, but you've got to take the head, and start down, that's one tactic, I reckon, and I'm pulling him into the house with me. And I feel bad about it. He's coughing, and light, and there's blood trailing back to the porch. But we're used to blood.

"Sorry, Dougie." I'm in his ear. "Dain's dead. See you soon enough, I reckon."

"Do the same," is all he says. Then he's still and pooling on the living room floor, and the flies already buzzing and no living hand to brush them away. But I've no time for sorrow.

I'm quick to Sobel's cellar.

The fella's all whistley breath. Time's running out, but there's two hours till night proper. He's still upon his bed. You could slap him about the head, there'd be no waking. But I'm cautious yet, in case all I know is a lie. They're canny buggers, yes. The room's dark, even with the door open; I'm quick to start the downward stroke. Right into the neck, it's rubbery and his eyes snap open, but I'm already cutting through all that sinew and tissue, and the head falls, its teeth a-chattering. Grab it by the hair and bring it to the porch, swing it out onto the road. It smoulders there. And I've got my first pair of deaths, and the bitterest taste in my mouth.

You're lucky to be a Day Boy. That's driven in from the beginning. *Privileged.*

Shit. Privileged to work your fingers to the bone, them first years all spent in terror. Cause your Master is death. Glorious, maybe, but death walking and brutish, for all the airs and graces. You can't pretty that up.

You're there to make sure it works. And when it all goes to hell, you're there to make sure it all burns. No one knows as much about killing Masters as a Day Boy. We know all the tricks, shall we say. The Masters set us up that way. We're not just limbs and eyes and ears, but insurance.

I can hear the Parson twins squabbling, playing a game. I shouldn't, but I get to the window, and I stare right in.

Monopoly. And it makes my heart ache, seeing them laughing and kidding. I block all the doors.

There's more tubs of oil around Kast's place than I'd ever ex-pected. Fuel for his burner. I roll a few under the house, quiet as, and split another, and one more, and I set a match to the slick.

The whole place goes up faster than I could believe, faster than kindling. There's screams, but I close my ears to 'em. One of those Parson twins bangs against the door, but I've blocked it good. And then those big tubs blow. And there's naught but wreck and ruin.

Kast got his premonition. Kast got his flames.

And I'm back riding. There's no point in stealth, just keep charging on as the sun plays its way down into the west.

Twitch is waiting at Tennyson's; there's no surprise after that fire, there's people everywhere rushing towards it, and me riding the other way. I slide off my bike, holding the blade. Twitch has got his knife out, and a scared, hurt look on his face.

"Just you and me," I say, the sun low behind me.

"No, just me," Twitch says, and he's on me with the knife, and we're rolling in the dirt, swinging and shielding and grab-bing at each other's throats. He's smaller than me and wiry as all hell, and I'm tired. The knife draws a line of blood across my back, a deep wound, but not deep enough. I'm already pulling away, then stabbing in. Cut him above the eye, and it's spilling and he's blinking, and I'm back in quick: I cut to kill.

He tumbles, throat gaping. And I leave him there. Tennyson's down in his hidey-hole, just beginning to stir.

Calling Twitch's name, and it's Thom's stake that I use to drive him to ruin. I run it straight through his heart, and leave that taipan blue-eyed and burning in his chest.

Just the knife and Certain's bag of ash in my hands.

I get to Egan's. Left him last, because he's alone. Purely strategic, even if he's the one I want dead first. But I'm quick to finding that he isn't there.

And I realise that there's only one place he could be. Back in my home, back hidden there. And I know for sure that he was the one that did the killing, of course he is. And I'm belting down those four streets to mine. Blood full in my head. That storm's building in the west, and I expect I'll be dead before it hits. But if I'm fast enough—fast enough—I might just—

And when I make it, he's standing on the verandah, looking down. And for a moment I can almost imagine that it's Dain. Not him.

I put my bike down. Then he speaks.

"What are you doing, boy?" And there I am standing and bleeding and sticky with my blood and the blood of the other Day Boys, and the dust and smoke of those Masters dead by my hand. And there's a crack of thunder, distant, but not that far.

Storm's filling the lands. Setting down its mighty legs, bellowing its great lungs out.

"Making revenge," I say in the silence that comes after.

"It's to be expected. Could have saved you time if you'd have looked in the cellar. Near killed myself, tearing open that roof. Had no time to do anything but hide. But it was worth it to kill the bastard." There's a joy in his features now. He knows it's done, and he wants to share his cleverness. He wants to play. The great battles have been fought, and now it's just him and a boy. "To ruin him and you. I should have done it a decade past. I tried to have it done in the City, of course, a little street assassination, but you were lucky, the both of you. And it would have been just that. Having failed, I almost made our peace, bringing you back from there. But then you killed my Grove. And so there's no forgiveness that I can find, just hatred. And now," he flashes me a smile, and the verandah creaks beneath him, "here we are."

I can see the Sun's marks on him. I can smell the rawness of his flesh, he isn't quite at the fullness of his kind.

"You're the last," I say.

Egan slumps a little. Doesn't bother hiding his surprise. "You killed them all? I thought you'd just come for me, thought you'd nut out my hiding place. Thought Dain would have taught you better."

He takes each step of that verandah with a little jump down.

Jump.

Jump.

Playful, like a cat that knows he has the mouse, but he's still not all awake. He opens his wide mouth and there's those rows of teeth. Then the first breaths of that storm hit, wind chimes start singing, and he's got my scent, the raw death of it, and he shivers a little. That weakness is a little bit of hope. 'Course, even weakened, he can take me.

Somewhere behind us, the sky flashes and rumbles. He blinks, scattered like that cloud-spread light.

There's nothing to do but charge, run fast as I can, arms out, knife swinging circle eights.

He's already stepped to one side. Like it's the easiest thing in the world.

"He's dead," I say again, and I fling that bag of ash open and into his face.

He howls a bit, but he is quick; most of it misses him. What doesn't burns and slides down his face, a ruinous sort of thing, all that beauty broken, but he can take it. He's had worse hurts, and all I've done is put the rod upon the beast.

"Seen one world's ending, I did," he says. "Been low and scrambling, chasing after the moon." He raises his hand east, where the moon will rise, but hasn't yet. His finger traces a spiral in the air, but I turn my head before it's done. "Been high and mighty, too. You think a little ash will worry me? Let the world fear my scarred old face for forever."

I take a slash out at him, and he knocks away my blade. I scramble at it. Scurrying away. And he slips through the dark and in front of me. So easy, and he's still just half awake.

Egan's blinking, standing there, one foot on the knife. But I have my other cutter, the little one, and I pull it free of my belt. Egan grins, and his seared lips crack, and I know it hurts, but he doesn't show it.

"Wouldn't have thought you had it in you. But then, Death is your shadow, isn't it? You killed my Grove with your stupidity, and you shall pay for it. Just like your Master. Him with all the apologies, the empty, *empty* words. You killed him, and such a low death is what you deserve, a drowning, a throttling. You'll get no teeth from me."

That's true, and maybe I do deserve it. Maybe that's what slows my swing, though I never thought I'd had the speed for it. Frankly, I'm done with life after all the killing I've just done. I don't even see him move, but I feel it.

He grabs my throat casually, then my back, and he lifts me up, and twists. Something tears inside, oh, but it is pain, and for the first time, I'm crying. He shakes me, more pain, and I'm dropping my little knife, and he's bringing me down to get a good look at me.

"Should have done this years ago."

Then there's a noise, a burning keening in my ears, and I'm on the ground, and his body's on the ground, thrashing and flaming, and Certain's holding Egan's head, like he'd cut it right off his shoulders. The eyes are rolling, the teeth a-snapping. Certain sets a light to it with unsteady hands, and it's quick to go up. He drops it all in a hurry. The mouth moving till there's nothing but bone that comes loose at the jaw. And that keeps burning.

Certain gives it a kick, and it shatters in a dandelion burst of ash.

"Damn fella goes on, don't he? Saw you riding for here, knew there must have been one hiding. Killing their own kind, who'd have thought to see a Master stoop so low."

I'm just lying there, curled in on myself.

"You hurt?" Certain asks; knows I am, but some silences you gotta fill.

Grainer runs up beside him, all I can see are his feet. "Is he hurt?"

I can't even nod my head, raise one hand a little, and Certain crouches down. "What do you think?" I say, and cough so brutally that I'm crying again, and tasting blood.

"Jeez, Mark, you made a go of it. A serious go."

"Yeah," I smile a bit, even smiling is a hurt. "None of 'em expected me, not a single one. It was all Egan's doing."

"Expected or not," Certain says, "they would have come for you tonight. It's how the world works. Maybe some day it won't, but that's not this one."

"I'm dying," I say.

"Maybe, maybe not." He picks me up. "Taking you to Mary's, she's waiting."

He says stuff after that, all the way into town, but I'm not listening. Rain's coming in, and the dark is silent but for the rain's whisperings. There's no screaming, no beasts moaning in the streets. Things will come creeping back in, but not tonight.

When I dream, I dream of his hand. Cold, closed around my fingers. He could never give me warmth. He could never give me love. But he kept me from the cold, even the ice in his heart. That was a strength of will. That was love. I don't know if I really appreciated it until later. But that's love, too. It don't matter that you don't understand it.

There's a wind blowing in from the west. Hot, hotter even than the sun it feels like, dry and strong, the sort of wind that sends paint to curling, and burns the grass to powder. Dry and dusty, like it's torched its way through the land. Winds blowing in from the west worry me. Been too many changes come with them, and I've had my share of them, surely. Can't have no more.

Except that's not the way the world works.

I've been a while getting better, don't know if I ever will. I've been wounded, and the wounding I've done is a deeper sort of hurt. I still have the run of the town. But Midfield's shrunk. All it has is boys and folks unbled, and people that whisper behind my back. I figure there's been debate about what to do to me. String me up? Cast me out? But I'm still here.

I went back home for a short while. Couldn't stay there, it felt too damn horrible, empty of everything that made it welcome. But I managed to stay long enough to get some clothes, and even look at Dain's given-up-on book.

It was a lifeless thing, not a single breath to it, and I could see why he'd discarded it. I don't know what was wrong with it, but something was missing, something wasn't there. Some things are better left to die. Not so much a cruelty, but a kindness. Still, I couldn't bear to see his papers ruined. I gathered them up, and gave them to Mary.

"What do you want me to do with these?" she asked.

"Keep them safe. Keep them in a box."

And that's just what she did.

Probably still there.

I stay at Mary's, sleeping in Anne's old room. Never saw inside it when she was here; now I don't really care to. But you've got to put your head down somewhere, and Mary's gentle. We've hardly had a cross word since I been here. I even help in her shop. Not much. Sweeping out the front, only till I'm sore. Slowly finding strength.

Certain comes to visit some days. We talk a little—Grainer's working out just fine—or we just sit. Don't have much talk in me.

Train's lingered several times, and when it does, I hold my breath, waiting for the sword to fall. But then it leaves again, tracking west or east. And I breathe. Masters came to speak to Certain, but they never came to me. And so I'm held, not moving forwards, not moving back. I was a Day Boy once, now I don't know what I am. And I dream of Dain every night. He stands there above my bed, just watching, never saying a thing. He's waiting to see what I do. I'm waiting, too. Maybe I'll die waiting.

One night there is a scratching at the window, the sound that I had thought forgotten, but never was, never could be.

"I do not seek entrance. You shall come to me."

I pull myself from the bed. Try to hide my hesitation, but there's no hiding from the likes of them.

"Hurry, boy! Did you think that there would be no consequence to what you had done? Through the dark I have come, through the secret ways."

I open the window, I've no choice. A darkness fills the window. Two bright lights shining in its heart, offering no true illumination. I shake and I shudder, the fits start their rising in me. And the Dark moves, reaches out, touches my face with old dry fingers. The fit falls from me like dust.

"You've reason to fear, for I am nothing but fear. But I've not come to kill you."

I know there's worse things than death, and that being left behind might be one of them.

"Why you here then?" I squeak.

The dark shape laughs, the bright lights wink out. "We used to call it cutting to the chase, boy. Dain honed you to an edge, didn't he? He was always the maker of weapons. The bombs and furies that are thoughts given free range. And that is why he was cast out. We feared that he might make that which would effect our destruction. That was his vanity: That was his true work, and it put the fear into us. And perhaps we were right."

I lower my gaze, but he can see my surprise, I hear it in his chuckle.

"Oh, we are not perfect. There in the dark, we sometimes forget that. There, where nothing changes, where the oldest men squabble and mark out ageless grievances, over and over. You have reminded us a little. Now, I did not come to eat you. I came to warn you. More will be coming, a new five to replace the old. Not today, not for a while yet, but they are being made ready. What you choose to do with such knowledge is up to you."

There is a great rustling of wings, a susurration as Dain might put it, and the Dark is gone, replaced by the lesser dark.

"What choice do I have?" I shout into the dark.

It says nothing back.

Mary comes knocking on my door. "You all right in there?"

"Just a dream," I say. Hell, it could have been a dream.

I can hear her hovering there, just outside my door, uncertain to the comforting of boys.

"Just a dream," I say again. And the floorboards creak her passage away.

I've always loved Midfield, but I and it have changed. We don't fit anymore.

Rob the auditor finds me on the edge of town, looking north to the next ridge along. He and Sarah. Riding in from some other edge. Maybe they've been here a day or so, though I doubt it. Both are stained with the passage of the sun. Rob drops from his horse, neat as a pin. Sarah doesn't get down. Just looks at me, hand curved above her brow to keep out the sun.

I don't say anything for a while. Get back to considering the edges of my world.

"Land falls away beyond that ridge," Rob says. "Flat as far as the eye can follow, nothing but grass and rotten stumps of trees. East of here there's forests. What do you think of that? More than you'd have ever seen along the train line."

"Didn't expect to see you here," I say.

"Didn't expect to come back so soon. But you go where you're called, even if that means some backtracking." He runs a thumb over the tattoo of the Sun on his wrist, spits a spit all speculative. "Heard you were out of a job."

"Maybe," I say.

He grins. "Maybe." He settles down on his haunches like a tired old man. "Don't look at me like that," he says. "There's miles plenty enough ahead in these bones, unless the world thinks otherwise. Mark, I don't dither. I don't hesitate, and I'm rare to give second chances. You want what I'm offerin', then I want a yes."

"After what I done? All those dead . . ."

"I know what you done, boy. Some lives possess a trajectory. They're a gunshot, aimed at birth. You've been heading towards us since you first bawled at your ma's breast. Ain't gonna kill you. There's been enough of that; besides it weren't your feud. These Masters fight. They grow sere as old thorns on their battles, and it'll be the death of their kind. There'll be new Masters soon, and do you think they'll be easy on the one that did for their brothers? You're a reminder—the tenuous way of things—and their kind don't like that. Stay here? You will shrink and be broken."

This town's not got much to offer me now. But it's given me more than hurt, and I'm not so dumb I can't be grateful. But he's right: Already I feel the town different, feel it putting its pressure onto me. The air's quickening out there, and growing stale here.

Might be time to be moving on. Sometimes leaving isn't running.

"Wasn't your fault. Situation like that, you fight or you run. Most times you die. But here we are. No one'll blame you, not one of us anyway. Only thing that'll kill you now is anger. Anger will bend you in ways that they won't accept. Stay angry and it'll be your death for sure."

"I've had enough of anger in me," I say, and I mean it. And I feel better for the words. The moment they pass my mouth. "I'm done with anger."

Rob shakes my hand. "You're a surprising quantity, my boy."

"He'll fit right in," Sarah says, and I turn, and look up at her. She winks at me.

Rob smiles, a little softness to all the severity of his face. "You ain't done growing yet, not by a long way. This horse ain't going to be an easy ride, but you're coming along."

"Do I get to say goodbye?"

"Life's one big goodbye," Rob says. "An unutterable farewell."

"Bloody poet," I hear Sarah mumble. Rob gives her a hard look, and she laughs. I don't.

Rob sighs and looks at me again. "From what I've heard, you got no one to say goodbye to."

"A day's all I need," I say.

Rob laughs this time. "A day, all that *you* can do in a day. A day's forever for you and no time at all."

"I'll follow you, if you let me do this," I say.

Rob nods, and he's grinning. "Some steel in you, then, boy. I can shape steel."

He considers. "We've work in the town next to this. Don't want you walking those paths alone. Like I said, you backtrack if you need to, and I'll do that for you. Two days, we'll be back. I hear you're staying at Mary's."

"Yes."

"We'll come for you the morning of the second day. You better be waiting."

"You've my word," I say.

Which is how I join with those whom, in a proper sort of world, I shouldn't. First step to becoming something fearful.

I say my goodbyes. I visit the graveyard where the boys are buried, because that is proper. There's no hard feelings that I can feel. We'd have all done the same. But it's awful quiet.

I lay a handful of red flowers on poor Grove's tomb. Always thought he'd be the one to do that for me. The world looked kinder on him, right up until the end. I breathe in that silence surrounded by my boys, and I feel the grief of what I've done. But it *is* done. They're dead, and I'm not. I could have run, but they would have caught me. My life was forfeit.

I'll be thinking on this forever. But now, when it's raw, all I can do is stand amongst those fresh-dug graves and whisper their names.

I'll take them with me, those names. Till someone whispers mine, and I'm down in the earth with them.

———

Certain's waiting for me at the farm. Grainer, too; the heat's kept them inside. And I think about that, how I'll be all in it, out in the places where there is no inside to hide in from the summer, or the winter, and the howling storms.

Certain goes to the cellar for cider.

"When you heading out?" Grainer asks, looking down at his hands (a good sight harder than they were, those palms, thickened and cracked by serious work). I don't ask how he knows I'm leaving. Everything's a surprise with Grainer, so nothing is.

"Tomorrow, maybe the next day."

Even here, amongst friends, it never does to be too specific. Grainer nods.

We look out across the dusty yard. Petri's curled up at my feet. She lets me rub between her ears, her tail thumpa thumpa thumping.

I squint up at Grainer. "You look after the old man."

"I will," he says.

"I might be back," I say. "I might check up on you."

Grainer shakes his head. "You won't be back. Someone else will: And I'll be here to greet him."

"Fair enough," I say.

Then Certain's there with the cider, and we sit, and drink, and complain about the damn heat.

———

Mary knows as well, and I wonder if I've written my intentions on my face. Never thought I was so obvious. We cook dinner together and eat in silence. Mary looks at me, from behind her plate and her knife and her fork. Chewing polite, and slow.

And it could almost be any other night since she took me in. But it isn't.

"You find Anne, you say hello," she says. "If the trail takes you that way. And I guess it will eventually."

I take a few more bites, and swallow. "How did you know?"

"Rob visited me. We were good friends once, and he asked if it were right to take you." Her lips thin, and then she smiles, and there's warmth in it. "He asked me. Like you're mine."

"What did you say?"

"I said it was your choice, that you're near enough a man."

I look at her, and take another mouthful. When I swallow it, I nod. "I don't think I'll get to the City any time soon."

"You'll get there eventually, and when you do, you say hello to my Anne, and tell her that I miss her."

I finish my meal, pack what little I have.

And then to bed and a sleep unexpected and deep. Me and the night turn oblivious for a while.

———

There's a knock on the door before that last dawn, barely a soft touch; a whisper of a knock, but I'm already awake. Sleeping light is not a habit I've broken. I pick up my bag. Mary's not up, don't want to wake her, it's easier if I don't, and I ease my way to the door and open it.

Rob nods. I leave the house for the fading dark. Birds are already singing.

"Good man," he says.

The roads are long, but I'll follow them. Thom and Anne are out there in the belly of the City in the Shadow of the Mountain. I've buried Grove, and Dain is gone. This town is a shadow to me. Nothing more than echoes.

My Day Boys carved a G into my arm, they marked me as a ghost, and there was truth in that; I've made ghosts of them all. I'm not a ghost myself. I am disembodied. Untethered. But there's life in me yet, and hope.

Dain and this town made me what I am, taught me what I need to know, but now I have to make my own mark in the world. Now, for better and for worse, the lessons ahead are my own. I might not have chosen to be a Day Boy, but I choose this.

Sarah smiles at me, and it's as warm a smile as I've seen these last months. "Are you ready?"

"Yes," I say, and I hear no hesitation in my voice.

Rob leads me to a horse. Grey coat, big eyes, they regard me with soft interest. "This is Kala. She's a sensible beast."

I pat her broad back, and yes, she's steady. Start to put my foot in a stirrup, and Rob settles a stilling hand on my shoulder. "We ain't riding today, boy. We're walking. By day's end, you and Kala will be best friends."

He shows me how to strap up my stuff. And then it's time to go. Before the sun rises and the land grows too hot beneath its hard thumb.

———

Every story should end with another step, and another leading out past the words.

You get to know somewhere by walking it. Feet know it first and once they do, the place opens like a flower, its smells, its shapes, its shadows. I've walked this town all my life, from that first walk, hand held by my Master. Can't believe that it ever felt so huge. It isn't: Towns have edges. They cut against the world, and the world is big, and the world likes to remind you. Sends its storms and its tumults.

Home's simply that: a brief respite. Home's the sense of safety, but only the sense of it. Can't dig deep enough to be safe, and if you could, you may as well stop breathing.

We lead our horses to the edge of town, and that nub of road that goes nowhere.

And we keep walking.

Acknowledgments

Well, this book is yours now, lovely readers.

This book, like all books, is born of quiet and chatter, solitude and friendship, generosity and jealousy, and all the grand and silly dichotomies that make up books and people.

Thanks again to Sophie Hamley, who quietly and persistently insisted that I finish it in a very troubled time. And thanks to Alex Adsett, who carried this one across the Pacific. Thanks to Diana, who read it when it wasn't quite what it is now, and told me true what she thought.

Thanks to Text and Mandy Brett, in particular, for taking a chance on the weirdness, and driving me to some sort of logic, and to editing the book with sensitivity, poetry and patience.

For the American edition, thank you to Liz Gorinsky for liking this enough to give it a new home. Thank you, too, to the rest of the team at Erewhon who have made this book a beautiful thing. I'd particularly like to thank Martin Cahill, Cassandra Farrin, Viengsamai Fetters, Lakshna Mehta, and Sarah Guan. Qistina Khalidah's cover, along with the type design by Samira Iravani and art direction by Dana Li, is, again, truly divine.

Thanks to my family, none of whom are monsters.

Thanks to my work family at The Avid Reader bookshop. Particularly to Helen Bernhagen, who has worked with me nearly twelve years' worth of Sundays, and to my boss Fiona Stager, who makes the place a refuge and a grand redoubt of stories and storytellers, who inspires us all, and provides a steady decent wage—nothing more important to a writer. And to Krissy Kneen, who is always an inspiration.

I wrote a fair chunk of this while half my face was paralysed, so thanks to the Bell's palsy as well.

And thanks to Terry Martin, who originally published a very different short story called "Day Boy" in *Murky Depths 4* all those years ago. It still sits as the heart of the book.

Thanks to Fiona, Essie, and Charlie, who weren't in my life when this was written, but who have taught me more of love and laughter than I ever could have hoped.

Finally, thanks to the town of Gunnedah, where I spent my boyhood, which is both Midfield and not at all, as all fictional places are one thing and another: back to dichotomies.

This book was written on Turrbal and Jagera land—always was, always will be.

Also by Trent Jamieson

THE STONE ROAD

"The novel, like its heroine, holds dear a loving, quarreling community, even as it understands that towns—like time and people—slip away like dust. *The Stone Road* is a cycle of mysteries, an invocation of kindness amidst decay, a promise to the living, and blessing for the dead."

—Kathleen Jennings, author of *Flyaway*

Furnace woke the day I was born. The earth shook, birds clotted the skies, and the dead, suddenly blinded, howled low and loud enough that almost everyone in Casement Rise heard them. Afterwards, a thin scratch of black smoke rose from behind the Slouches, the low hills west of town.

Furnace had been lit, and soon it began to call: a deep humming in the earth and the air. A deep humming that burned right through the body.

Nan sent three men that way to find out what caused the smoke, what it meant. Good men; strong and trustworthy. They did not come back for weeks, and when they did, they were changed. Quieter, sullen, whispering of a promised land. They called it Furnace—so did everyone, after that—and they soon left again, going back to Furnace. Three others went with them. Those six were not the last to be called, but no one else came back.

My life was bound with Furnace, and that was a bleak and thorny tangle of a thing, worse than the angry mysteries of my mother.

I was born mad, she said. Born with teeth, and I bit Dr. Millison's hand as he cut my cord, tasting blood before milk. Suckled hard, and gave pain before I shed any tears. That was her version, anyway. I was a baby. It was all heat and light and touch in my infant mind. I knew nothing of my own ragged birth or the earth's agitation. Didn't know when Furnace called my dad, and drew him away from my mother, who took to drink and nights of crying not long after.

I knew nothing about all this until the dead man spoke, and I was older by then. Before that I was walking, talking, singing, and crying, always with Nan, thinking the whole world was all about me, the way children do.

The dead man grabbed my leg, as hard as you could imagine, his fingers digging deep into my skin. He pulled me down to the black earth, and whispered, "Finally! I gotcha! The light burns down here, but you I could see. Listen. There's a hungry fella coming for you. Listen to me. Listen." His breath was hot, his eyes white, the pupils pinpoints scratching for sight.

I didn't listen; I howled.

I don't remember what else he told me, but I will never forget Nan's response: the sudden sourness of her sweat mingled with tobacco, like it had turned all at once to fear; the way she yanked me from his dead grip, swift but gentle (and she could be anything but gentle. There was a part of me that watched, distant and cold, oddly satisfied as she struck the dead man hard with her walking stick. Then he was gone, like he had never been there at all.

But my leg stung, and his fingerprints would mark me for days. The first touch is like that.

"Keep your feet clear of the earth, Jean! You must keep your legs up. Higher, now. Higher, Furnace take you! You're not ready."

I cried, and she held me steady, and stared hard into my eyes. I stared back—I was never one to look away—and she smiled at that a little. Nan always respected strength, even as she hunted out weakness. I sniffed and snuffled, and the tears came. She rubbed her thumbs across my cheeks.

"This has started too soon. The dead are always talking, and there are so many of them now, but you shouldn't hear them. Not yet. I'm so sorry, child."

She didn't sound sorry; she sounded angry, perplexed. Maybe other things as well, but what do children know? She held me up from the earth, hard on her hip, her other hand tight around her walking stick, until we were home. I wasn't a baby anymore, and Nan wasn't a young woman, but she carried me all the way, and she didn't falter.

From then, until I was much older, I was forbidden to walk barefoot outside. Even in boots, Nan told me, I had to be careful wherever the earth was clear of grass. Because that's how the dead speak. That was how Nan and I heard them: up through the earth and the soles of our feet.

That is the first thing I distinctly remember, that dead man's touch. From that point on, memory came to me clear and true, at least with most things.

Furnace called others in our town, but even then I was heading to the Stone Road. I was called to death. Nan did her best to keep me from it—keep me from the town, too—and saw to my education. I learnt more from her tales of the town than I ever did from walking through it. I rarely walked outside without her company, and hardly saw anyone on my own. And I guess it worked, for a while.

Then it didn't.

On my twelfth birthday, a man came to visit, uninvited.

Twelve is a lucky number, though it didn't turn out so lucky for me. I suppose that's no surprise; it was my birthday, after all.

There was a party. There had been cake, and fairy floss made from an old hand-wound machine that Aunty Phoebe brought out with great delight every time someone in town had a birthday, whether they had a sweet tooth or not. Nan's friend Jacob had come over with his placid pony, May, both pony and man possessed of infinite patience. He let me and the other children ride her even though I was a bit old for such things. I'd received from my aunts, who were generous that way, exactly three books, all of them printed by publishers in the Red City, all of them adventures. I liked that kind of book a lot. In truth, I'd rather have been reading them than playing party games.

I was the only one who saw the man, at first.

He came up from the creek, dressed in a cloak of leaves, walking daintily, like a cat crossing a puddle. He moved so gracefully that it was hard not to be captivated. I held my breath, watching him. It was the sort of grace that threatened to become chaos, but never did.

I might have run if I had more sense. Instead, I watched, waiting for it all to come undone. He was the most interesting thing I had seen that day. Which was why it was all the odder that no one else seemed to see him.

However, they did move to let him pass, with troubled looks on their faces that rippled out from his passage. Soon enough, everyone was frowning like someone had been sick in front of them, but no one was ill. Lolly Robson *had* thrown up on himself from all that fairy floss, but that was hours ago, and his mother had taken him and his brothers home—much to their horror, and his shame.

Even though it was my party, the guests were happy to leave me alone. My birthdays had a reputation for hazard. I was different. The other children weren't grabbed by the dead when they walked barefoot. Their nans didn't get up before dawn, and go out into the dark doing whatever it was that mine did. Seeing to problems, she called it. I just saw it as a secret. But I didn't ask. I'd given up on asking. I never got an answer, just reproach.

I stood alone, a bit distant from everyone, watching the adults and their reactions to that graceful man's approach.

He was swift, though he didn't hurry, just walked right up to me. "Miss March," he said. His voice had a chill to it. "I believe it's time we met."

He smelled of rot and river water, with a deeper scent of smoke. That last one was familiar: It filled the town whenever the wind blew in from the west over the Slouches, carrying the smell of Furnace with it, and giving me migraines. One was already coming on. Why did he smell like that? It brought back memories, things I thought I'd forgotten from my most babyish years. That smell. A chair. My nan holding me.

I was frightened, but he positively beamed at me, as though I was the cleverest, most enchanting thing he had ever seen. "I came to say happy birthday. Why, it's my birthday, too, don't you know?"

"Happy birthday," I said, and he clapped his hands.

"She speaks!" He touched my face. I flinched—his fingers were clammy, the smell of smoke rising harder against the rot. I moved to step back, but he grabbed my wrist. "Thank you for the birthday wishes. They're much appreciated, Miss March. I was beginning to think you were a mute." He glanced at my boots. "You're half-deaf as it is, wearing those. What's your grandmother doing? You take those heavy boots off sometimes, I bet? Don't you? You're not *all* timid."

He crouched down, and peered into my eyes. I tried to shut them, but I couldn't. I tried to yank my hand from his, but he held it, steadily. He kept up his study of me. "Right. Don't talk too much, now. It's better if you keep your mouth shut, and listen."

His eyes shone gold. They were quite beautiful, but there was something wrong in them: a shadow, and a hunger of sorts. How did he know my nan? He certainly thought little of her when it came to me.

"Don't you want to know how old I am?" he asked.

When I shook my head, he seemed ready to slap me. I knew that look, though I mostly saw it on my mother's face. I flinched.

Instead, he smiled. "I'm twelve," he said. "How am I twelve when I'm a man? Do you know?" His grip tightened, and his mouth unhinged. His teeth were dark and sharp, his breath smelling of ash. "How am I twelve when I feel so old?"

I shrugged. How could I possibly know the answer? He came even closer, close enough that our lips almost touched. The world buzzed and popped, and my heart lost its rhythm, turning into a painful clenching. All I could smell was smoke. Time stilled. His hands that threatened violence lifted, and he reached up and pulled a golden coin out of my left ear. I swear, I'd felt it swell there.

There was a cruel delight in his eyes, almost as though he hadn't expected that to happen. He winked. "Birthday magic," he said. He pressed the coin into my palm. "This is my gift to you. If you want it."

I nodded, clenched my fist around it. He smiled like he was truly happy. "I'm so very pleased," he said. "Magic is the key to a good friendship, they say."

"Get away from her." And there was Nan. Face bloodless, full of fury. "Away."

"I only came to wish her happy birthday." He sounded surprised, almost offended.

"You weren't invited."

"I should have been."

Nan held her walking stick like a club. "Get away from her." She didn't shout it, just said it cold and calm. In that moment, I was more scared of her than him. I'd not seen her like this before. A little moan passed my lips.

The man laughed. "You've coddled her, Nancy. Why? You weren't treated so gently. She's a mouse; a tiny, frightened mouse. Look at her, not a single bruise. At least, not from you. And there you are, weakening, weakening, and she's never been tested. Doesn't even suspect the troubles coming her way."

I looked from him to her. What troubles? But Nan wasn't looking at me.

"Get!" She swung her stick, and somehow missed.

"You shouldn't do this," he said. "You should have invited me. We've had our chats, but she's my concern now."

"Go," Nan said, and swung again.

He danced backwards, out of reach.

"Happy birthday, Jean," he said. "It's going to be an interesting year."

Then, without a hint of hesitation, he turned, so gracefully, and dived at my grandmother. What she did next was not at all graceful, but it was precise. She swung her stick, and there was such a loud crack that my ears rang. The world stopped buzzing, and the graceful man was gone, with nothing left of him except a pile of leaves that Nan quickly threw a match into.

She grabbed my shoulders, looked in my eyes like she was hunting something there. I wanted to turn my head, but that gaze held me. What was she looking for?

"You still in there?"

"Yes," I said.

Something loosened in her. "Did he hurt you?"

I realised I had pissed myself, and I started to cry, full of shame. I knew that he had wanted to hurt me, though I didn't know why.

I shook my head. Behind her, far too many people were staring at me. The children had stopped playing. Some folks were leaving, herding their children before them. I couldn't see my mum. Later she'd come home, smelling of liquor, and she'd hold me, her eyes hard, like it was all my fault, like I'd called trouble down on me, and she was comforting me despite herself. But she'd hold me anyway, and I'd let her.

Nan leant down by the burning leaves, not much more than ash now. She jabbed at them with her walking stick, and they fell apart.

"Go clean yourself up," she said, tapping her stick against her heel. "You're safe now."

I didn't believe her. I didn't know what to believe, but I knew I wasn't safe. Troubles were coming, no matter what Nan said.

I suppose I shouldn't have been surprised. Every birthday of mine was a challenge. Mum and Nan would grow tense the day before; they'd start whispering, stopping before I entered the room. Who could blame them for being so anxious?

When I turned one, the townsfolk say, a big grey bird the size of a dog with a beak like a hawk came, and sat on my window. When I reached for it, it tried to peck out my eyes. But I was quick, and I laughed and swatted it away. That bird went and ate Mrs. Card's tiny dog, Beatrix; so I heard. Nan never spoke of it, but my Aunty Liz told me.

On my second birthday, a column of fire burned right in the heart of town. It died away as soon as Nan went to it. No one else could have banished such a thing, or so Jacob whispered to me one evening when I asked him about my birthdays. "Your nan's special. So are you."

"What about my mum?"

"Of course. She is, too." But he made the circle of the Sun upon his palm, and people don't do that unless they've said something bad. Then the conversation stopped, and I didn't learn what that special thing was.

On my third birthday, there was a storm so hard-edged that buildings fell right over, and four people went missing, blown out of town like that girl and her dog and the twister in the storybooks (though some say that all they did was go to Furnace). I never thought it odd that the world could, on a whim, just yank people away. That's what I grew up with.

When I turned four, the sun was sealed up by the moon, and there was a distant howling, like a hundred wolves had been set loose upon the land. The howling didn't last long, falling away to a silence that was, somehow, far worse. That one I remember: The land grew so still it made me cry. Nan held me until the sun returned. The memory remains so clear to me.

My fifth birthday was marked by a cloud of locusts that ate most of that year's crop. They called that year Jean's Famine, though no one would say that to my face. Nan discouraged it, but I still heard it when no one thought I was around.

On my sixth, three people were found dead in their homes. Whispers of a man without skin, a monster, went around town.

On my seventh, there was a distant ringing, and a rope appeared, hanging from the sky. The farmer, David Preston, decided to climb it, despite Nan warning him not to. Soon after, the ringing stopped, and we watched David's head fall to the earth. People blamed us, particularly his brother Myles, who has been punishing us ever since.

When I turned eight, a tall tree in the park flowered with sweet-smelling stone fruit that made anyone who took the smallest bite sick for weeks. Somehow that fruit ended up finding its way into every kitchen, lurking in every pantry. Myles came at the tree with an axe, but Nan wouldn't let him chop it down. She consumed the fruit herself, staying at its base throughout her sickness. From that point on, the tree stopped producing fruit, and instead shone white and ghostly. Townsfolk called it White Tree, and were banned from going near her.

Nine, and something stole the Robsons' best cattle. Took all Nan's skill to stop a war.

On my tenth, there was a fire upon the river, a twining flame that raised itself high, like a demon, or a twister. It didn't make a sound, but it set the birds restless. No one was stupid enough to swim to it, which pleased Nan, so we stood upon the banks, and watched it burn, town on one side, birds on the other.

On my eleventh birthday, nothing happened, but a few weeks later Jim, the trader, arrived, and said that there had been an insurrection in the Red City, and five Masters had been dragged out into the day. A terrible death for them: The sun set them alight and screaming at once.

The Council of Teeth, the rulers of the Red City, were swift in retribution. They feared a loss of face almost as much as open rebellion. I remember Nan demanding that Jim be specific about the date, then looking at me with a grim horror, a look that I'd never seen her give me before. It went away quick, but I didn't forget. Since that dead man's touch, I'd not forgotten anything.

All these things happened, and the town saw me at the heart of them.

Nan said that there were bad occurrences every day, some you needed to look for, others you didn't, and my birthdays weren't that special. I didn't quite believe her, but felt lucky that, except for the bird, none of these things really happened to *me*, until the graceful man and his golden coin.

My coin, now. I didn't tell Nan about it. Something stopped my mouth. I took it to my room, and hid it beneath my bed.

Every night I'd look at it, and I'd smell smoke, and the hint of a headache would drift behind my eyes. Sometimes the coin would burn hot in my hands, and the next day I would hear of so and so, gone west, gone to Furnace. Despite the horrible prick of my guilt, I never told anyone about that coin. Not when I was twelve, or for a long time after.

Well, I told *someone*.

There was one person I could talk to about that coin, though he wasn't really a person anymore.

That evening, while Nan and Mum held a whispered conference in the kitchen, I snuck outside, sat on the edge of the stairs to the verandah, slipped off a shoe, and touched a single toe to the earth.

The dead boy was there. Sometimes he wasn't, and I'd lift my foot up straight away, lest an angry man start talking or moaning about the blinding light, and the closed gate. I had no patience for the other dead; they scared me. But I liked to talk to the little dead boy.

The dead below couldn't see where they were, but they could see me, and Nan. The boy had forgotten his name, but he remembered other things.

"Jean?"

"Yes, it's me."

"Good. Your nan, she's a terror!"

"I was nearly killed today."

"Don't you horrify me so, Jean! Nearly killed on your birthday? Your birthday, it's always your birthday!"

"I'm all right now."

"What happened?"

"There was a man, a graceful man."

"Oh, the one that treads so lightly out of the west! The one that catches us like fish. I don't like him. Keep away from him, Jean."

"I will," I said, wondering why he'd never mentioned him before. "But he gave me a coin."

"I wouldn't take a gift from him."

"Too late."

"I suppose you must keep it, then."

"He reminded me of the chair," I said.

"Oh, that was a ghastly thing."

"Yes," I said, and shuddered. Not wanting to think on it.

"Did you have a good birthday?"

I thought about that instead. "Until then, yes. I think."

"Was there fairy floss?"

"Yes."

The dead boy sighed, the sort of sound that could break your heart with sadness. "Was there cake?"

"Yes."

"What was it?"

"Chocolate, of course!"

"Oh!"

"Do you remember chocolate?"

"I've forgotten so much down here," he said. "It seems so long ago, all those foods and sweets. But I'll never forget chocolate."

That made me sadder than I cared to admit. "Would you like a story?"

"Yes, for a little while. If you don't mind."

I looked around; no one was about, so I opened one of those adventure books, and started to read to him. There were pirates and everything. The dead boy helped me with the difficult words, and I forgot about the graceful man.

But Nan didn't.